S0-BMT-620

Morgan took her in his arms and held her against him, then turned her face up to him. When his lips touched hers, Jessie met him with a desperate need of her own. For a moment, she forgot he was a man she didn't trust, a man she hardly knew at all. She needed his touch, the pressure of his hands about her waist.

"Guess I ought to say I'm sorry, that I picked a real bad time to do that. I'm not sorry at all, though, Jessie."

"No," Jessie smiled, "I know you're not. And neither am I..."

*Also in the LONE STAR series
from Jove*

LONGARM AND THE LONE STAR LEGEND
LONE STAR ON THE TREACHERY TRAIL
LONE STAR AND THE OPIUM RUSTLERS
LONE STAR AND THE BORDER BANDITS
LONE STAR AND THE KANSAS WOLVES
LONE STAR AND THE UTAH KID
LONE STAR AND THE LAND GRABBERS
LONE STAR IN THE TALL TIMBER
LONE STAR AND THE SHOWDOWNERS
LONE STAR AND THE HARDROCK PAYOFF
LONE STAR AND THE RENEGADE COMANCHES
LONE STAR ON OUTLAW MOUNTAIN
LONGARM AND THE LONE STAR VENGEANCE
LONE STAR AND THE GOLD RAIDERS
LONE STAR AND THE DENVER MADAM
LONE STAR AND THE RAILROAD WAR
LONE STAR AND THE MEXICAN STANDOFF
LONE STAR AND THE BADLANDS WAR
LONE STAR AND THE SAN ANTONIO RAID
LONE STAR AND THE GHOST PIRATES
LONE STAR ON THE OWLHOOT TRAIL
LONGARM AND THE LONE STAR BOUNTY
LONE STAR ON THE DEVIL'S TRAIL
LONE STAR AND THE APACHE REVENGE

WESLEY ELLIS

LONE STAR

AND THE TEXAS GAMBLER

A JOVE BOOK

LONE STAR AND THE TEXAS GAMBLER

A Jove Book/published by arrangement with
the author

PRINTING HISTORY
Jove edition/June 1984

ISBN: 0-515-07628-7

Chapter 1

Jessica Starbuck stalked impatiently before the station, keeping to the narrow strip of shade as best she could. In spite of the early rain that had marked her arrival, the day promised to be a scorcher. The brief morning shower only added humid air to the bayou country heat. Visible waves of moisture rose from Jefferson's muddy streets and clung to the crowns of yellow pines.

Jessie knew the region well and wasn't surprised. Spring in East Texas lasted twenty minutes at best. If you missed the fun, too bad—the calendar moved ponderously into summer and left you behind.

Setting down her leather valise, she searched the broad street for anyone who might be Tobias R. Pike. She'd never seen him before, but that was no reason he shouldn't have spotted her. The train had been in for a good quarter hour, and there weren't that many women traveling alone.

Jessie sighed, pulled a kerchief out of her sleeve to pat her face, then dabbed her neck and the vee of flesh exposed below. The bodice of her blue cotton dress was modest enough, but failed to hide the full swell of her breasts. A pair of burly loggers hooted their approval as they stomped by.

Jessie hid a grin, studied the street once more, and retrieved her valise. "To hell with this," she said aloud. "You can find *me*, Mr. Pike!"

Lifting her skirts, she scurried across the street toward the center of town. A wagonload of timber rattled by, two black teamsters urging their mules through the mire. Past them, dark smoke billowed over a row of brick warehouses masking the river. The smoke, and a sudden throaty whistle, told Jessie a sternwheeler was just pulling in or leaving town. Jefferson had

1

changed since she'd been here with her father, a good ten years ago. Jessie knew the reasons why, but the change itself was clear to any stranger after a few short minutes in town. Horses, carriages, and wagons filled with goods still plied the streets, but the smell of prosperity was gone. Jefferson's day in the sun was over, and everybody knew it.

"Uh, Miss . . . Miss Starbuck?"

Jessie stopped and glanced to her left. A short, portly gent in a drab gray suit and a black bowler was gesturing frantically from the darkness of a partly open door.

"I'm Jessie Starbuck," she replied cautiously. "Do I know you?"

"Well, uh—not actually," the man said nervously, tipping his hat to show a fringe of graying hair. "You, ah—do, I guess, in a sense. I'm Tobias Pike, Miss Starbuck, your, ah—general manager here in Jefferson."

"Oh, well, in that case . . ." Jessie smiled. "I'm pleased, Mr. Pike. Guess we missed each other at the station."

"Yes, yes," Pike said hurriedly, "terribly sorry about that. Would you, ah, care to step in out of the sun, Miss Starbuck? Awful hot out there."

The broad, gold-lettered sign on the door read: D. POTTER, SADDLES, BRIDLES, & RIGGING. Jessie frowned at Pike. "In *there?* I don't need any saddles, at least not at the moment."

"Well, no, now of course you don't, dear lady." Pike shot her a sickly grin. "I thought, that is, I—"

"What, Mr. Pike?" Jessie sighed and stepped past him into the store. She'd seen enough frightened men in her life to know she was looking at one now. Oily beads of sweat peppered his face and a tic pulled at the corner of his mouth. The man's tiny eyes, buried in folds of fat, never stopped darting about.

"All right," said Jessie, "something's wrong, Mr. Pike. Why don't you just tell me what it is?"

Pike swallowed and wet his lips. "Oh, now, no reason to be alarmed," he assured her. "I simply thought the, ah, gravity of the situation—"

"I'm aware of the situation, Mr. Pike. Has anything changed? I mean, since I got your message to come?"

"Well, no—"

"You're certain of that?"

"Oh yes. Yes, of course." Pike wet his lips again. "I thought it might be best if we—if we talked in a more *private* setting

2

than, say, the hotel, or the Starbuck office. Just a sort of—cautionary measure, you understand."

"Oh? A measure against what?"

"Nothing, nothing, dear lady." Pike spread his hands and tried another smile. "One, ah—never knows, though, does one? In many ways, Jefferson is a very small town. And there are elements here that—uh, yes. People notice things. The wrong kind of people, you see. They, ah—ah—"

Pike's voice trailed off. Jessie stared, her puzzlement at Pike's behavior suddenly turning to anger. "So you thought we'd *hide out* in a saddle shop, right? If anyone's after me, maybe they won't figure I talked to you."

Pike blanched. "Miss Starbuck, I *assure* you such a thought never occurred to me. It is *your* safety that is uppermost in my mind!"

"Uh-huh. Sure." Jessie's green eyes narrowed until Pike looked away. "I will see you at dinner, Mr. Pike. Promptly at noon, in the *public* dining room of the Excelsior Hotel. Do you think you can manage that?"

Pike blinked. "Uh, certainly, Miss Starbuck. N-noon it is. And I assure you again, dear lady—"

"Don't," Jessie warned him. "I've had about all the assuring I can stomach." Grasping her valise, she stalked out of the shop and left Pike standing.

At least, Jessie conceded, Pike had managed to get her a decent room. More than decent, really—the spacious quarters were the best the elegant Excelsior Hotel had to offer. Gilt mirrors scattered about the walls made the room seem even larger. Polished hardwood floors were covered with fine carpets, and the sofa was patterned silk. There were marble-top tables, a large armoire, and a cherrywood bed large enough for four. The sight of the enormous bed amused her. "Now what do they figure I'm going to do with *that?*" she asked no one in particular.

Tossing her valise on the bed, she paused to remove the pins from her hat. Laying the blue sunbonnet by the valise, she shook her head free. A thick tumble of blond hair fell past her shoulders. A beam of morning light danced through the curtains, turning her tresses to burnished copper. The hair complemented her startling green eyes, and skin the color of cream. A perfectly straight nose was set above a wide, generous mouth

3

that curved slightly at the corners. Her features were strong and determined—or girlish and full of mischief, depending on her mood of the moment.

Jessie glanced longingly over her shoulder at the polished brass tub in the corner. Hurrying to the sofa, she quickly removed her shoes and stockings, then stood again to work the buttons of her dress. Even before she signed the register in the lobby, the Starbuck name had worked its magic. At her mention of a bath, the manager snapped his fingers and set his people running. By the time he'd personally escorted Jessie to her room, the tub was filled and steaming. Close by was a bottle of fine Möet champagne in a bucket of ice, a thin-stemmed crystal glass, and a copy of the *Jefferson Jimplecute*.

"A swallow of that would go real fine," Jessie sighed, "but not before this." Stepping out of her gown, she unhooked the cream-colored chemise underneath and let it fall in a froth about her ankles. As she crossed the room, gilt mirrors caught her naked image. The glass reflected a tall, slender-bodied woman with full, uptilted breasts tipped a dusky shade of rose. A tiny waist flowed to the curve of her hips past a perfectly flat belly to incredibly long legs. As she crossed the room, the mirrors caught a quick flash of color between her thighs—a delicate, silken touch of strawberry-gold.

Before she stepped in the tub, Jessie loosed a red garter holster on her thigh and laid it on a towel close at hand. Silver and ivory flashed from the small pistol inside. Wrapping a kerchief about her head, she sank gratefully into the water. A deep sigh escaped her lips as she closed her eyes. It was the first time she'd allowed herself to relax in two days. Even now, the strain was still there, the tension in every muscle and tendon refusing to let her go.

It had all happened so quickly.

Two weeks before, she and Ki had been in Fort Worth, the scene of the latest of the raiders' daring strikes. This time they'd hit a well-guarded train right in the yards, killed six men, and carried off a hundred thousand in gold. The robbery had taken less than eight full minutes. By the time the law arrived, there was nothing to see but corpses and a railway car opened up like a can of beans.

Then, four days later, they'd struck again, sending Jessie and Ki to the little town of Hope, in the southwest corner of Arkansas. The raid there was a near copy of the one in Fort

4

Worth. Twenty thousand in gold, and two men dead. The robbery was number seventeen, and the total take was now well over four million dollars. Over the past six months, the raiders had hit banks, trains, and freight offices in Texas, Louisiana, Missouri, and Arkansas. They struck with unerring accuracy and faultless timing, and the loot was always the same—gold, sometimes in coin, but usually in the form of small, easy-to-handle ingots. The robberies had another feature in common: nearly every one affected the Starbuck interests in one way or another.

Jessie knew exactly who was behind the raids. She had no proof and didn't need it. The outlaws were too polished, too perfect. They knew where the gold would be, and when, and likely how much. They were getting rich quick, and hurting the vast Starbuck empire in the bargain. Jessie's financial managers were burning the midnight oil, juggling funds and transferring accounts across the country. The word was already out: Starbuck is in trouble. People who did business with Jessie's various interests were beginning to balk. If Starbuck couldn't pay, then Starbuck credit would go next. And when that happened—

"It's them, all right," Jessie had told Ki. "It can't be anyone else."

"Most likely you are right," Ki said calmly.

"Most *likely!*" Jessie exploded. "Most likely frogs are green and rabbits jump. I *know* it's them, Ki!"

It has to be, she thought. *I can almost smell them.* Gently she kneaded sore muscles in her shoulders, the action raising the firm tips of her breasts above the water. Jessie knew her enemy well. She and Ki had met them head-on more times than she liked to remember. And before that, her father had fought them half his life. As a young man, Alex Starbuck had begun his prosperous career with a fleet of trading vessels to the Orient. There he'd come up against a wealthy Prussian business cartel. They were ruthless men, determined to make their fortunes at any cost. They struck out at Alex, and Alex struck back. Ships were hijacked and warehouses burned. It was a harsh, deadly game with no holds barred. Jessie's mother, Sarah, was murdered. And finally, Alex Starbuck himself was struck down by cartel assassins on his own Texas ranch, the Circle Star. Suddenly, Jessie found herself heiress to the vast Starbuck fortune—and the terrible legacy that went with it.

5

Not long after her father's death, she learned that the faceless men of the cartel were after more than the Starbuck holdings. Their ultimate aim was to undermine the economy of America itself, leaving the young United States open to exploitation and ultimate control by the only men in the world who held sufficient power and wealth—the members of the cartel.

A Western Union message had arrived while Jessie and Ki were still in Hope. On the surface, it was innocent enough—an advisory concerning bulk timber shipments from Jefferson to Fort Worth. Decoded, the innocuous words carried a far more portentous meaning:

WE HAVE EVIDENCE THAT STOLEN GOLD IS BEING FUNNELED TO AN AREA IN THE BIG THICKET. URGENTLY ADVISE YOU COME AT ONCE. TOBIAS R. PIKE, JEFFERSON, TEXAS.

"That doesn't make sense!" Jessie protested, slapping the message with her hand.

Ki's almond eyes stared past her. "Maybe it does," he answered. "The Thicket's a good place to hide."

"Sure, if you're an outlaw running from the sheriff. But hauling tons of gold in and out of that place? Why, Ki? Lord, gold's not worth a thing if you squirrel it away. I can think of a dozen better ways than that to carry it off. And so can the cartel. 'Cross Texas to Mexico, down the Red River to the Mississippi—"

Ki shrugged. "This Pike thinks you're wrong."

"Yes, he does," Jessie muttered, "which means I've got to find out why."

The next day, Ki journeyed to Shreveport to follow up the only lead they had, that several possible gang members had been spotted there the week before. Jessie finished up in Hope, and three days later caught the Texas & Pacific south from Texarkana. Ki would meet her when he was through, taking a river steamer north through the Big Cypress Bayou, to Caddo Lake and Jefferson.

Maybe he's on to something, thought Jessie. *Shreveport's more likely than the Thicket. You could get where you wanted to from there. Down the Red River to the Mississippi, and on to New Orleans. That makes a lot more sense . . .*

Jessie shook her head and stepped gingerly out of the tub. Choosing one of the Excelsior's oversized towels, she closed

6

her eyes and rubbed the smooth fabric over her body. The bath and the warm morning air made her sleepy. She opened her eyes and glanced longingly at the big cherrywood bed.

"No, damn it," she muttered half aloud, "a nap won't do, no matter how good it sounds." It was likely ten-thirty or later; she'd have to unpack, see if someone could press the wrinkles out of a dress, and get ready for Tobias R. Pike.

Pike puzzled her no end. From Hope, she'd wired one of her people in Galveston for his record. He was good—as sharp and competent a manager as you could ask. Yet there was something terribly wrong. He'd sent her an urgent message, then balked—turned right into a frightened mouse. Something had clearly scared the man badly. What? Jessie wondered. It had to be something pretty bad. Pike had fifteen years with the Starbuck interests. Now, in one morning, he'd made a fool of himself, risked his job in front of his boss. If a man would do that—

Jessie was deep in thought. It was a moment before it dawned on her that the door had opened silently behind her. She whirled about and froze, sucking in a breath and dropping her towel in the bargain.

"Wh-who are you?" she gasped. "Get the hell *out* of here, mister!"

The man stared, his features reddening. "Uh, sorry," he said quickly, "guess I got the wrong room."

"I *know* that, damn it—now turn around and go!"

"Yes'm, sorry." He half turned, pausing to let pale gray eyes trail over the curves of her body. "My God," he said in wonder, "you are the finest-looking woman I ever saw, and that's the truth—"

Jessie went to her knees, jerked the ivory-handled derringer out of her garter holster, and aimed it with both hands. "You better hope I am," she said darkly, "'cause I'm the last naked lady you're ever going to see!"

The man blinked, turned on his heel, and slammed the door behind him. Jessie let out a breath and came shakily to her feet. Lowering the weapon, she stared at the impassive face of the door. She could still feel the man's gray eyes, boldly caressing her flesh . . .

7

Chapter 2

"Guess you know the old Jay Gould story," said Pike. "'Bout everyone does. I can get the manager to show you the register if you like. Know him real personal, he won't mind at all."

"Thank you," said Jessie. "I know the story, Mr. Pike."

"Really something, isn't it?" He paused to chew a mouthful of food, then chase it with half a glass of wine. Somehow, Jessie noted irritably, Pike had recovered almost at once athe sight of the Excelsior's lavish menu. Jessie settled for cold beef and tomatoes, whil her portly manager ate his way through potatoes, greens, duck, and reast pork.

"He was right here, you know," Pike went on. "In this very hotel. Spoke to the man myself. Wanted to run the T&P through town. Folks here in Jefferson turned him down flat. Said, 'No, Mr. Gould, we've got steamboats here. What do we need a railroad for?'" Pike threw back his head and laughed. "Old Gould was fit to be tied. Signed the hotel register. January second, 1872, it was. Third name from the top, and it's still right there. Drew a little flyin' jaybird, then wrote out 'Gould.' And at the bottom of the page he added: 'End of Jefferson, Texas.' Said grass'd grow in the streets, and bats'd roost in the churches. Damn close to right he was, too. Oh, pardon my language, ma'am."

Jessie leaned forward across the table. "Mr. Pike," she said evenly, "I didn't come here about Jay Gould and the railroad. You sent me a very puzzling—a very *alarming* message. I would like to hear the rest of *that* story, and I'd like to hear it *now*."

"Well, uh—yes, by all means," Pike sputtered, dabbing a linen napkin at his face. He peered over his shoulder briefly, then faced Jessie again. "Few days before you got here," he said softly, "there was an Injun shot in a brawl. Down in Murder

8

Alley, on Line Street near the river. Name was Black Lizard, one of the old Caddos—not many of them around anymore. This particular Injun was a bad one, been in trouble before. Law got on the scene quick for a change, 'fore whoever did him in had time to rob him." Pike paused and raised a pudgy finger for effect. "Now, what this fellow had on him, Miss Starbuck, were six four-ounce ingots of twenty-four-karat gold. All of it ninety-seven-percent fine. And every single bar stamped with the Circle Star brand."

Jessie let out a breath. "Do you have those bars, Mr. Pike?"

"Not likely, I don't." Pike made a face. "They disappeared quick in a couple of lawmen's pockets. But the deputy who *told* me about 'em is a friend. Did a big favor for him once and knows I'd never let on to his boss. He wouldn't lie to me. Miss Starbuck. If he says it was Starbuck gold, then it was."

Jessie bit her lip in thought and squinted across the linen-topped tables to the curtained windows beyond. "And is that all? Do we know any more?"

"We do indeed," said Pike. "My friend, upon my urging, discovered a little more. This Caddo worked for a spell for one of the loggers. That's where the Thicket comes in. He hadn't been in town a day 'fore he was killed, but folks who ought to know said he came right from the Thicket and he was running plumb scared. He didn't mean to *stop* here, you see. He was just passing through, headed north."

Jessie nodded understanding. "And you think perhaps he stole the gold in the Thicket—"

"And whoever he stole it *from* caught up with him," Pike finished. For an instant, the fear he'd shown that morning touched his eyes again. "They were simply unlucky that the law happened to be close by. Otherwise we'd know nothing at all."

Jessie did a few quick figures in her head. "That's close to a thousand dollars in gold. Of course, he couldn't get that for it himself, and neither could whoever wanted him dead."

"What are you saying, Miss Starbuck?"

"Nothing," Jessie said with a shrug. "Just that it's not unusual for a man to steal gold and run—or for someone else to kill him for it. Still, Mr. Pike, I'm inclined to agree with you. The coincidence of Starbuck gold turning up at a time like this is too much to swallow. I'd guess the thief was killed because he knew where the gold came from—not because he had it."

9

Pike seemed pleased that his employer agreed. In celebration, he poured himself another generous glass of burgundy, shaking the bottle to get the last dark drops. "There's more, of course," he told her, downing the wine in a swallow. "I, ah—I've put in a great deal of time on this, Miss Starbuck. A great deal of time."

"I appreciate that," Jessie said without expression. "And of course that's no less than I'd expect from such an experienced and loyal manager as yourself."

"Well, yes, goes without saying." Pike flushed and cleared his throat.

"Now. You just said there's more. What is it that you have?"

Pike leaned forward, his black-agate eyes narrowed to slits. "Corroboration, Miss Starbuck. Cor-*rob*-oration." He thumped out the syllables on the table. "I did not let the matter lay with my knowledge of the Caddo and his ill-gotten gold. No, my dear lady, I did not. I sought *corroboration* and I found it. In the person of one James Cooper, who confirms the story entirely." Pike sat back and looked pleased.

"And this Cooper?" Jessie asked patiently. "Who is he and what does he know?" She was beginning to understand Tobias Pike. He had been a frightened man when they'd met, but part of his manner then was likely due to the time of day. Pike was a man who needed drink to keep going. He'd held off his morning libations to meet the boss with clean breath, and earned himself a good case of the shakes.

"James Cooper," Pike went on, "is an old and trusted employee of yours, Miss Starbuck. Family's worked for the Starbuck Steamship Company since, oh, a few years after the War. Very honest and dependable fellow, for a colored. I went straight to James, I did, soon as I learned about the Injun. James Cooper's family has lived in the Big Thicket more than forty years. James knows the place like the back of his hand." Pike leaned forward confidentially. "He didn't want to talk about it, Miss Starbuck. Likely wouldn't, to any other white man but me. And Cooper says there *is* something funny going in the Thicket. A big camp, deep in the worst part of the place. Lots of men going in and out by night. Most of 'em white, says James, but they've got some Caddos workin' with them."

Pike paused to let the words sink in. Jessie sipped her wine and set it down. "And Mr. Cooper would show us this place?"

"Absolutely. Of course, he'd have to be protected. Wouldn't want to risk his family's safety."

10

"And I wouldn't ask him to, of course, Mr. Pike, the sooner we get on to this, the better. I want to meet Mr. Cooper. I'll leave the arrangements and the security to you, and—"

"There's more," Pike interrupted. "Something that might help a great deal. James's third cousin, or uncle or whatever, is Jacob Mose."

"Who?" Jessie shook her head. "I don't know the name. Should I?

"If you lived in East Texas, you would, dear lady. Everybody here has heard of Jacob Mose, white and colored alike. He's sort of a legendary figure, a man the coloreds call on when they get in some kind of trouble. Of course, a lot of the stories about him are pure hogwash, to be sure. But he *is* a man with some power among his people." Pike cleared his throat. "In truth, one must admit the, ah—white man's justice does not always favor the coloreds. 'Course, most of the rascals deserve what they get, you understand."

"Yes," Jessie said dryly, "I understand the course of justice very well, Mr. Pike."

"At any rate, James couldn't say whether Jacob Mose would help. He's not all that fond of white folks. If his aid could be enlisted, however—and I'm not sayin' it could—"

"I guess we'll have to leave that to Mr. Cooper," said Jessie. She paused, brushed her hair off her shoulders, and looked at Pike. "I don't wish to embarrass you in any way," she said plainly, "but there's something I very much need to know. And I'm afraid I must insist you give me an honest and straightforward answer. This morning you did everything you could to avoid being seen with me. You haven't seen fit to tell me why, so I guess I have to ask. Perhaps you have a very good reason. If so, I'd like to hear it. Are you in danger because of what you've learned? If you are, I quite understand, Mr. Pike. It means I'm in danger myself. And if I am, I'd like to know it."

Pike flushed and instinctively reached for his glass. Finding it empty, he nervously tapped the table. "I, ah—apologize for my behavior," he said softly. "Truly, Miss Starbuck. Inexcusable. Yes, no question about it."

"That doesn't answer my question, though, does it?"

Pike frowned. "The answer, ma'am, as straightforward and honest as I can give it, is that I truly don't know." He looked right at her, and this time she knew she was seeing the real Tobias Pike. All the bluster and false courage were stripped

11

away. "Jefferson is a very fine town, Miss Starbuck, but there is an element here—riffraff, thieves. Since I—since I found out about the Injun—"

"You've felt as if someone's aware of what you know? Is that it?"

"Yes, yes, exactly," Pike said quickly. "Ma'am, I know my job and I don't mind saying I do it well. But I am—not a man of great courage, and I'm not ashamed to say it. This sort of thing is not to my liking at all. Still, I felt obliged, when this matter came to my attention—"

"You've done very well," Jessie said warmly. "I have an idea your information will prove most valuable indeed."

Pike brightened a little. "As you say, ma'am, that's my job, of course."

"And you don't *know* anyone's aware of the fact that you have the information you do. Sometimes our nerves play tricks on us, Mr. Pike."

"That's, ah—certainly true," Pike said dryly. Jessie could see he didn't believe that was so in the present case.

"What I'd suggest is that you get word to Mr. Cooper that I'd like very much to see him. That I would assure him that I—oh yes?"

Jessie turned as their waiter appeared at her shoulder. With a slight bow, he placed a bottle of Möet champagne in an iced silver bucket at her side. "From the gentleman over there," he said politely, nodding toward a corner of the room. "He trusts you'll accept this with his compliments." The waiter placed a white calling card on the table. Jessie picked it up and read the name on it: JEFFREY HAMILTON MORGAN, ESQ. Then she glanced curiously in the direction the waiter had pointed. A tall man in a well-tailored black suit and string tie nodded at her and smiled. Jessie felt her face color, and jerked back to face the waiter.

"You may tell Mr.—Mr. *Morgan* that I do *not* accept his gift," she said sharply. "That I—no, wait." Picking up the card, she glanced boldly in the man's direction, tore the card neatly in half, and dropped it in the bucket. "Now. And thank you for your trouble."

The waiter bowed and moved off. Jessie hid a smile behind her linen napkin. *Nervy son of a bitch, even remembered it was a Möet by my tub. Wonder when he found time to look at that?*

12

"My—my God," blurted Pike, "you don't—*know* that man, do you?"

Jessie frowned at Pike's suddenly stricken features. "No, not really. Should I? I gather that you do."

"He's one of them," Pike said intently. "The crowd I was talkin' about. Name's Black Jack Morgan. A gambler, and God knows what else. If anything crooked's going on in East Texas, you can bet Morgan's got a hand in it!"

"I'm not a bit surprised," said Jessie.

"What?"

"Nothing, Mr. Pike. If you're finished, why don't we leave? I need to drop by the Planter's Bank, and I'm sure you've got plenty to do."

"Yes, yes, by all means." Pike stood at once, clearly glad to be away. Jessie decided his first order of business would be several stiff belts to calm his nerves. She followed Pike into the lobby, keenly aware that the man named Morgan trailed her with his eyes.

Pike held the door to the street and let her pass. "I'll be— pleased to see you to the bank," he told her. "I mean, be glad to do that, Miss Starbuck, glad to do it."

"No, thank you," she replied. "I saw it this morning. Know right where it is."

Pike tried to hide his relief. "Well, as you wish, ma'am, as you wish."

Out of the corner of her eye, Jessie saw a big wagon loaded with blocks of ice. A dozen small boys shouted at the driver, begging for a free sliver to share. The teamster waved them off and shook his reins.

"You'll get word to James Cooper, then? I'll meet him wherever he wants."

"I'll find him," Pike assured her, "and I know a place to meet."

"Good. And thank you, Mr. Pike. You've done very well indeed."

"My pleasure, Miss Starbuck. My pleasure, indeed. I only wish I could ha— *Oh Jesus God, no!*"

Pike's face went slack with horror. Jessie turned and saw a dark-haired man step quickly from behind the ice wagon and jerk the shotgun to his shoulder. A cry stuck in her throat and she threw herself to the ground. White light exploded from the gun's twin barrels, a second thunderous roar following quickly

13

on the first. The blasts struck Pike full in the face, tearing his head nearly away, and hurling him through the Excelsior's large front window. Glass shattered and a woman shrieked. Jessie raised her head in time to see the killer turn and sprint rapidly down the street.

"Get down, damn it!" A strong hand pushed her roughly back. Three shots roared from a Colt only inches from her head. The man above her cursed and thrust the weapon under his coat. Lifting Jessie up, he rushed her quickly off the street and back into the lobby. Jessie stared and saw it was Morgan. She started to speak, then caught sight of Pike.

"Oh *God!*" She turned quickly away and clasped a hand to her mouth.

"Miss Starbuck," Morgan said quietly, "I think you and me could use a drink, and I'm not talkin' about French champagne . . ."

Chapter 3

Ki stood on the low afterdeck of the *Texas Star* as the big sternwheeler backpaddled laboriously to midriver. Dark water boiled under the hull, sucking up Red River silt from the bottom. Ki watched the tangled forest of masts, derricks, and high black smokestacks pass by. In a moment the boat was clear, and he could see the whole array of squat vessels crowding the Shreveport wharves. Nearly a dozen steamboats were nosed inshore, packed so tightly that a man could walk the Red River from the railyards clear to Travis Street without once wetting his boots. Waterfront smells hung on the humid air: woodsmoke, grease, raw stacked lumber, lard, and stiff hides.

The sharp blast of a whistle cut the morning. For an instant the deep drumming of the engines came nearly to a halt. The vessel drifted, the sternwheel stopped. Then the plank deck trembled and the *Texas Star* churned forward upstream.

Ki stood watching till Commerce Street and the wharves passed 'round the bend, then he made his way forward past the cargo and the boilers, under the high derricks. Climbing the short staircase, he paused on the hurricane deck, searching for his cabin. Several passengers stood looking over the river. Two portly gents in expensive, English-cut suits and planters' hats argued over the current price of cotton. Past them, keeping well to themselves, a man and a woman watched the shore. The man was somewhat older than his companion, as tall and proud as an aging pine. He was dressed in a tailored frock coat of finest blue cotton, and a red silk vest. Silver hair puffed from under a broad-brimmed Stetson. Ki nodded as he passed, and the man nodded back. The young woman by his side followed Ki a long moment with her eyes. She was a delicate,

15

slender beauty with hair the color of butter, a saucy little nose, and lips set in a pout. Startling blue eyes touched Ki, and roamed boldly over his body. Ki met her gaze, then regretfully turned away. She was trouble looking for someone to happen to, something he didn't need at the moment.

Turning to port, Ki passed one of the big twin stacks and walked aft. Number Three was more like a closet than a cabin. Inside, there was a barrel-backed chair, a basin, and a pitcher. On the wall hung half a mirror and a mounted kerosene lamp. Ki tossed his satchel on the plain wooden bed and heard it crackle. When he pressed the mattress with his hand, his suspicions were confirmed. The ticking was filled with cornhusks or straw—likely some of both.

A door slammed shut in the cabin next door, and a woman's high-pitched laughter reached Ki through the thin paneled walls. He wondered if it was the girl with the pouty mouth. Pausing before the mirror, he rubbed his jaw and decided he needed a shave. The thought brought a grin to his face.

You don't need a shave, he said to himself. *You're thinking about that girl.*

Ki was anything but vain about his appearance, but he was used to women's glances. Men often noticed the slight difference in his features, but women saw something more. The boldest of them studied him with open curiosity, wondering about the sharp planes of his cheeks, the sweep of raven hair that fell to his collar, and the brown, penetrating eyes that lifted slightly at the corners—this last, a gift from his Japanese mother. Those who were bolder still considered the lean, wiry frame beneath his clothing, and wondered what pleasures such a man might have to offer.

Ki straightened his tie over the pale blue cotton shirt, and ran a hand quickly over the wide lapels of his jacket. He longed to shed the stiff, confining clothes in favor of his accustomed loose-fitting apparel. Still, he mused, you couldn't travel the river looking more like a deckhand than a passenger.

Leaving the cabin again, he stepped outside and sniffed the air, wondering if the *Star* served breakfast. He'd grabbed up his belongings right at dawn, missing the morning meal. The *Texas Star* was building steam, the only vessel headed for Jefferson. Jessie would be surprised to see him so soon, but there was nothing to do in Shreveport. There were plenty of

16

disreputable characters in town, but none matched the gold raiders' descriptions. He hoped Jessie's trip had been more useful than his own.

The sharp blast of a whistle caught his attention. A large sternwheeler was headed downriver to the port the *Texas Star* had left behind. The *Star* answered the greeting with a quick blast of her own. Passengers waved and called to one another.

Ki stepped to the railing and squinted at the countryside to port. Already the last neat patches of furrowed ground had given way to tall trees and thick second growth. Climbing the shore was a bone-white tangle of dead trees, a jam over ten feet high. Ki knew such tangles were a constant Red River hazard. The ones you could see wouldn't hurt you, but a log lying just beneath the surface could rip out a boat's belly in an instant.

Leaving the railing, Ki moved down the narrow stairwell to the main deck below. Just as he reached the bottom, a dark figure came out of nowhere and raced by as Ki stepped aside. Three burly men ran by after the first. Two clutched short wooden clubs in their fists. The third was a thick-chested man the size of a bear. Heavy slabs of muscle threatened to burst his blue seaman's jacket. One ham-sized hand was doubled in a fist; the other gripped an ugly-looking blacksnake whip.

Ki glanced curiously after the group, then followed them aft past the boilers. Before he reached the open deck, a terrified yell reached his ears. An instant later he saw them. An angry black man struggled on the deck. One of the burly men sat solidly on his chest, pinning down his arms. The other squatted over his head, beating him methodically with a club. A man in a seaman's jacket stood calmly aside and grinned.

Ki didn't stop to ask the reason for the scene; the odds told him all he cared to know. Before the man could raise his weapon again, Ki ran forward and kicked him solidly in the chest. The fellow grunted and went sprawling. Ki grasped his companion by the collar, jerked him to his feet, and turned him around. The man blinked in surprise. Ki's right hand came up in a wedge, chopping short and fast like the blade of an ax. The blow took the man where his shoulder joined his neck. He staggered back numbly, pain contorting his features, then fell to the deck and screamed.

Ki sensed the man behind him, ducked and twisted aside,

17

and knew he was half a second late. The blacksnake whip lashed angrily about his legs. Ki stumbled, caught himself, and rolled. The leather coil snapped free. The big man smiled, snaked the whip along the deck, and lashed out again. Ki came to his feet and danced quickly aside. The blow stung his arm and tore his jacket. Before he could move again, leather sang in a whisper and caught him hard. Sharp pain lanced up his thigh and Ki gritted his teeth. The man was good. He'd seen a few men who could handle such a weapon. If you knew how to use the deadly leather, you could cut a man to ribbons, choose the spot you liked, and peel his flesh like a surgeon.

Ki saw his choices in an instant—turn and run, or get inside the man's reach, past the tip of the flail that could slice him up and kill him. For Ki, it was no choice at all. When the whip lashed out again he let it come, stepping back just enough to let leather slap the deck. As he'd guessed, the man took a quick step forward as he dragged the whip back for another blow. Ki moved forward in the same instant. The man leaped back and brought the leather down hard. The whip stung Ki's legs and ankles. Ignoring the sudden pain, he rolled in a ball and twisted, slamming his palms to the deck. The action brought his body off the ground, knees bunched nearly to his chest. The man was fast and saw it coming, but this time Ki was faster. His legs snapped out like pistons, his boots catching the man full in the belly. The man bellowed as tortured air left his lungs, and he sailed across the deck and hit the aft bulkhead hard. The whip went flying.

Ki was on him in an instant. An ordinary man would be out of the fight, but Ki knew this one wasn't finished. Even as he brought the firm wedge of his hand down hard, the seaman warded him off and lashed out, catching Ki's chest with his knee. Ki went after him, clutching at the man's sturdy legs. The seaman kicked free, turned, and faced him in a crouch. Pain twisted his heavy features. Tiny black eyes flared in anger, gauging the distance to the whip. Ki circled warily, giving himself room. The seaman jabbed out with his right and stepped quickly to the side. Ki watched the cords of muscle in the other's beefy neck. He knew the right was a feint, and let the big left hand brush his cheek. Before the man could step back, Ki landed three punishing blows to his face. The man staggered and spit blood.

18

Ki moved in relentlessly. His fists smashed again and again at the barrel neck, pummeled the heavy features. The man stumbled, but caught himself and swung blindly with his right. The blow surprised Ki and sent him reeling. The side of his face went numb. He shook his head to bring back feeling, wiped stinging sweat from his eyes. The seaman came at him, roaring like a cornered beast, his ruined face dark with blood. Ki sucked in a breath and raised his hands.

Enough is enough, he thought darkly. *This time, friend, you're going to—*

"Look out, mister—behind you!"

Ki caught the blur of motion to his left, ducked, and felt the club whisper past an inch from his ear. The black man came in fast, grabbed Ki's assailant in his arms, and kept going. Ki had no time at all for a second look. The seaman was on him again, big fists flailing the air. Ki twisted on his heels and thrust his feet at the other man's thigh. The blow staggered the man, who howled, then pulled himself erect and met Ki coming. Ki's stiffened left slashed him across the nose; his right came in fast and landed just above the temple. The seaman's eyes glazed. He stared straight ahead for half a second, then dropped to the deck and didn't move.

Ki turned swiftly. The black man stood above a silent, prone figure. Fists still curled in knots, he grinned broadly at Ki. Ki returned the greeting. The first man Ki had felled still groaned in pain on the deck. The black man had soundly whipped the second.

"I assume these boys aren't friends of yours," Ki said.

The black man laughed. "Ain't none of 'em friends of mine, mister. That fella there you whupped, he's the meanest bastard ever come down the river."

"Not now he's not."

"He wakes up, you and me both gonna—" The man stopped, looked up sharply and backed off.

Ki turned to face the man striding toward them. He was a gaunt, sharp-nosed man with angry red features and a mane of white hair. A river captain's peaked cap topped his head, and tarnished gold buttons dotted his dark blue coat. He stopped before Ki and let his eyes sweep the carnage on the deck.

"What the hell happened here, mister?" he demanded. "I want an answer, and I'll have it fast!"

19

Ki wiped dirt off his face. "These three men were beating up that one over there," he explained. "I joined in to lend a hand."

The captain frowned past Ki. "Beatin' up who? You mean the nigger?"

Ki looked straight at him. "I mean the man over there. The only one standing besides us."

For the first time, Ki noticed that several crewmen had moved up close behind the captain. Curious passengers lined the upper deck, staring in awe at the sight below.

"And you figured that was your business, now did you?"

"Yes. It was my business. There were three of them. I didn't like the odds."

The captain's face went dark. "Mister, you are a *passenger* on this vessel. That means you get to ride, eat, sleep, and look at the scenery all you please. It *don't* mean interfering with the runnin' of this boat."

"No. You don't understand. It has nothing to do with the boat. Those three were beating up another man. They would have killed him, Captain, if—"

"All of which is none of your goddamned business if they did!" Water-blue eyes stabbed Ki and held him. "The man you tore up there is my first mate, mister. Keepin' the crew in line's what he gets paid to do. If he was doing what you say, I figure he had a reason."

"Cap'n, I wasn't doing nothin' at all," the black man protested. "Mr. Jake there, he and them others—"

"Shut up, boy!" the captain roared. "Damn it, I didn't ask you." He raised a trembling finger and pointed forward. "Get up where you belong. I'll deal with you later!"

"Stay where you are," Ki said softly. His dark eyes never left the captain's. "Sir, what do you intend to do with that man?"

"Whatever the hell I want to do, friend. Now you get your ass *off* the afterdeck."

"No. I don't think so," said Ki.

The captain stared, as if he couldn't believe what he was hearing. "Howie! Get somebody to haul Chad and Joe back, and get Jake to his cabin. Lewis, get over here."

A tall seaman with pale features and a slack-jawed smile came quickly to his side. The captain's hand snaked to the man's belt, drew a long Smith & Wesson, and aimed it directly

20

at Ki's belly. "Get this *gentleman's* baggage," he said evenly, "and tell the wheelhouse to heave to around the bend." He grinned nastily at Ki. "Afraid we made a little mistake, mister. Your cabin ain't available anymore."

"Now look!" Ki protested.

The hammer clicked back on the pistol. "We don't have a lot of room on the *Texas Star* for niggers," the captain said quietly. "Black ones, or yellow ones neither."

Chapter 4

Ki stood on a sandbar and watched until the *Texas Star* chugged around the bend. Before the big sternwheeler disappeared, the girl with the butter-colored hair waved goodbye. Ki didn't bother to wave back. A swarm of angry gnats circled his head. His boots were filling with water, and the sun turned the river to hot brass.

"Mister, I'm real sorry I caused you all this trouble. Real sorry, sir."

"I'm not a mister or a sir," Ki said evenly, "and you've got nothing to be sorry about." He grinned then, and offered his hand. "My name's Ki, what's yours?"

The black man accepted his grip. "I'm Silas. Silas Johnson, Mr. Ki. I—" Silas caught himself and shook his head. "Sorry. Misterin' folks is a hard habit to break."

"I guess," said Ki. "But the War's been over some while, Silas. Time some of those habits got broken."

"Uh-huh." Silas gave him a searching look. "You in East `exas, friend. Black folks goin' to be niggers a *long* time 'round ..re."

Ki could think of no answer for that. He followed Silas through the shallows and up the bank to firmer ground. Great cypresses spread their searching roots into the river. A moccasin nearly as thick as Ki's arm showed its pale white belly and slid lazily into the water. Only a few yards back from the river, the light changed abruptly from searing white to a soft, misty gray-green. Heavy Spanish moss bearded the trees, and lush ferns covered the ground.

"You have any idea where we are?" asked Ki, "or where we ought to be going?"

"Know right where we are," said Silas. "Off the Red River, couple of miles into Big Cypress Bayou. Lake Caddo's north-

22

west, and Jefferson's on the ass-end of that." He looked at Ki and grinned. "Ain't exactly what you was asking, though, is it? 'Less you want to hike south and start over, we be following the shore to Brown's Landing. Ain't more'n two or three miles, I don't reckon."

"And we can get a boat there?"

Silas grinned again. "Lot less of a boat, but the folks there is better'n what we left."

"I'm agreeable to that," said Ki.

The two miles north seemed longer than Ki figured they should be. Dry ground was hard to find, and though Silas knew the country fairly well, the pair had to backtrack more than once.

Ki had changed to more comfortable clothing, trading his traveling wear for loose-fitting cotton trousers and a shirt, and rope-soled slippers. He liked the feel of his worn leather vest, but the day was too steamy for that. Lifting a pair of razor-edged *shuriken* throwing stars from his vest, he dropped them in his pants pocket and put the vest away. Before he closed the satchel, he slid the slim *tanto* blade and its lacquered sheath in the waist of his pants, and covered it with his shirt.

Ki knew Silas Johnson had glimpsed his weapons, but the man made a show of looking away, telling Ki plainly that he knew how to mind his own business. Ki instinctively liked his new companion. Silas had a gentle, easygoing manner, a habit of pausing and looking about, then moving off slowly on the path he'd chosen to follow. His engaging smile and patient brown eyes matched the tall, gaunt figure, spare features, and hollowed cheeks. On the surface, he seemed the last man on earth who'd be a danger to another. Ki, though, had seen the man in action, the quick spark of fury in his eyes, the dark corded muscles that knew how to lash out and stop a man cold. Silas was strong, and he was fast. For good reason, he kept those qualities to himself unless he had to bring them to bear.

For nearly an hour, Silas led Ki beside the bayou, under tall pines and thick-trunked oaks. Finally he stopped and wiped sweat from his brow.

"Be a little piece yet," he said. "Gettin' somewhere ain't real quick around here. We can get something to drink at the landing. Don't trust the water here. You can find yourself a fever without trying."

"I can wait," said Ki.

23

Silas raised an appraising brow. "Yeah, I guess maybe you can." He thought a long moment, then nodded. "I'm grateful for what you done back there. You brought yourself into my trouble. Ain't many men would."

"Three's about all any one man ought to have to handle."

"Ain't that the truth." Silas shook his head. "You know *why* they was tryin' to kill me? Wasn't just no roughin' up, it was some more'n that. Thing is, you see, I can read. And write a little, too. Mr. Jake, he's the mate—the fella you cut up bad? He don't like uppity niggers too much. Made the mistake of lettin' him see I know my letters."

Ki stared. "They were going to kill you for that?"

"Hell," Silas said soberly, "man like that'd do it for a whole lot less." He looked away and squinted at the shadowy path ahead. "See, there ain't but a few colored deckhands can read any at all. What the boss man does is stick playing cards on boxes and barrels—show the hands what they supposed to unload where. Like, Marshall's the king of diamonds, Longview's the ace of hearts, and ol' Jefferson's the king of spades." Silas stopped and grinned. "'Stead of being dumb, I plumb forgot. Mr. Jake seen me readin' one of the crates, and that's when the cat's fur flew."

Ki started to speak, then swallowed his anger. Silas caught his expression. "Best be going, I guess. Landing won't get no closer, you and me standing here."

At first sight, Ki thought the *Annie B*. had probably sunk and taken root in the muddy landing. A longer study showed him the boat was sound, or likely sound enough, though a good coat of paint would do wonders. It was a small sternwheeler, less than half the size of the *Texas Star*. None of the riverboats sat more than a yard above the water, and this one didn't measure up even to that. Ki decided the shallow draft helped the illusion that the vessel was nearly ready for the bottom.

Silas read the concern in his features and showed Ki a broad grin. "Told you it wasn't the *Robert E. Lee*, now didn't I?"

"That's what you said, and you were right. It's not even close."

"Get us upriver, and that's what counts. Been makin' this run a good thirty years."

"I'd have guessed sixty."

Silas laughed, and led them out of the trees into the clearing.

24

Brown's Landing was a patch of dappled water, a small inlet choked with water lilies. A narrow plank wharf buffered the ancient vessel from the shore. Back in the trees, on slightly higher ground, Ki spotted a rough-timbered shack on stilts. A tin-pipe chimney poked through the roof, and the smell of fresh coffee was heavy on the air. Silas walked a few steps closer to the house, then stopped, raising a hand in warning. An instant later, a heavyset black man stepped from behind a tree, brought a shotgun to his waist, and clicked back the hammer.

"Now, what's your business here, gennulmens?" he said quietly. "Let me hear you talkin' real quick." He was a big man, well over six feet tall. Solid slabs of muscle banded his broad bare shoulders and thick neck. His chest threatened to burst the bib overalls that stretched across his frame.

"It's me, Mr. Clay, you remember?" said Silas. "Silas Johnson. I come by here a couple times last year with your brother."

"You mean Josh?"

"No, sir. Who I mean is Henry."

"Uh-huh. An' how's Henry doing? You see him lately, have you?"

Silas let out a breath. "Mr. Clay, your brother Henry's dead. I reckon you know he is."

"Yeah. Reckon maybe I do." The muzzle of the weapon didn't waver. "An' who you got with you, Silas Johnson? Ain't never seen *him.*"

Before Silas could answer, the door of the shack opened and a girl walked toward them through the trees. Ki watched her come out of shadow into the sun, and felt his pulse quicken. She was a tall, rangy girl dressed in tight, faded denims and a worn cotton shirt. A broad snakeskin belt with a tarnished brass buckle cinched an impossibly tiny waist. The waist curved gently into high, pointy breasts that flared boldly below her open collar. Ki found it a pleasure to watch her walk. She moved barefooted on long and slender legs, covering the ground with the easy grace of a cat. She held her back straight and let her arms hang loose. All the motion in her body seemed to flow from some well-oiled machinery in her thighs. There was an aura of pride about her that intrigued him. She was a back-woods girl, but she walked with the calm assurance of a queen.

"It's all right, Charlie." She stopped beside the big man and laid a small hand upon his arm. "I remember Silas, too." She studied Ki's companion, a sparkle of amusement in her eyes.

25

"What you and your friend been doin' all morning, wrestling bull 'gators? Lord, man, you look beat on a rock and hung out to dry." Ki liked her voice. It was a soft, lazy drawl spiced with a touch of mischief.

"Somethin' close to it," grinned Silas. "We had us kind of a time, Miss Annie." Silas quickly explained what had happened aboard the *Texas Star,* and why he and Ki were walking instead of riding. For the first time, the girl turned her attention to Ki. The sudden gaze startled him, stirring deep emotions he couldn't name. Her eyes were wide-set, an intense shade of blue as dark as deep water. The pupils were half hidden, masked by lashes as black and thick as the tumble of hair that framed her face.

"You're welcome here," she said simply. "If you can pay your passage, fine. If you can't, you can lend me a hand. I've damn little business, but what's here is heavy, and there's no one to do it but me and Mr. Clay. We'll be stokin' up 'bout four, and leaving when the day cools off." The lazy eyes flickered, and she gave Ki a long, appraising glance. "By damn, I wish I'd been a bird. Would've given five dollars to see Jake Marshall lose a fight." Her full lips curved in a smile, then she turned to the big man beside her. "Put that shooter away and get moving, Mr. Clay. Let's see if that boiler's going to blow or make steam."

Ki could easily have paid the low passage for both himself and Silas Johnson, but it was clear that the girl needed strong hands and backs nearly as much as she needed money. Hanging his shirt on a limb, he joined Silas and Charlie Clay loading dockside cargo aboard the *Annie B*. There was no more time to talk to the girl, but that didn't stop him from looking. Once or twice, he was certain she glanced his way. But with the dark and lazy eyes that looked everywhere at once—and nowhere at all—how the hell could he tell?

"Does she run this outfit herself?" he asked Silas. "Just her and Charlie?"

"Has now for 'bout five years. Her pa, old Amos Brown, run it 'fore that. Since the fifties or so, I reckon. She don't make much. But she don't quit, neither."

Ki helped Silas lift the last heavy kegs aboard the *Annie B.*, then stopped and rubbed the ache out of his back. Glancing up, he saw the girl on the upper deck, moving hurriedly for-

26

ward. The sun touched her unblemished flesh and turned it gold. An extra button on her shirt had worked loose, and bright beads of moisture glistened in the cleft between her breasts.

Ki said under his breath, "The way that lady walks ought to be against the law."

Silas caught his muttering and grinned. "Likely is, somewhere, don't you reckon?"

Chapter 5

Ki guessed it was after six, probably close to seven. A moment before, the bearded trees and marshy islands passing by had caught the muted reds and golds of evening light. Then, in only an instant, darkness swept in and clothed the bayou in murky shadow. Charlie Clay and Silas got the lights going quickly aboard the *Annie B*. Pine knots burned in metal drums fore and aft, and amidships along the shallow decks. High atop the vessel were large oil lamps with metal reflectors and colored glass—red for larboard and green for starboard.

The lights didn't relieve Ki at all. Another boat could see them clearly enough, but he couldn't imagine how the lights helped the vessel find her way. Only yards ahead of the *Annie B.*'s bow, the water was pitch black. One big snag you couldn't see, a jam that hadn't been there the trip before...

Charlie Clay greeted his question with open scorn. "A man don't have to *see* the river," he told Ki. "Man either knows it or he don't." And that, plainly, was that.

Moving aft past the cargo and the wheezing, thumping engines, Ki climbed the stairwell to the wheelhouse perched on the upper deck. The girl looked over her shoulder and saw him, then turned back to the wheel.

"Permission to come aboard," said Ki. "Uh, is that the way you say it?"

Annie gave him a throaty laugh. "No, Ki, that is *not* the way you say it. You're already aboard, looks to me. Thing you need to say is, 'Permission to come topside, Captain.' Only you're already up there, too."

"Oh." Ki pretended to back off. "Guess I better go down and start over."

"Just get in the wheelhouse," she said, grinning, "and stop distracting the captain."

28

"Aye-aye, ma'am." Ki shot her a half-salute and stepped in. The little box atop the vessel was hardly big enough for two. As he ducked his head through the door, his shoulder brushed lightly against her cheek.

"Oh!" The girl started, the sleepy eyes going wide for just an instant. Color rushed to her cheeks and she looked quickly away. "Not—not much room in here, I guess. Doesn't take but one to steer."

"No. I guess it doesn't." Ki's throat was suddenly dry. He knew what had surprised her, for he'd felt the same sensation. When they touched, it seemed as if they brushed each other with fire. The heat of her flesh raced through him and brought every nerve alive.

"Have you—have you been on a sternwheeler before? Well, hell, of course you have." She gave a quick little laugh. "Just got kicked off of one, didn't you?"

"I've been on the Missouri. And the Mississippi too."

"Yeah, so have I. Once." Annie sighed. "That's *real* river-boatin', you know? This isn't much. Not anymore. But it's all we got left. Can't even get up the bayou to Jefferson anymore, 'cept this time of year, in the spring, when the floods upriver raise the water. You know 'bout that or not?"

"No. No, I don't." Ki watched the pulse in her throat, keenly aware of the musky scent of her body. He saw her catch her breath, and knew she felt his eyes.

"The—the Great Raft," she said quickly. "You heard about it, I reckon. Used to jam the Red for near two hundred miles. Been going on as long as anyone can remember. Backed up and turned hundreds of thousands of acres into bayou and swamp. Ol' Captain Shreve, the one they named the town after, he cleared the Raft 'bout fifty years ago and opened trade a thousand miles upriver. Only the Raft started formin' again fast, backing water clear into Cypress Bayou—where we are right now. Let the steamboats through to Caddo and Jefferson, and started things happening." She shook her head and sighed. "Lord God, my pa used to have a dozen boats on the river. We had one of those big white houses in Jefferson. And I had me a pony, I remember. Should have seen the town then. Wasn't anything like it anywhere in Texas. There was fifteen steamboats at a time, tied up night and day. Travelin' clear down the Red to the Muddy and New Orleans. *The Danube, Red Cloud, Bessie Warren.* I can't even remember 'em all . . ."

29

The girl's voice trailed off. Ki knew the rest of the story. Engineers had blasted the Raft again in '73, and all but killed steamboat traffic to Jefferson. A year after that, Jay Gould ran his railroad past the town and left it high and dry.

"It isn't just here," he said gently. "The Missouri's not much anymore, and I don't guess the Mississippi will last, either. It's a railroad country now."

"Yeah, but I don't have to like it," she said tightly. He was standing close behind her, close enough to smell her hair. She knew he was there, and didn't move away.

"Annie, how long can you keep this up? I mean, you can't just—" He checked himself. "Sorry. Guess that's none of my business."

"No, that's all right—really. And the answer is, I'm damned if I know. Long as I can, I guess. Don't know anything else. Don't much *want* to, either."

"I can understand that."

"Wouldn't know how to act, away from the river."

"That's not true at all . . ."

"What? Why do you say that?"

Ki slid his hands along her arms and gripped her shoulders. Annie gasped, then gently relaxed against him. "I said it because I think you're a woman who'll end up on her feet wherever you are. Here on the river or anywhere else."

"And—and just what kind of a woman you think I am?" Ki caught the slight quiver in her voice. "I'm—I'm not even sure myself. I—"

Ki turned her quickly about to face him. With a sigh, she went suddenly limp against him, lazy eyes closed, full lips moist and nearly touching his own. Ki moved his hands to her waist and pulled her against him.

"Oh Lord," she moaned, "you don't know how much I— damn, what am I *doing!*" Her eyes went wide and she pushed him firmly away. Turning back to the wheel, she squinted anxiously over the bayou and brought the boat quickly to starboard.

"Everything all right?"

"It is now." She gave him a rueful grin. "Talk about distractin' the captain—" Leaning out the side window, she shouted down below. "Mr. Clay! I need you up here now. Right smart, Mr. Clay!"

In an instant the big man was scrambling up the stairs and

30

lumbering like a bull across the deck.

"Take the wheel, Mr. Clay," Annie said primly. "I'll be down below if you need me. Only don't." Without another glance, she shook black hair over her shoulder and pranced quickly toward the stairs. Big Charlie Clay gave Ki a dark scowl. Ki beat a hasty retreat.

She was waiting on the port side forward, her cabin door open. Pulling Ki inside, she shut the door and leaned back against it, breathless.

"Oh Lordy," she laughed, "I don't think I did that well at all, did I? Charlie's looked after me since I was born, and he still thinks I'm a little girl."

"He doesn't think I'm a little boy," said Ki.

Annie stood straight, took a deep breath, and came to him. Locking her hands loosely about his neck, she shook her head in wonder. "God, who are you? I don't even *know* you and I—I don't know you, but I do." She paused, and her dark, lazy eyes stared desperately into his. "When it happened up there, when you touched me—"

"I know. It just happened. I don't know why, but it did."

"I haven't known a lot of men, Ki. I mean—not real close. Haven't been many I *wanted* to know. I know *you*, though, and that's kinda scary. I never saw you before today, and I've known you forever. Just touchin' you now, being this close—" Tears welled up in her eyes and she buried her head in his shoulder. "Oh, Ki," she cried out, "I know you've loved me before. I don't know where or who I was then, but it's so. Love me again, Ki, please! *Love me good, right now!*"

Ki gently kissed the sweet-salty tears from her cheeks, ran his hands softly over the raven tumble of hair. Annie molded her body to his. Her breath came in rapid bursts of heat against his throat. Ki slid his hands down the small of her back, past the tiny waist to the swell of her hips.

Ki grasped the slender circle of her waist and pulled her hard against him. Annie's neck snapped back and her mouth fell open. Tiny pearls of moisture peppered her brow. Her breasts threatened to poke through the fabric of her shirt; her body lashed wildly against his own with a fury she couldn't control.

Suddenly, Annie's honeyed skin flushed with heat. A ragged cry escaped her throat, and her body went rigid. The sweet joy of release coursed through her slender form. She sucked in a

31

breath and sagged limply in his arms.

Ki lifted and carried her to the small bed in the corner, and laid her down gently.

Strong little hands came up to pull him hungrily down to her. The softness of her lips met his, and she let the tip of her tongue flick rapidly into his mouth. Ki trailed his fingers past the hollows of her cheeks to the tangle of her hair. His mouth slid from her lips to the tip of her nose, past feathery lashes to her ears and the warmth of her neck. Annie sighed and closed her eyes.

Ki pulled away a moment and watched her, marveling at the sight of her slender figure. A kerosene lamp burned low in a bracket on the wall. The light touched her flesh and turned it the color of gold. Once more he was struck by the haunting memory that this had all happened before, that they'd loved each other, held each other close in another time and place. There was room for such ideas in his Oriental heritage. His samurai master, Hirata, had taught him that each single being travels again and again through life, and Ki believed it might be so. If it was, he was certain this girl had been a part of his existence before, perhaps many times.

"I know what you're thinking," she whispered.

"Yes. I know that you do."

"I'm glad, Ki. I don't pretend to understand it, but I'm glad I found you again."

He bent to take her in his arms, but she wriggled gently free, slid out of his reach, and came to her feet. "Just sit right still and watch," she said softly.

Moving around the bed, she stopped before him and grinned. One lazy eye was shadowed in a veil of coal-black hair. Without looking away, she rested her hands on her thighs, moved them provocatively past her belly and her waist until they cupped the swell of her breasts. Annie bit her lip and closed her eyes. Her hands kneaded the firm mounds of flesh, the tips of her fingers coming to rest on the hard little nubs that pressed against her shirt.

"Want to see any more?" she teased. "Or is that 'bout enough?"

"I, uh—guess that's plenty," Ki said dryly.

"Liar." Annie shot him a wicked grin and loosed the buttons of her shirt. When she was done, her hands slid past the column of her throat to let the shirt slip past her shoulders.

32

Ki sucked in a breath. Her breasts were as firm as a very young girl's, set wide apart and high. The taut, creamy globes flipped up abruptly into proud, saucy little nipples tipped a dusky shade of coral. Annie bit her lip, unclasped the brass buckle of her snakeskin belt, and undid the buttons of her tight denim pants. For an instant she stood before him, the faded garment clinging to the high, sweet curves of her hips, the flat vee of her belly naked to his eyes. Then, easing her hands beneath the cloth, she slid the denims down her legs and quickly kicked them free.

Ki stared, and felt himself harden even more against his trousers. Annie was more breathtaking than he'd imagined. Her body was lean and lanky, the firm and slender form made of velvet-soft curves and lazy angles. The narrow waist flared to the bones of her hips, then swept in hollowed shadow to the flat plane of her belly and the proud silken mound just below. Her long, tapered legs seemed to go on forever. Ki followed the lovely lines down to delicately slim ankles and tiny bare feet.

"My God," he breathed, "you are—something to see, lady."

"Like it, do you?" she asked softly.

"You know I do, Annie."

"It's all yours," she whispered. "Take what you like, Ki. I want you to love me all over, any way you like. Taste my nipples and make them hard, put your—put your fingers deep, deep inside me and—oh, *yes!*"

Annie shrieked and flailed her long legs as Ki swept her up and carried her back to the bed. She pulled him down upon her and they landed together in a tangle. Annie wrapped her legs about him to hold him down, but Ki sprang free, came to his feet, and ripped his shirt over his head, then kicked his trousers away.

Annie sat up straight and stared at his rigid member. "Come here quickly, please!" she begged breathlessly.

Ki stood beside her bed and grinned. "We've got plenty of time, Captain. Unless you'd rather go topside and do a little steering."

"Oh, I'm going to do me some *steering*, all right," she said darkly. "You just watch and see if I don't!" Before Ki could back away, one lean hand snaked out and circled his erection. Annie pulled him firmly to her, scissoring her legs tightly about his waist. Ki grabbed her arms and stretched them wide, pinning

33

her to the bed. Annie cried out as his mouth found her breasts. He drew the firm nipples into his mouth, relishing the musky taste, the lovely pliant flesh against his tongue. Annie groaned and writhed beneath him. Ki let loose her arms, and she snaked her hands quickly past his waist to grasp his hardness. Her fingers worked eagerly at his manhood to bring him closer. A cry stuck in her throat as she thrust him into her warmth.

Ki felt the moist and honeyed flesh close hungrily about him. The fragrant scent of her desires assailed his senses. Annie thrust joyously against him, her slender legs pounding the small of his back. Ki plunged himself inside her again and again. With each new stroke, the girl caressed his swelling member with velvet flesh. The heart of her pleasure tightened about him, teasing him closer and closer to sweet release.

"Take me now," Annie cried hoarsely. *"Take everything I have!"*

Once more, Ki drove deeply into the furnace between her thighs. Annie's slender body held him fiercely in its grip. Her neck arched back, the dark and lazy eyes squeezed shut. Her mouth opened wide to take the hard thrust of his tongue. Ki reached down and gripped the firm flesh of her bottom. Annie gasped and arched her back off the bed. Rigid nipples teased his mouth; a bright rivulet of sweat puddled in the hollow of her belly.

Ki thrust harder and harder, slamming her body against the bed. Suddenly, Annie shuddered and went rigid. Ki felt her body tremble, felt his hardness swell inside her.

Annie screamed . . .

The flesh of her loins convulsed about his erection, triggering explosions in them both that sent them soaring to delicious heights of pleasure.

Annie sighed and went limp beneath him. Ki held her close, cradling her head in the hollow of his arms.

"Oh, Ki," she whispered softly, "that was—damn, I don't know what!" She slid out of his grip, turned and folded her arms over his chest, and stared down into his eyes. "It's good to love you again. It truly is."

"Yes, it is, Annie. Very, very good."

"How long you figure it's been?"

"I don't know. I only know that it's so."

She grinned, and the lazy blue eyes flashed with mischief. "I can tell you one thing, mister. It isn't going to be that long again."

34

Ki touched the tip of her nose. "And just how long do you think it will be?"

Annie cocked her head and listened. "Charlie Clay's bringing us into Caddo Lake. We left the bayou a little spell back."

"Now how do you know that?"

"We captains have got a feel for things, friend."

"I know. I felt some of them a minute ago."

"You did, huh?" Annie grinned and kissed him soundly. "Well, lean back, Ki, 'cause you've got a lot more feelin' to go. We don't hit Jefferson till morning, and you're going to be plumb busy till then."

Chapter 6

Black Jack Morgan led her quickly past the carnage in the lobby to a far corner of the Excelsior's dining room. Jessie was too shaken to argue. Morgan hailed a waiter and ordered whiskey for himself and brandy for her. When the drinks came, Jessie downed hers at once. The potion set a fire in her belly, and sent the liquid warmth to every part of her body.

Morgan watched her with concern. "You all right? That's a pretty stiff drink for one swallow."

"I guess maybe it is." The brandy's heat flushed her face. "It was your idea, remember? You said I needed a drink." She sat back limply in her chair. "Lord, you were right, too. All I've got to do now is keep it down!"

Morgan nodded and sipped his whiskey. "The law'll want to see you, soon as they get to thinkin' straight. I figure it'll take a while to find you back here. Give you a chance to catch your breath."

"You've had some experience in that, have you, Mr. Morgan?"

"What's that?"

"Avoiding talks with the law. From what I hear—" Jessie bit off her words. "Hell, I'm sorry. I had no business saying that. I'm grateful for what you did. I'm not thinking too straight at the moment."

Morgan grinned. "No problem, Miss Starbuck. I owe you an apology, too. That makes us even." Jessie flushed in spite of herself. She couldn't forget the way his steel-gray eyes had swept boldly over every inch of her naked body.

"I'm sorry," he said plainly. "I really did get the wrong room. There was a poker game next door, and—"

"I believe you, Mr. Morgan."

Morgan drew a cheroot from his vest, studied it critically,

36

and put it back. "The business that happened out there—maybe you don't want to talk about it now. If you don't, that's your concern. If I can be of any help—"

"No. I'm all right now." She looked curiously at the lean, sharp-planed features, the strong, slightly crooked nose and the firm line of his jaw. He had the look of a man who'd never let his face betray his hand. Tobias Pike had hinted that Morgan was a great deal more than just a gambler, and Jessie couldn't say he was wrong. If Morgan was involved with some of Jefferson's shady citizens, the cool gray eyes would never betray it.

"I do mean that," Morgan repeated. "If I can be of any service at all."

"Seems to me you already have been," said Jessie. "More than enough, Mr. Morgan."

The gambler waved her off. "No more than anyone else would have done, Miss Starbuck. I was there, that's all." He sipped his drink and looked at Jessie without expression. "Any reason you figure someone'd do a thing like that?"

Jessie matched his look with her own. "To Mr. Pike? Why, I haven't the slightest idea. Pike was my employee, but I didn't exactly know him. Not until today. Obviously someone in town knew him a lot better."

Morgan's brow arched a good quarter-inch, but he didn't press the question.

"You live here and I don't," Jessie said. "Did you know him at all?"

"Some. And I don't exactly live here, Miss Starbuck. I'm a gambler by profession, and gamblers don't settle too long in one place."

"So I understand."

"I *did* know him, though. Pike and I didn't run in the same pack, but I've seen him once or twice." Morgan paused for just an instant. "I know he worked for you. And so does everyone else."

Jessie came alert. "And what's that supposed to mean?"

"What? That Pike worked for you? Nothing special, why?"

"The way you said it, I thought different."

"Ah, I see." Morgan nodded in understanding. "You think maybe the fact that he worked for you *did* have something to do with his death."

"I didn't say anything of the sort!" Jessie's green eyes flashed

37

in irritation. Damn him, he'd turned her question around, put *her* in the hole she'd been digging for *him*. "If someone didn't like the Starbuck name, they should've shot *me*, Mr. Morgan. I'm a good deal closer to it than Pike was. That fellow with the shotgun had his chance. He'd could hardly have missed."

"Yeah, I kinda noticed that myself." Morgan gave her a thoughtful look. "You care for another brandy?"

"No, I'm—just fine."

"Look, Miss Starbuck, if I said something I shouldn't—"

"Now why would you think that?"

"Well," Morgan said absently, "maybe 'cause you been tryin' to tie that napkin in a knot for the last couple of minutes. I kinda thought—"

"Well, *don't* think, Mr. Morgan." Jessie refused to show her anger. "What's *wrong* with me, if anything is, ought to be plain enough. Seeing a man get his head blown off isn't what I do every afternoon."

Morgan winced. "Damn it all, I didn't mean to ask a bunch of fool questions. You're right. It's not my business at all. I'm sorry. Really."

"Your apology is accepted."

Morgan forced a grin. "I think we're in a rut, Miss Starbuck. We've got more apologies between us than the Caddo's got snakes."

"I guess maybe we do," Jessie agreed.

Morgan brightened. "Tell you what. Let's put all the apologies aside and start over. If you're feeling up to it, I'd be honored to buy you supper this evening." He held up a hand before she could protest. "You don't have to answer now. And if you accept, I promise we'll dine someplace far from the Excelsior Hotel."

Jessie laughed. "If I *did* accept, that'd certainly be a condition, Mr. Morgan. Only I don't really think right now I could—" Jessie stopped, stared past his shoulder, and came to her feet. *"Ki!* Oh, Lord, am I ever glad to see you!"

Morgan turned curiously as Ki strode across the room to their table. He was dressed in faded cotton garments that looked quite a bit the worse for wear. One cheek was badly bruised, and there was a wicked welt on his neck.

Jessie gave him a hug and pecked his cheek, then held him away and frowned. "Uh-oh. What's the other fellow look like?"

"Worse, I'm pleased to say." He glanced past her at Black Jack Morgan.

38

"Oh, Ki, this is Mr. Morgan. Ki is an associate of mine, and a friend."

"Jeffrey Morgan." The gambler stood and squeezed Ki's hand.

"A pleasure, sir," Ki said, nodding.

Morgan looked at Jessie. "I'll leave you two to your business, Miss Starbuck. Hope to see you later. And you too, sir."

"My thanks again," Jessie said warmly. "I'm very grateful, really."

Morgan nodded and hurried off. Ki followed him warily with his eyes. "Who's that?" he asked.

"I'm not quite sure," Jessie said distantly. "That's a very good question." Her face brightened again. "Now sit down and tell me what you've been up to. I didn't expect you this soon, but I'm awfully glad you're here. Nothing in Shreveport, right?"

Ki shook his head. "Not much. I would have been here this morning, but my boat wasn't the best. The engines quit in Caddo Lake and we drifted a couple of hours." He paused then, and his eyes clouded with concern. "Jessie, what happened out front? Everyone in town's outside the hotel, and there's blood all over the place. They say a man was killed."

Jessie cleared her throat and looked at the ceiling. "Yeah, well—that's what happened, all right." She looked warily at Ki. "It's a long story, but the man who got shot was Tobias Pike. I was, well—sort of there with him at the time."

"What!" Ki nearly came out of his chair. "My God, are you all right?"

"I'm here," she said wearily. "Guess that's better than poor Pike." She leaned over the table and grasped his hands. "Ki, I don't know exactly what's going on here, but we're on the right track."

"So I see," Ki said soberly.

"Look, I'm all right. Now just listen. I've learned a lot in a short time, but I'm not sure what any of it means." Quickly she told him all that Pike had said about the murdered Indian found with Starbuck gold, and his tie-in with the Thicket. She related what Pike had told her of James Cooper and his connection with the mysterious Jacob Mose. Finally she told him of Pike's murder, and how Morgan had appeared on the scene—leaving out the fact that they'd met, in a sense, before that.

Ki listened intently. When Jessie was finished, he clenched his teeth and glared. "This whole Thicket business doesn't make sense. Not any more than when we talked about it in Hope.

39

It's one of the best hiding places in the country, but so what? Whoever's running this operation—the cartel or whoever—doesn't *need* to sneak gold around in a swamp."

"I know," Jessie agreed. "It hit me the same way, Ki. But someone brutally murdered Pike. Right in broad daylight in the middle of town. And Pike *knew* someone was watching him. The poor man was frightened out of his wits."

Ki's almond eyes narrowed. "And that killer could easily have turned his shotgun on you."

"No, that's not exactly true," Jessie said distantly. "He could have killed me if he wanted, but he didn't. Morgan saw that, too. And it's something I simply don't understand. If they knew Pike had something on them, why didn't they kill him *before* I got here—before he could ever pass on what he knew?"

Ki let out a breath. "That puts a question on top of a question, doesn't it? Why not kill you too? If they were waiting for Pike, they knew you were with him, and that he'd had a chance to tell you what he knew. The information is much more dangerous in your hands than it ever was in his. All he could do was pass it on. They know who you are, and they surely must know you'll act on what you know. You won't sit still and let them bankrupt the Starbuck holdings." Ki stopped and gave her a look. "They *ought* to know by now. You've never turned your back on them yet. Even when it wouldn't have been a bad idea, Jessie, to act with a little more caution, a little more—"

"Ha!" Jessie grinned and squeezed his hand. "Feels to me like a little Oriental wisdom coming on."

Ki cleared his throat. "The idea never crossed my mind."

"Good. 'Cause I could mention a few times when caution wasn't exactly *your* cup of tea!"

"Only my mother was Japanese," Ki said solemnly. "Sometimes the blood of my American father takes over. Once or twice I have acted in a reckless, even perhaps a foolhardy manner."

"Oh, that's the *American* side, huh?"

"Yes, of course. It's certainly not the Japanese."

"Well, don't look now, but your American side of the family's been at it again. You never did tell me where you got those knots and bruises."

Ki flushed. "It's a long story, and not too flattering. Jessie, look, about this business with James Cooper—I may be able

40

to help. There was a black man on the boat. Silas Johnson. A good friend now. With Tobias Pike dead, this Cooper won't be real eager to help. I'm sure Silas would talk to Cooper if he's around."

"Great!" Jessie beamed and pushed back her chair. "Get yourself a room, and stow your satchel. Rest, or get cleaned up, or whatever you want to do, then go out and give it a try. If we can find Cooper, the trail's not dead. I'll meet you back here about—"

"Hold on, Jessie." Ki gave her a narrow look. "If you're going to meet me back here, you're thinking about going somewhere else."

"Well, yes. The Planter's Bank, for one. So?"

"So you've already forgotten what we talked about two minutes ago," Ki snapped. "Someone killed that Caddo Indian to shut him up. They murdered Pike right in front of your eyes. Remember?"

Jessie sighed. "What do you want me to do, Ki? Hide under the bed?"

"Good idea. Why didn't I think of that?"

"Because it's foolish, that's why. They know I'm here, Ki. They likely knew when I left Hope and took the T&P, and even what seat I had. We've talked this over before," she said gently. "I'm not going to hide. It's too late for that. And as you said yourself, they could have killed me easily, if that's what they wanted to do."

"They could change their minds, too," Ki said darkly.

"Ki—"

"All right," he sighed, "come on. At least let me walk you to the lobby."

The lawmen were waiting politely by the desk. Jessie told them she'd only known Pike a few hours, and had no idea who'd want to kill him.

"And how long have you known Black Jack Morgan?" asked the older of the two.

Jessie didn't care for the look that went with his words. "About half as long as I've known Tobias Pike," she said coolly. "Why do you ask?"

The lawman backed off. "No offense intended, Miss Starbuck. It's just that, well, if you ain't been in town too long, you might not know Mr. Morgan isn't real—respectable, you

41

might say. Oh, he dresses like a gent, but looks can be deceiving, now can't they?"

Jessie let out a breath. "Yes. They certainly can. Thanks so much for the advice." Leaving the two with an icy look, she stepped out of the lobby and into the street. To her left, workmen were boarding up the window Pike had flown through.

Jessie squinted into the sun and crossed the street. Behind her, across from the Excelsior, was the big stone Federal Building. The Planter's Bank was at Walnut and Austin, and she started in that direction. Far above the trees, a white heron flapped against a bright and cloudless sky. Jessie saw the brick warehouses in the direction of the wharves. So many of them were empty, so many companies moving on.

Maybe this is the last year for Starbuck here, too, she said to herself. *Likely we could use the money better somewhere else.*

The thought reminded her that she'd have to drop by Tobias Pike's office. Whether Starbuck stayed or not, someone in the company would have to pick up the reins.

"Miss—over here!"

Jessie looked around, looking for the source of the male voice that had just summoned her. "Who's calling me?" she demanded sharply. "What do you want?"

"Ma'am, I mean you no harm, honest to God I don't."

Now Jessie realized that the voice was coming from an alley to her right, and she squinted, peering into its concealing shadows. "If that's true," she said, "show yourself. I don't favor talking to men I can't see."

A lighter shape separated itself from the comparative blackness and, without leaving the alley, stepped forward just enough so Jessie could see that it was wiry little man with a drinker's bulbous nose. He must have been sixty or older, and had matted white hair and a stubbly growth of grizzled beard. The blue suit he wore was neat and reasonably clean, though a bit threadbare; it had been well-tailored when it was new.

The man held up his hands as if to show that they were empty. "I'd like a word with you, is all. I'm a—I *was* a friend of Tobias Pike's. A good friend, miss."

"All right," said Jessie, "what is it you want to tell me, Mr.—?"

"Baxter. Jaybird Baxter's what they call me." He showed her a practiced smile. "Been so long, I don't even remember why."

"And you were a friend of Pike's."

"More'n that," he said cautiously. "We were sort of—business associates, you might say."

"What kind of business?"

"Ah, business you don't exactly keep books on, Miss Starbuck. You know?" He caught her expression and winked. "Don't take me wrong now. I know he worked for you. Our business had nothing to do with yours. Tobias never mixed his, ah, personal and public enterprises." He paused then, sniffed the air, and checked both sides of the street. "The thing is, miss, I know some of what he was doing. And I don't take kindly to the folks that did him in." The rheumy blue eyes looked right through her. "I know where the Indian's woman is hidin' out."

Jessie held her breath. "What Indian woman is that, Mr. Baxter?"

"Ha!" Baxter grinned again. "You're a cool one, miss, and that's wise. Very wise indeed. I was you, I'd do the same. Can't be too careful when you're—" Baxter suddenly went rigid. As he glanced past Jessie, all the color drained from his face. Turning on his heel, he darted down the alley and disappeared.

Jessie whirled around quickly, trying to find what had frightened him off. The streets were nearly empty. There was a freighter's wagon, and three men on horses. Past them, two ladies strolled along, and farther down the street—

Jessie stopped and moved to her right for a better view. A tall man in a dark suit was moving hurriedly away. Jessie only saw him for a moment. She couldn't be certain at all, but it looked like Black Jack Morgan.

★

Chapter 7

Ki spent only a moment in his room, long enough to leave his satchel and slip into his leather vest. Moving hurriedly down the stairs, he left the Excelsior by the back way and walked to the wharves. On the way, he passed a narrow-front store selling drab workmen's wear. When he left, his features were covered by a broad-brimmed straw hat, used and frayed. With his clothes still sweat-stained and dirty from his trek along the bayou, he decided he'd blend in well with the dockside crowd.

For a while, Ki roamed through the neighborhood adjacent to the wharves, stopping to look in windows and wandering idly down one narrow street and then another. A stall was selling lemonade, along with tender strips of beef wrapped in bread. He bought himself a meal and walked along eating. Half an hour later, he was almost certain no one was dogging his path. Stepping up his pace, he made his way to the spot where the *Annie B.* was docked.

Annie and Charlie weren't in sight, but Silas was on deck, cleaning up the space where the cargo had been unloaded. "My, that's a fine-lookin' hat," he said soberly. "Must've set you back a pretty penny."

"I'm working on being Jefferson's Mr. Astor. Do you have a minute to talk?"

"Got nothin' else but. Miss Annie and Charlie Clay took off on business. What you need, friend?"

"Help," Ki said plainly. "Help from someone I can trust."

"And you figure that's me?"

"If it were something I had to figure, I wouldn't be talking. Would you like a job, Silas? Starting out at a hundred dollars, cash money?"

Silas sat up straight and gave him a wary look. "Ain't sure

44

whether I would or not. Money like that, you lookin' to burn down the town, or blow up the T&P?"

Ki grinned. "Jefferson will burn down by itself. And I could get some rivermen to blow the railroad for nothing." He eased the straw hat over his brow and leaned back against a keg. "The hundred's for two things: First, you're a man I can trust; and second, there's risk involved. Right now, and however long this business takes. If it goes on longer than we figure, the pay will be higher. After tonight, we'll likely be taking a trip south, down to the Thicket."

"Uh-huh," said Silas, "I'm listening."

Ki left very little out, omitting only the cartel's involvement; he could go into that when there was time. He told Silas that he worked for Jessie, and that the two of them were looking for the men who were stealing Starbuck gold. There was a black man who might or might not still be around town—a man who had information they desperately needed. Finally he said the killings of Tobias Pike and the Caddo were part of the picture.

Silas raised an eyebrow at that. He knew about the Caddo, and news of that morning's murder had spread quickly along the docks. "You all got yourselves a mouthful of trouble, seems to me."

"You want to chew some of it?"

A smile creased Silas's dark features. "Why, hell, yes I do. Beats carryin' bales of cotton and kegs of nails."

"Just so you know the risk. It's there—you can bet on it."

Silas pulled himself erect, the motion cording the muscles in his arms. "You seen the job I had before. Wasn't all that safe, you might recall."

Ki grinned. "No, I don't guess it was. You think you can find James Cooper?"

"If he's black and he's here, I can find him." He paused then, and looked straight at Ki. "I can, and you can't. And you're smart enough to know it. Take it wrong if you like, but I got to ask. You come to me 'cause you trust me, or 'cause I got the skin for the job?"

"Fair enough," Ki nodded. "The answer is yes to both questions. Only a black man can find James Cooper and get him to talk to me. If that was all I wanted, that's all I would have told you. I want you for the rest of it too. That part doesn't call for any special color of skin."

45

Silas bit his lip. "Sorry. You never give me cause to put that kinda shit on you, Ki."

"No, but you've got good reason, I expect."

Silas clasped Ki's hand. "Reckon you know some of 'em, too. Bein' part yellow slant-eye nigger and all—"

Ki laughed. "There's been a couple of times. Last one seems like only yesterday."

"You got a good memory." Silas nodded down the wharf. "Our friends on the *Texas Star* are kinda neighbors. Got in the night before us, in case you didn't notice. If you got nothin' to do till I get back, you might want to drop by and have tea."

"I'll think about that." Ki stood and walked Silas to the railing. "Watch yourself, damn it. No one followed me here—which doesn't mean they aren't keeping an eye on the boat. They know who I am, and they know I'm with Jessie. If they don't know I'm with you, they soon will."

"I'll keep that in mind," Silas told him. With a nod over his shoulder, he stepped onto the dock and ambled toward the dockside buildings, as if he had no place special to go.

Ki whiled away the afternoon, staying out of sight aboard the small sternwheeler. He expected Annie and Charlie at any moment, and waited for the sight of the girl's lazy, angular stride along the docks. The hours crept by, and neither of the two returned. It was nearly seven before footsteps sounded on the deck. Ki walked out of the galley, where he'd built himself a roast beef sandwich.

"I found him," Silas said soberly. "Sure as hell wasn't easy." He moved past Ki to the galley table, where he sliced himself a piece of meat and doused it generously with pepper sauce. "James Cooper is one scared rabbit. Didn't want to be found a'tall. He'll talk to you, Ki. Ain't real happy 'bout it, you understand, but he'll do it. Told him you'd give him some money and help him get clear of those other folks. Figured you'd back me on that."

"I should have thought of it myself." Ki swallowed the last of his sandwich. "When are we going to do it?"

"Right now," Silas said plainly. "Longer we wait, better chance there is our cottontail might find himself another hole."

The sun fell quickly over the town, leaving Ki and Silas in late-evening shadow. Ki was grateful for the darkness, and

46

wary of it. The night was impartial; it hid your own movements and your enemy's as well.

For a while Silas led them aimlessly through one narrow street after another, past darkened buildings and houses showing squares of lonely light. When Ki was certain they were alone, Silas turned abruptly and left the heart of Jefferson behind. Ahead lay a cluster of small houses that belonged to the town's black population. Hounds barked and jerked at their ropes as Ki and Silas passed. Woodsmoke and cooking smells hung in the sultry air.

Silas held up his hand, and Ki came quietly to his side. "James Cooper's in a house 'bout six doors down. I'm tellin' you now, so's we won't have to say nothin' again. The house has got a little ol' oak by the side. Dead, with no leaves on it. Dog next door, but none at the place we're going. We come up to the back, and knock four times soft."

"And Cooper lets us in?"

Silas's eyes narrowed. "*Better* be him lets us in."

Ki nodded and let Silas lead. The small dirt yard behind the house was pitch black. Motioning Silas to watch his back, Ki drew his *tanto* blade and knocked four times. Nothing. Ki waited, and knocked again. Something was wrong—he could sense it, almost smell it in the air. Signaling Silas to him, he gave the knob half a turn and pushed the door aside. Again, nothing. No sound, no hint of movement inside. Not even a—

Suddenly Ki went rigid. The overpowering odor stiffened the hairs at the base of his neck. Searching his pockets, he found a box of matches. Shielding them with his body, he set the box afire and tossed it into the house. The flare of light sent quick, twisted shadows up the wall, then faded back to darkness.

"Run," he said sharply. "Get out of here fast, Silas. *Go!*"

Silas needed no further invitation. Turning on his heel, he sprinted out of the yard, leaped a pile of split firewood, and ran for the dark grove of trees just ahead.

"No, this way!" Ki caught up with him quickly, grabbed his arm, and urged him down a narrow street. "Use the darkness, but know what's in there first. Stay close to me and don't stop. They're here—I don't know where, but they're close."

"Shit, man—" Silas stopped him and turned him around. "What the hell you *see* in there?"

"A man," Ki snapped. "Stripped and nailed to the wall.

47

Someone split him up the middle. I smelled him when I opened the door."

"Good God A'mighty—" Silas let out a breath. "This afternoon I'd have took this job for 'bout twenty. Don't feel a goddamn bit overpaid no more."

Ki raced from shadow to shadow, with Silas on his heels. His trained samurai senses searched the night. He could feel them, almost see their ghostly shapes, read the death-thoughts in their minds. Two of them—no, three—ranging the darkness on either side, staying just away, like sharks on the edge of a school of fish. He saw, now, that the two on either side were unimportant. The third, though—

For an instant Ki could almost see his face, feel the tiger scent of his breath. The brief flash of insight was *kime*, the sense that had no name. It came and then it was gone, but Ki had seen enough. The glimpse of his enemy's power turned the blood in his veins to ice.

My God, what is it? What's out there?

"This way," he told Silas. "We're only a few blocks from the water."

Silas looked puzzled. "Middle of town's still lit. We go your way, we goin' to get caught in the dark."

"Those three don't care about the light," Ki said grimly. "They'd kill us in the mayor's front parlor."

Before Silas could answer, Ki guided him down a narrow alley, paused to sniff the air, then turned and moved to the left, toward the wharves. They were close now, the two that didn't matter a block behind, herding them toward the other. Ki could sense the man's presence, drawing nearer every moment. His face was dark and clouded, blurred in constant motion, as if the anger in his heart had spawned a storm about his features.

They could have killed us back there, waited while we walked in and found James Cooper. He didn't want that, he wanted the hunt . . .

Ki's mind raced. Silas was a fighter, but he couldn't face the man waiting ahead. Silas wouldn't know, wouldn't understand what he was. The man with the storm in his mind would kill him in a breath—

"Silas, wait." Ki drew his friend to him. "There are two of them, right behind us now. Take the one on the left. Leave the other alone, if he'll let you. I'll handle the one ahead."

48

"How you know there's three?" Silas asked sharply. "I ain't seen nothin', or heard nothin' either."

"I know, damn it, now go. Keep those bastards off my back." Silas nodded and disappeared. Ki let out a breath. The other was close now, waiting just ahead. *He knows me. Knows exactly where I am*—

Ki stopped and stood perfectly still. The slim *tanto* blade was already in his hand. He heard the sounds of the river, the creaking of a boat against its moorings. The smell of stagnant water reached his nostrils. Rotten fruit. Woodsmoke. Man sweat—

The blur of motion touched the edge of his senses, whipped past his throat, and sparked the wall behind. Ki leaped desperately aside, knowing he was just a hair late. The second blade came at him in the shadow of the first, silver slicing the night. Pain brushed his ribs. Ki threw his body to the ground, came up in a crouch, and thrust his blade up fast. A curve of steel met his own, and numbed him to the shoulder. Ki's blade clattered to the street. His foe pressed in for the kill, slashing deadly arcs in the air. Ki backed off, dropped to the street on his shoulders, and lashed out with his heels. The blow caught the other on his hip and set him spinning. Ki sprang to his feet and came in under the man's blade. His stiffened fingers jabbed for the throat in the *shoto-uchi,* the knife-hand strike. The blow was incredibly fast. Ki could smell his enemy's death, feel the windpipe snapping under his fingers—

Suddenly the man was gone. Ki's deadly hand struck air. He staggered to catch his balance and turn before the other could cut off his life. Steel kissed his cheek. A fist caught the small of his back. Ki turned in a fighting crouch and caught a blow to the chest, another to the face. His neck snapped back and blood filled his mouth. The blow sent him sprawling and saved his life, rolling him free of his enemy's lashing feet.

Ki brought himself erect and wiped his face. For the first time he caught a glimpse of the other's face, the hard, wiry shape of his body. Ki sucked in a breath and stared. The man's features were nothing like his own, but his body was the same. He could almost sense what the hands would do next, where the blade would strike. The man was naked to the waist, his flesh coated with sweat. When the muscles in his belly went rigid, Ki could feel the great strength there himself. Fighting the man was like facing death in a mirror.

Ki's foe stepped to the right, turning the point of his blade in easy circles. Ki moved back, past the edge of the brick building. His feet touched the worn wooden planking of the wharf. The dark bow of an old sternwheeler nosed to the dock. A pine-knot fire cast shadows, thirty yards to his left.

Suddenly the man before him moved. This time Ki felt him coming. The blade sliced air, but Ki was gone. Leaping over the humming steel, he kicked the man in the chest. The other was fast, but Ki was faster. Before his feet touched the ground, his hands were moving. He chopped the man relentlessly across the face, the edge of his hand as hard as the blade of an ax. The man grunted and went down, rolled and kicked out desperately to stay alive. Ki moved in to take him, jerked back his foot for a killing blow—

A quick, terrified scream split the night and brought him up short. Two men burst out of the alley not ten yards away, sprawling in a tangle on the docks. Ki cursed himself for glancing away from his opponent. The man was on his feet, coming in fast. Ki circled him warily, watching the man's hands, the straining cords in his neck.

Footsteps pounded behind him, then another pair, heavier than the first. Ki risked a look over his shoulder. It was Silas and, lumbering along beside him, the powerful figure of Charlie Clay, a shotgun gripped in his fist. Ki attacked his foe. The man kicked out and danced deftly aside. From the corner of his eye, Ki saw Charlie come to a stop. His legs dug into the dock and spread wide; the shotgun came up fast—

Ki saw it coming, saw the man's mouth tighten in a grin, the blade leaving his hand and whipping air.

"Charlie, look out!"

Charlie's finger tightened on the trigger as the blade made circles in the air. Charlie jerked and went sprawling. The shotgun exploded at the sky. Ki threw himself at the killer, gripped him about the chest, and sent them both rolling. The man twisted in Ki's arms, and Ki felt himself falling. Dark water closed over his head. He kneed the man hard, wrapped strong thighs about the other's slender waist. Ki's back hit the muddy bottom. He found a throat and squeezed, thumbs digging hard into delicate tissue. The man clawed blindly at Ki's face, fighting to break the deadly grip. Ki's lungs were nearly bursting. Still, he held on grimly, not daring to give an inch. Air bubbles rose from the man's mouth in a muted cry. He writhed against

50

Ki, twisting and turning to wrench his body free. Ki held on, his chest screaming for air.

Suddenly the man jerked sharply to one side, twisting his waist from Ki's grip. Ki moved to avoid the kick he knew was coming. The man's feet caught him in the chest with a force Ki had never imagined was there. Air drove out of his lungs, and his mouth sucked water. His head struck something hard. Pain filled his skull; he clawed for the surface, but something cold and slick held him back. He realized, then, with a sudden deadly calm, that the hurt in his head was gone, that he didn't really need fresh air anymore . . .

Chapter 8

"You don't mind me saying so, Miss Starbuck, I'm more than pleased you decided to come. I don't guess I thought you would."

"You didn't?" Jessie batted her eyes and smiled. "Why, Ah'm suhprised, Mistah Morgan. A man of yoah confidence and experience?"

"God help me." Morgan groaned and looked at the sky. "If you're an empty-headed belle, Miss Starbuck, I'm the Queen of England."

Jessie looked him over, "No, too tall. Reckon you're someone else."

"I hope to hell I am."

Jessie couldn't help laughing with him. Morgan was a likable companion, and a strikingly handsome man in the bargain. Whether or not she could trust him was something else. Tobias Piké, Jefferson's town lawmen, and finally the mysterious Jaybird Baxter seemed to think he was carrying the plague. Was it really Morgan she'd seen, Jessie wondered. *Someone* had scared the old man out of his wits. Still, in all fairness, she couldn't be sure. Tall men in dark suits weren't all that hard to find. In the end, she decided to accept the gambler's invitation to supper, partly to find out something more about him—and partly, she admitted, because she plain wanted to see him again.

After taking care of business at the bank, she'd found the Starbuck offices close at hand. The place was in total confusion, and Jessie brought it quickly back to order. Picking the calmest clerk in the room, she put him in charge on the spot, warning him not even to breathe unless he checked with Galveston first. On the way back to the Excelsior, she found a pale green gown

52

she thought would fit, and told the owner of the shop to send it to her room.

Ki wasn't back, and Jessie really didn't expect him. Finding James Cooper wouldn't be easy, even if Ki's friend was willing to help.

I know where the Indian's woman is hidin' out . . . Baxter's words still stuck in her mind. If the old man did know something, she'd have to follow it through. But where the hell would she find him? There were hundreds of old codgers down on their luck, and most of them looked exactly like Baxter.

"That fellow who works for you," Morgan said suddenly, "he's part Oriental, isn't he?"

"Ki's mother was Japanese," said Jessie. "And he doesn't just *work* for me, Mr. Morgan. He's a good friend as well. He, uh, tries to keep me from getting in too much trouble," she added with a grin.

"Looks like a man who could," Morgan said evenly.

The sun was disappearing over the trees when they left the center of town and started for the wharves. Jessie decided that Morgan heartily approved of her new dress. More than once she'd caught his eyes roaming freely over the bare swell of her breasts and the curve of her shoulders. He'd already seen much more, but it was clear that he wasn't finished looking.

"I suppose," Jessie said finally, "you can stop calling me Miss Starbuck if you like. And I'm getting tired of 'Mr. Morgan.' What do you like? Black Jack or Jeffrey?"

Morgan winced. "How about Jeff? My mother calls me Jeffrey, and folks who bet against me use—that other."

Jessie gave him a mischievous grin. "And you don't exactly care for it, eh?"

"No. Not much."

"Price of fame, I guess."

"Price of something," Morgan muttered. "You hungry at all?"

"Starved." She gave him a curious glance. "You haven't said where we're going, unless I didn't hear."

"I didn't say. It's a surprise."

"Uh-oh. I've heard that somewhere before."

Morgan laughed and guided her along. "Yeah, I'll just bet you have, at that. Oh, one thing. Since you do such a fine Southern lady imitation, your name where we're going is— wait—Annabelle. Miss Annabelle Lee."

53

"I'm damned if it is," Jessie said darkly.

"Don't be such a grouch," he told her. "You're going to like it, whether you want to or not."

Morgan led her along the wharf toward the half-dozen sternwheelers nosed into shore, and stopped abruptly before the second. "Well, here we are," he grinned.

Jessie stopped and put her hands on her hips. "If you think I'm going clear to New Orleans for supper, mister, you better think again."

"Where we are going," Morgan explained patiently, "is straight to the dining salon of this vessel, where you'll have the pleasure of the best down-home bayou cooking you ever tasted." He held out his arm in a gallant pose. "You joining me, ma'am?"

"Hell, why not?" Jessie sighed. "All I can do is get sold and shipped off to some rich fellow's hacienda in South America."

"Isn't a one of 'em could afford you," said Morgan.

"Why, what a nice thing to say—I think."

The sternwheeler's dining salon was long and narrow, furnished with a big oak table large enough for a dozen people. Now it was set for only two, with a white linen cloth, candles in silver holders, china, and sparkling crystal. The candles bathed a corner of the room in a warm and friendly glow.

"My, my, I'm impressed," said Jessie. "And, Lord, something smells wonderful! What on earth is it?"

Morgan grinned, helped her to a chair, and seated himself. As if on signal, the door opened behind him and a tall, elderly black man in a crisp white jacket entered the room with a trayful of covered china dishes.

"This is Miss Annabelle Lee from Atlanta," Morgan said soberly. Miss Lee, this is Mr. Bill Simon, the best riverboat cook on the North American continent."

Bill Simon smiled. "Pleased to have you with us, Miss Lee."

"Thanks," said Jessie, peering anxiously at the array of covered dishes. "My pleasure, and from the smell of that food, I'm not wrong. Oh Lordy, look at that!"

Bill Simon served her plate as Jessie watched in awe. In a moment she was looking at generous helpings of wild duck with plum sauce, hush puppies, and hot grits with butter and honey.

"Now *that's* what I call food," said Morgan. "But you've got to try this first. Right, Bill?"

"Right, Mr. Morgan. If I do say so myself." Holding back a grin, Bill uncovered another dish and served Jessie a large helping in a bowl.

"Oh yes," moaned Jessie, "you're right. This definitely comes first."

"Crawfish cooked in butter and garlic, swimmin' in a fine wine sauce," said Bill. "Hope you enjoy it, miss."

"Mr. Simon, don't you worry," Jessie assured him. Bill Simon disappeared, returned to fill their glasses with a white Bordeaux, then vanished again. Jessie sampled the dish, then closed her eyes and moaned. "Lord, Jeff, you're right. Where has that man been hiding?"

"Old friend of mine," said Morgan. "I ride this boat downriver sometimes. For—professional reasons, you understand. Or just for the hell of it, if Bill's cooking."

"I think I'd like to *live* here," said Jessie.

"Be a good idea, if you wanted to weigh about two hundred pounds and waddle like a duck."

"I don't," laughed Jessie, "but it sure is tempting. Jeff, this is really some of the finest food I ever—" Jessie stopped, her fork in midair, as the door at the end of the room opened. A man stepped in and nodded at Morgan, then turned and doffed his tarnished cap at Jessie. "Miss," he said with a smile, "it is my pleasure to have you aboard. I cannot recall when such beauty has graced this table."

Morgan laughed aloud, threw down his napkin, and squeezed the older man's hand. "Miss Annabelle Lee, Captain Josiah Stewart, master of this vessel. Watch this old sea dog, he's got a woman in every port."

"*Did* have," the man sighed. "*Did* have, Morgan, in younger days. Bill treatin' you two all right?"

"The food's marvelous, Captain," said Jessie. "Won't you have a glass of wine with us?"

"No, no," Stewart protested. "Love to, dear lady, but I've business to attend to." Jessie thought the man looked every inch a riverboat captain. He was lean and silver-haired, with a weathered face and stern features. "Are you visitin' us here in Jefferson, then?"

"For a day or so," said Jessie. "So far, this meal is the high point of my trip."

"Bill's a fine cook, that's for certain." Captain Stewart folded his arms behind his back. "I've got some real good coloreds aboard. Hard workers. Won't tolerate anything else." He grinned knowingly at Jessie. "Lady of your breedin' will understand that, of course."

Jessie's green eyes narrowed. "Understand exactly what?"

"Why, the problems you have with the nigrah, of course."

"No. I *don't* have problems like that, Captain Stewart."

"Then you're most fortunate, I'd say. Most fortunate indeed. Found a bad egg in *my* bunch just yesterday morning. Big buck wouldn't take the whipping he had coming, and I had to put him off, him and some Chink who couldn't mind his own affairs. Put 'em both ashore in the wilds, is what I did. I will not tolerate such business aboard the *Texas Star*. No, ma'am, I will not."

"What?" Jessie sat up straight. *"What* did you say?"

"Captain Stewart—" Morgan caught the fire in Jessie's eyes. Stewart ignored the warning, and glanced curiously at his guest.

"I beg your pardon, miss? What I said, clearly, I supposed, was—"

"Yes, I think I got it, all right." Jessie rose, picked up her crawfish stew, and walked quickly behind Morgan. Stewart looked bewildered. Jessie stopped a foot away, then calmly jammed the bowl in his face.

Stewart yelped and staggered back, slapping at his face and the front of his jacket. "God *damn* it," he cursed, "what's wrong with you, woman? You had no call to do that!"

"You're wrong," snapped Jessie. "I've got all the call in the world. Now—you've got fifteen minutes to get your gear off this boat. If you're still here then, I'll have you tossed in jail."

Stewart dabbed his face with a napkin and shook his head. "Wh-what the hell are you jabbering about? I'm the *captain* of this vessel!"

"Wrong again," Jessie told him. "You *were* the captain. You're not anymore. My name's Starbuck, mister, not Annabelle Lee." She cast a stony look in Morgan's direction. "And if memory serves me, the *Texas Star* belongs to the Starbuck Steamship Company."

Stewart's face went slack. "What the hell is this?" he roared at Morgan. "By God, if this is your idea of a joke, you son of a bitch—"

56

Jessie stepped to the door, slammed it behind her, and stomped across the deck to the wharf. Picking up her skirts, she stalked furiously toward the town.

"Jessie, wait!" Morgan caught up and grabbed her arm. Jessie shook him off and kept going. Morgan walked in silence beside her until the Hotel Excelsior was in sight. The center of town was brightly lit. Pineknot gas burned in high glass globes on ornate lampposts, turning the streets yellow-white.

"Look," Morgan said soberly, "I didn't have any idea your friend got kicked off the *Texas Star*. Hell, you figure I think that's funny?"

"You knew that boat was mine," Jessie said furiously.

"It was a joke," Morgan protested. "On you and Stewart both. He'd find out you were the owner, and you'd learn you were having supper on your very own boat. Wasn't any harm meant, and—"

Jessie stopped and raised her hand. "What was that? Did you hear it?"

"I don't know, someone shootin' off a gun." He turned her around to face him. "Listen, Jessie. I got off wrong with you right from the start. And I'll be damned if I'm doin' any better. I've sailed with Stewart a dozen times. I never saw him whip his hands. If I had, I'd have done something about it. And Bill Simon is an old friend of mine, damn it."

A shout went up somewhere down the street, past the hotel. Men on foot ran past, headed in the direction of the wharf. Jessie frowned and looked after them.

"You should have seen Stewart's face," Morgan said darkly, "when I told him he'd put the wrong man ashore."

"Ki didn't even *tell* me what happened," she said. "And you can bet he knows the *Star* is mine. All of our vessels have the word 'star' on their names somewhere. He knew all along and didn't do a thing." She turned to Morgan and touched his arm. "I'm sorry. It's not your fault, you couldn't have known."

"It was a lousy idea," Morgan said tightly.

"No, it was a good idea that turned out badly. I ought to apologize to Bill Simon. I shouldn't have wasted that crawfish on Stewart."

Morgan thought for a moment. "You got a head chef or something at the Starbuck Steamship Company? Someone that oversees the whole thing?"

"No, I don't think we do." Jessie's face brightened. "Jeff,

57

that's a fine idea! You think Bill'd like it?"

"Bill would be delighted, and he'd make a perfect head chef. Besides being a great cook, he's a real snob."

Jessie laughed, then stopped and looked curiously past Morgan's shoulder. Men with lanterns were walking up the street from the wharves, talking excitedly among themselves.

"What is it? What's going on?" Morgan stepped forward and stopped one of the men.

"Killings down at the docks," the man shouted. "Four men dead. They're bringing the bodies up now!"

Morgan turned back to Jessie. "Come on, I'll get you back to the hotel."

"No. No, wait." Jessie wanted to turn and flee, but something held her. A flatbed wagon led by a mule rattled out of an alley down the street. By the light of the men's lanterns, she could see the lifeless bundles in back, jerking with the rhythm of the wheels.

"Jessie, come on," urged Morgan. "This is nothing you need to see."

"No, I can't go. I can't—"

"Jessie? Jessie Starbuck?"

Jessie stopped. A tall, slender girl rushed toward her out of the shadows and grasped her shoulders. "I'm Annie, Miss Starbuck, Annie Brown. You don't know me, but I know you."

"What? What is it?" Jessie stared at the girl's terrified eyes, the tears that stained her cheeks.

"Don't go over there," Annie moaned. "Don't do it, Jessie!" A ragged cry tore from her throat, and she flung herself into Jessie's arms.

58

Chapter 9

Jessie wrenched herself free, her face twisted in pain and disbelief. "No, no—it's not him, it's not!"

"Jessie, don't!"

Annie and Morgan tried to stop her, but Jessie stumbled blindly past them to the wagon. Men turned at her piercing cry and stepped aside. Jessie held Ki's head to her breast, hot tears scalding her face. Finally, Morgan and Silas Johnson gently pulled her away. Morgan held her to him and Jessie buried her head in his shoulder.

"Everything's going to be all right," Silas said softly. "You're goin' to be just fine now—"

"No!" Jessie cried out. "No, that's not so! Nothing's ever going to be all right again!"

A crowd had already gathered when the wagon reached the doors of Harlow Quint, the town mortician. When Quint and Jefferson's lawmen tried to lay the four bodies in one room, Annie Brown came down on them in a fury. The men backed off from her anger, and Ki and Charlie Clay were stretched on tables in a parlor by themselves. The two dead outlaws were left out front for the public to see.

"Jessie," Morgan said quietly, "I'll stay with you if you like. Whatever way you want."

"Thank you," she told him. "I'd—I'd like to be alone with him." Morgan nodded and stepped aside. Jessie looked past him to Annie. The girl stared over Jessie's shoulder as if she didn't see her at all.

"Won't nobody bother you, miss," Silas said firmly. "We'll see to that."

"Thank you," said Jessie, "thank you so much..."

• • •

59

A kerosene lamp cast a cone of gloomy light, leaving most of the room in shadow. The two bodies lay on low wooden benches, hastily covered with blankets. One figure was considerably smaller than the other. Jessie moved quickly to it and peeled back the blanket.

"Ki," she whispered, "it's me. I'm alone."

Ki opened his eyes, sat up cautiously, and gave her a weary grin. Jessie held him close, kissed him soundly, then backed off and braced her hands on her hips. "Friend, I hope you've got a real good reason for this business. I never wanted to go on stage, and I still don't."

"I don't think you'd have any trouble getting a job."

"That's because you purely scared the hell out of me," Jessie said flatly. "Ki, what *is* this all about?"

"Listen, I'm sorry, Jessie. I had to do it like this. I told Annie to warn you."

"She did. Whispered that you were all right, but I had to pretend you weren't." Jessie let out a short breath. "Frightened the daylights out of me, anyway. That's why you got such a good performance." She looked up then, and glanced curiously at the body nearby. "Ki, do you mind telling me who *that* is? He's, uh—really dead, isn't he?"

Ki's smile faded. "His name's Charlie Clay. Annie's known him all her life. He was a good man, Jessie."

"Oh, Ki, I'm sorry." She read the pain in his features. "What *happened* out there? Who was he? And—who's Annie? And the black man guarding our door? I'm sorry, I don't understand *any* of this!"

Ki let out a breath. "I got kicked off the *Texas Star* with Silas. That was when I met Annie and Mr. Clay."

Jessie gave him a rueful look. "I know about the *Star*. You should have said something, Ki."

Ki looked surprised, but didn't pursue it. He told her about Annie and Charlie Clay, then brought her up to date on the night's events. Jessie felt a chill touch her spine when she learned how they'd found James Cooper.

"It was a trap," Ki said soberly. "Someone got to Cooper first, then waited for us to come. Silas stopped two of them. I was fighting the other, and Annie and Charlie heard the noise from their boat. Charlie came running with that shotgun of his, and spotted me and Silas in trouble." Ki stopped and looked away. When his eyes returned to hers, Jessie felt a moment of unreasoning fear. It was as if he'd really died, and the man there before her was his ghost.

"He's fast," Ki said absently. "Fast and incredibly good. He threw that blade and killed Charlie before I could—before I could even move. And he damn near finished me off, besides." He paused then, and took her hand. "That's why I decided to play dead. We almost killed each other there in the water. He *thinks* he finished me off—he didn't have the air left to stick around and see. Silas got me out and nearly pounded me to death, getting the water out of my lungs. He carried me back to Annie's boat before the dock got crowded."

"And when you came to," Jessie finished, "you decided to play possum."

"Yes. Jessie, the men Silas put away were hired hands. One of them probably gunned down Pike. The other, though—he's a cartel assassin, no question about it. You don't pick up talent like that on the street." He stared at her, his dark eyes sparking with anger. "They're determined to keep us out of the Big Thicket. Whoever gets in their way is going to wind up dead. I don't know how they know that Cooper talked to Pike, or that he intended to talk to me. Silas is certain no one followed him this afternoon."

"If the cartel's assassin is that good—"

"Right," Ki agreed. "Silas would never know. But I didn't tell him that."

Jessie was silent a long moment. "I've got an idea where you want to go with this. But you tell me."

Ki showed her a half-smile. "Don't give me that look, as though you disapprove already. You haven't even heard what I have to say. First, I'd suggest you get me buried properly. Without any help from that mortician, if it's all the same to you. I'll get out of here tonight, back to Annie's boat. After the funeral tomorrow, I'll go downriver with Annie and Silas. Silas and I will go ashore somewhere, get horses, and head south for the Thicket. Maybe we can find this Jacob Mose. At any rate, we'll do some looking on our own."

"Uh-huh. And?"

"And what?"

"What am *I* supposed to be doing all this time?" she asked sharply. "Tending to my knitting?"

Ki had to grin. "That's an interesting picture. I'd like to see that."

61

"Well, don't hold your breath. Look, friend—"

"Just let me finish, all right? I don't expect you to sit on your hands, Jessie. I know you better than that. Look—if they think I'm dead, and that you're not headed for the Thicket yourself—"

"No, that won't work. Even if you were dead, they know I wouldn't give up. *Especially* if you were dead."

"Right. And what *would* you do? If I were really dead, Jessie?"

"Oh, come on, Ki—"

"No, tell me. It's important."

Jessie took a deep breath. "Get some help and go after those bastards," she said grimly. "Find out what's in the Thicket—"

"But that would take a while, wouldn't it?" Ki suggested. "You wouldn't want them to see just exactly what you were up to, if you could help it."

"No. No, I wouldn't."

"So you'd go down to Galveston, maybe, or Houston—or, even better, over to Dallas or Fort Worth—*away* from the Thicket to throw them off, give yourself a few days to get something going. They'd keep their eyes open, but they wouldn't worry about you for a while. And that'd give me a chance to catch them off guard. They sure as hell won't be worrying about *me*. When I find something, I'll get to a Western Union office and send coded messages to you at half a dozen places."

Jessie folded her hands. "You've got this all thought out, haven't you?"

"You think it's a bad idea?"

"No, damn it, I *don't* think it's a bad idea. But I know what else it is, Ki because I know how that devious mind of yours works. For some reason, the cartel hasn't tried to kill me. You figure they don't want me dead, or they'd have finished me off by now. So—I get away from here and get busy, and they leave me alone and see what I do. Meanwhile, you dash down to the Big Thicket and take 'em *all* by surprise. You and Silas Johnson."

Ki looked at the ceiling. "The way you put it—"

"Is exactly the way it is," Jessie finished. She reached down suddenly and kissed him on the mouth, a bright tumble of hair brushing his shoulder. Ki looked astonished, and Jessie almost laughed.

62

"All right, we'll do it your way. I just want you to know that I am *not* fooled at all. I'll be waiting for that wire. And *you* wait until I get there with help, understand?" Her green eyes suddenly turned soft. "I love you for what you are, Ki. And for trying to keep me out of trouble."

"It's a full-time job," he said soberly. "And I'm not very good at it, Jessie."

"Shut up and lie back down. I'll see you in a few days, friend. Take care of yourself. And don't get snakebit, either."

Jessie covered Ki's face with the blanket, then turned and opened the door and stepped out of the room. A small man with spectacles was waiting past the solid barrier of Silas Johnson and Jeff Morgan.

"Ah, Miss Starbuck," he said earnestly, "I share your grief, madam, I surely do. I promise you we will, ah—take care of the deceased in a dignified manner."

Jessie looked at him straight in the eye. "What you'll do, mister, is keep your hands *off* the deceased. Period. You got that straight?"

The little man looked bewildered. "Why, ah, there are certain preparations—"

"For me. Not for you. My friend was a samurai warrior. I'll need a bolt of white silk. About three yards ought to do. And a dozen white candles in silver holders."

"Well, of course. In the morning, I'm sure we can make whatever arrangements you'd like."

"Tonight, not tomorrow," Jessie said flatly. "Now, mister." She turned to Silas Johnson. "I know you were his friend. Would you help me now, please? I'd like you to be Ki's guard of honor. That means no one else is to see him or touch him until he's in the ground."

Silas nodded. "Yes, ma'am. I reckon that'll be just the way it is."

Jessie looked past him to the lawmen she'd met at the Excelsior. "If you two gentlemen have any objection to *this* gentleman carrying out his duties, you'd best tell me now."

"No, no, not at all," the older of the two said quickly. "Whatever you want's just fine, Miss Starbuck."

"Good. Now someone run out and get me that silk. This has been a trying experience, and I don't intend to hang around this place all night . . ."

● ● ●

Jessie waited in the shade of the big oak. Jeff Morgan sat in the carriage a few yards away, smoking his cheroot. In a moment Jessie saw the other carriage approaching down the narrow country road. Silas Johnson stopped his horse, and Annie Brown stepped to the ground. A dozen black men and women had followed the carriage down the road; now they stepped up and each one solemnly shook Annie's hand, then turned and walked back in the direction from which they'd come. Jessie left the shade and met Annie, taking the slender girl in her arms and holding her close for a long moment.

"Let's walk a little, all right?" Jessie said quietly. Annie nodded. Neither one spoke till they were well down the road.

"Was it a nice ceremony?" Annie asked finally.

"Yes, Ki would've liked it. Tell him I spent a small fortune on flowers. Did everything go all right last night?"

"He got back to the boat in the middle of the night. He's certain no one was watching. He and Silas filled the coffin full of bricks from the alley. No one else got near him, Jessie. Not from the moment you left the room."

Jessie grinned. "Awful waste of good silk. You and I both could've had a couple of dresses from that." She stopped then, and held Annie firmly by her shoulders. "I'm sorry, Annie. I shouldn't be joking at a time like this. My loss isn't real, but yours is."

Annie shook her head, and her eyes filled with tears. "No, really. We got to smile, Jessie. It's the only way to keep goin'. Charlie Clay died doin' something he wanted to do. He was a good man. A *real* good man." She brushed back tears, and her face suddenly clouded with anger. "You know that son of a bitch mortician wouldn't *touch* Charlie at all? Had to send him to the black undertaker, and bury him in the black cemetery. 'Course, Charlie wouldn't have wanted to be anywhere else, you understand. But it's the damn *idea* of it, Jessie. That ol' man *raised* me, just the same as my pa. Whenever I skinned my knee or got scared of the dark, he'd just hold me till I got all better. He never noticed I was white. And I sure never thought about him bein' different from me. *Damn* those bastards!"

After a while, Jessie walked the girl back to her carriage. Silas Johnson shook hands solemnly with Jessie, and then with Jeff Morgan. Silas laid his shotgun on the floor of the carriage and drove Annie away.

"Come on," Jessie said after a moment. "I think you need to buy me another drink."

Morgan started the horse down the road. "I wish I could say something that would help. I'm sorry about Ki, you know that. Nothing can bring him back, of course. I just—" Suddenly, Morgan jerked the horse to a stop and turned his gaze intently on Jessie. "I've no business at all interfering in your affairs right now, but damn it all, woman, I'm going to speak my mind whether you like it or not. You're in some kind of trouble. I don't know what it is, but I'm not a fool. Tobias Pike's dead, and so's your friend, and three other men besides. All in the same day *you* get into town. What the hell is going on here, Jessie? And what can I do? Looks to me like you could use a friend or two. You've damn sure got one right here beside you, if you need it."

Jessie stared, then tears filled her eyes. She was crying for Annie Brown, and for Charlie Clay and James Cooper and Tobias Pike—one man she'd hardly known, and two she'd never met at all. Morgan took her in his arms and held her against him, then turned her face up to meet his. When his lips touched hers, Jessie met him with a desperate need of her own. For a moment she forgot he was a man she didn't trust, a man she hardly knew at all. She needed his touch, the pressure of his hands about her waist. Finally she pulled away and looked into his light gray eyes. Morgan let out a breath.

"Guess I ought to say I'm sorry, that I picked a real bad time to do that. I'm not sorry at all, though, Jessie."

Jessie smiled. "I know you're not. And neither am I..."

Morgan promised to see her for supper, after she'd had a chance to rest. Jessie said she didn't want to leave the hotel, and he told her he'd arrange to have the meal brought to her room. Jessie agreed, and left him in the lobby.

When she opened the door to her room, she saw a folded piece of paper lying on the floor. Jessie picked it up and opened it. The message inside was written in a clear, precise hand with a scratchy pen:

Miss Jessica Starbuck,

I am grievous sorry for your loss. Please accept my sympathies, dear lady. Perhaps I should not intrude, but

65

I feel it is my duty to tell you again that I know where the Caddo Indian's widow can be found. I will have two horses three-quarters of a mile north of town at five in the morning. If you are interested, I must ask that you come alone. I regret, Miss Starbuck, that I must ask for fifty dollars to meet certain expenses. If this meeting intrudes too quickly upon your mourning, I shall certainly understand.

Your obedient servant,

James R. Baxter

Jessie dropped the note on the table. "Oh Lord, Ki," she sighed. "you're not going to like this, I know. It's exactly what you *didn't* want me doing—only, damn it, I don't see how I can let Jaybird Baxter slip by."

Chapter 10

Black Jack Morgan arrived promptly at eight. His plain black suit was freshly pressed, and the white silk shirt was clearly right off the shelf. The pearl-gray vest was from a tailor in New Orleans, and his boots had been handcrafted in Fort Worth.

"My, my," said Jessie, "if you don't look fine, Mr. Morgan." She took his flat-crowned Stetson and set it aside, then reached up to kiss his cheek. "Fresh shave too," she grinned, "and you smell good besides."

"Told that fella not to put anything on me," Morgan grumbled. "They don't feel right if they're not shakin' something out of those bottles. My God, Jessie Starbuck, who *cares* what I look like?" He let out a breath in appreciation. "Lady, you are just as pretty as you can be!"

"Jeff—it's the same dress I wore into town," Jessie scolded. "I didn't pack much for social wear."

"The dress is just fine," Morgan said plainly. "It's the woman wearing it that I'm talking about."

"Well, thank you, sir." For a moment their eyes met. Then Jessie looked away and moved quickly across the room. "I've got a little brandy, or would you rather have some bourbon? Supper ought to be along soon."

"Bourbon will be fine."

Jessie handed him his drink, then poured herself a brandy. Morgan waited till Jessie took her seat, then joined her on the sofa. After a moment he placed his empty glass on the table in front of the divan.

"Are you all right, Jessie? Did you get any rest this afternoon?"

"Some. I'm doing the best I can. I—don't think the shock of what happened to Ki has really hit me yet."

"I think you're doing remarkably well," he told her.

67

You noticed, did you? I was afraid maybe you would...
"I've got to," she said aloud. "Don't have any choice."

"You going to stay here awhile?"

"Awhile, I guess. Not too long. I've got a lot to do."

Morgan caught her hesitation. He looked at her curiously, then rose to pour another drink. Staring intently at the glass, he downed the amber liquid in a swallow.

"I'm going to ask a question," he said abruptly. "If you don't want to answer, then don't." The steel-gray eyes seemed to bore right through her. "You don't trust me much, do you?"

Jessie tried to look blank. "Jeff, why would you say a thing like that?"

Morgan swallowed his irritation. "Don't insult me, Jessie," he said gently. "I'm full-grown and I'm not simpleminded. I know what you've likely heard about me 'round here. If you've talked to any of Jefferson's fine and noble citizens." Morgan made no effort to hide the trace of scorn in his voice.

"All right," said Jessie, "I'll tell you straight and honest. They say you're a gambler, but that you don't stop there. That you're mixed up with bad people in Jefferson. Whatever crooked's going on in town, Black Jack Morgan's got a hand in it."

Morgan's expression didn't change. "Do you believe that?"

"If there's a dark side to you, Jeff Morgan, I haven't seen it. You've been very good to me."

"That's not an answer, is it?"

"No. How could I give you a real answer? All I can say is what I see. I'd like to think that what I see is what's true. It probably is, but I've been fooled once or twice."

Morgan allowed himself a grin. "Fair enough. You want to hear the truth about Black Jack Morgan?"

"Yes, I think I do."

"It's no big secret. I'm a gambler, Jessie. A gambler and nothing more. Trouble is, I'm a damn *good* gambler. I'm good, I play straight—and I win." Morgan looked right at her. "I'm sure I'm not telling you something you don't already know, but high-stakes poker draws all kinds of people. Churchgoing merchants and fat bankers'll sit down with the biggest thief in East Texas, and never bat an eye. All they care about is winning. If they do, I'm 'good ol' Jeff.' If they don't, I'm a goddamn crook." Morgan smiled again. "You ought to hear what the bad ones call me when *they* lose."

"What's that?"

"*Dead* Black Jack Morgan."

Jessie flinched. "I'm glad you can laugh about it."

"Have to. Laugh, and never button your coat." He raised the corner of his jacket to show her the short-barreled Colt .44 in a cross-draw rig, set just above his hip. Jessie had seen the weapon once before, when he'd taken three quick shots at Pike's killer.

"Kind of a big gun for a gambler," she said.

"I told you. I get a lot of big losers."

When the waiter knocked discreetly, Morgan rose quickly, touched the butt of his gun, and made sure the man was delivering supper for two and nothing more. The steaks were large and perfectly grilled. Along with fresh hot bread and several side dishes, there was a good Bordeaux from the Excelsior's ample cellar. Jessie decided she wasn't eating at all like a lady in mourning, but she was too hungry to care. Jeff Morgan could think what he liked.

Morgan, however, was too wrapped up in his own appetite to concern himself with Jessie's. Pushing his plate aside, he stood and groaned aloud. "Lord, what I need now is a walk down to Shreveport and back."

Jessie smiled. "Would you like some coffee? Or some of the hotel's peach ice cream?"

Morgan made a face. "Don't even talk about food, all right?" He walked to the window and gazed out, then lit a thin cheroot. He'd said very little during supper, but Jessie had caught him looking her over more than once. It wasn't hard to read the man's eyes. The two had held each other that morning, and exchanged a bold kiss that promised a great deal more. Morgan's look told her he hadn't forgotten, and Jessie's memory was just as good as his.

Now she sat on the sofa and watched him stare out at the street. He hadn't turned to face her in a good ten minutes.

"Jeff," she said finally, "are you all right? Have you got something on your mind?"

"Yes," he said without turning. "I—no, it's nothing at all, Jessie."

"Oh. Well, fine."

He turned then, let his eyes touch hers and move quickly away. "I think—I think maybe I better be going. Gettin' kinda late, I guess."

69

"Jeff?"

"Yeah, well—you've been through a real hard time and I don't want to intrude. Let's see, where's my hat? Look, I sure do appreciate the—"

"Jeff Morgan, what the hell is wrong with you?" Jessie stepped into his path and stuck out her chin. Her green eyes sparkled with flecks of gold. "All evening long we've been looking each other over, as though we both had a fair idea what course came after the steaks. Now don't tell me that was all in my head."

Morgan cleared his throat. "No. It wasn't in your head, Jessie."

"Then what?" she demanded. "Are you waiting for me to *ask*?"

"Good Lord, no. I just—"

"Maybe you like real shy, retiring ladies. Like Miss Annabelle Lee. Bet she'd never be so—*foahward,* as to let *Mistah Moh' gan* know her feelings—"

"Damn it," Morgan said, flushing, "stop that now. You—you got me all wrong."

"And just how did I manage to do that?"

Morgan looked at his boots, then faced her squarely. "Jessie Starbuck, there's nothing I want more than to come over there and take you in my arms. I just figured it wasn't the right time. I was afraid that if I showed intentions like that so soon after—after your loss, you wouldn't think much of me."

Oh Lord, thought Jessie, *this mourning business is going to get me in trouble yet . . .*

"Jeff, that's real sweet of you," she said carefully. "It surely is. Except that I, uh—need someone close more than ever right now. Can you understand that? I *want* you to stay, and I want you to love me. I don't think I can put it much plainer than that."

Morgan's eyes got wide. "By God, you don't have to, lady." He tossed his Stetson across the room, crossed the few steps between them, and took her in his arms. Jessie laughed and slid her hands around his neck. Morgan touched her chin and raised her face to meet his own. Jessie closed her eyes and relaxed in the strength of his arms. When his mouth touched hers, a tremor of excitement swept through her body. She parted her lips to welcome the hard, probing thrust of his tongue. He explored every corner of her mouth, tasting each sweet hollow

70

of delight, stroking her lips ever wider. His touch seemed to heighten the fires within her. With a sharp little cry, she let her neck go limp, making her mouth a cup for him to drink. Morgan groaned and pressed her to him. Jessie let the pink tip of her tongue flick past his lips, matching his hunger with her own. The taste of his mouth sent fresh waves of desire racing through her body. His kiss seemed to smolder in her belly, burn the tips of her breasts. Morgan let his lips caress her cheeks, trail through the tangle of her hair past the soft column of her throat.

"Yes—oh yes, Jeff, *please!*" Jessie whispered. Releasing her grip about his neck, she brought her hands to the bodice of her dress and quickly loosed the buttons. While her fingers worked impatiently at the task, Morgan brought his hands down to her waist, then boldly slid his palm across her belly to stroke the proud curve of her mound.

Jessie gasped and opened her eyes wide. Clutching the front of her dress in both hands, she ripped the cloth aside, tearing away the bodice and the creamy chemise beneath.

Tossing her fiery hair over her shoulders, she cupped her naked breasts in her hands and offered them lovingly to his mouth. She watched his steel-gray eyes drink her in, saw the tanned flesh of his cheeks go taut with hunger. A cry choked in his throat and he clutched her breasts in his hands, drawing the rosy nipples into his mouth.

Jessie moaned as his tongue gently caressed the sensitive flesh, swelling the dusky circles into hard little nubs. She squirmed beneath his grip, arching her back and grinding her breasts against his mouth. Morgan's tongue kneaded her nipples into satiny points of pleasure. Now even the touch of his breath made her gasp. He knelt on the rug and his lips left her breasts and trailed down the hollow between her ribs to the gentle curve of her belly.

"Oh, Jeff—yes!" Jessie cried out and gripped his shoulders hard, knowing what was coming, relishing the joy of his mouth moving closer to her pleasure. Morgan paused and grinned, his kiss just inches from the soft line of down below her navel.

"Don't guess this gown is worth keeping now, is it?" he said softly. "Might be best if we just stripped that lovely body of yours naked—"

Jessie went rigid as his hands pulled the gown over her hips and past her thighs. Gripping her by her waist, he lifted her

71

off her feet to let her kick the tatters free.

"My God, Jessie, you're—I've never seen anyone as lovely as you."

"Like what you see, do you?" Jessie put her hands on her hips and gave him a saucy grin, thrusting her belly out boldy toward his face. "Don't know why you're all excited, Mr. Morgan. I look just like I did when you, ah—got the wrong door. *If* that's what really happened—"

Morgan didn't answer. He reached out and touched the red garter holster on her thigh. Jessie placed her hand over his, and slid the silver derringer down her leg.

"Now," she said softly, "I don't have on anything at all. Does that suit you, Jeff?"

Morgan smiled and moved up to face her on his knees, touching his lips once more to the swell of her belly. His hands found the soft curve of her back, the delightful swell of her bottom. His mouth brushed the feathery edge of her treasure, the heat of his breath a hot brand against her thighs. Jessie closed her eyes, waiting for his touch. Her pulse beat rapidly in her throat.

Morgan let his tongue brush gently over the luscious silken nest. The kerosene lamp across the room turned Jessie's flesh to honeyed cream, the downy mist between her legs pale gold with a touch of rose. He kissed the long plane of her thighs, moving nearer but never touching the delicate flesh close by.

Jessie came up on her toes. Tension corded the columns of her legs. Her fingers moved hurriedly down to guide him, to offer him all she had. With trembling hands she stroked her flesh aside, opening herself to his kiss. Morgan's lips found the satin-petaled flesh. His tongue flicked out to tease the musky treasure, taunt the hard little pearl that glistened within. Jessie's whole body trembled. Morgan's tongue probed deep inside, thrusting again and again, tasting the sweet spice of her flesh. Jessie felt the warmth within her grow. It flowed like a hot and sugary syrup from her belly to the rigid points of her nipples. Rivulets of moisture streaked the hollow of her belly.

"Now," Jessie whispered, raking her nails against his arms.

Morgan's hands gripped the swell of her bottom. Suddenly he thrust his tongue against the rigid little nub that was nearly bursting for his touch . . .

Jessie screamed and arched her back, gritting her teeth against the rising wave of heat that surged through her body. She

72

exploded again and again, letting the hungry fires caress her. She tossed back her hair and laughed with joy. One final, almost agonizing swell of pain and pleasure spasmed her thighs, and she fell back limply in his arms.

Morgan lifted her easily and carried her to the oversized bed in the corner of the room. Jessie felt deliciously warm and sleepy. Through a veil of tousled hair, she saw him standing by the bed. Now the black suit and fine silk shirt were draped across the sofa. He sat beside her and ran his fingers over the high swell of her hips, the narrow circle of her waist. Jessie smiled with pleasure at the hard-bodied figure, the lean planes and angles of his shoulders. She saw the musculature of his belly, the black matting below. Snaking a hand across his leg, she gave him a mischievous grin and grasped his swollen member.

"Oh my," she sighed, "I do believe the bottom half of you is about as pleasurable as the top. Lord, Jeff, that was just—lovely! More than that, only I haven't got the words to say it right."

"I was there," he told her. "You don't have to, Jessie."

"Mmmmm, you were there, for sure," she purred softly. "No question about that. And you sure are here right now. Goodness! Are you going to keep getting bigger? You've got to stop sometime. At least I *think* you do." Her small hand gently stroked his erection, one finger sliding in a circle about the tip.

"Jessie, I won't stop gettin' bigger if you keep doing that!"

"What kind of threat is that?" she laughed. "I, uh—know something that'll work even better. Would you like to guess what it is?"

"To hell with guessing," Morgan said tightly. "I *know* what it is." Without warning, he edged his hands beneath her and flipped her roughly onto her belly. Jessie shouted and kicked her legs in the air. Reaching past her head, he grabbed two pillows and eased them beneath her waist.

"Oh yes, yes!" Jessie cried. "Oh, I *love* that, Jeff!" She snuggled her belly comfortably atop the pillows, and spread her legs and twitched her bottom in a delightful invitation. Morgan crawled quickly between her creamy thighs. Laying his hand gently at the base of her neck, he let his fingers trace the curve of her back and come to rest lightly between her legs. Jessie trembled as his fingers moved in a slow, lazy circle at

73

the heart of her pleasure. She groaned and gripped the sheet tightly in her fists. Morgan teased her relentlessly, letting his hands caress her thighs and brush the supple flesh between her legs. Then, without warning, his fingers slid gently inside her. Jessie cried out and jerked her bottom up hard to grind against him. His touch sent joyous spasms racing through her body, triggering fires that threatened to overwhelm her.

"Don't—don't tease me anymore," she gasped. "I can't take it, Jeff."

"You want more, do you?" he said tightly. "Then *tell* me what you want!"

"Oh God, I want *you!*"

"Tell me, Jessie!"

"Take me, damn you!" Jessie screamed. "Put—put all of it in me now. *Take everything I've got!*"

Morgan eased her thighs still farther apart, then rammed his shaft deep inside her. Jessie cried out with pleasure. The soft coral petals between her thighs opened like a flower to welcome him in. Morgan gripped her slender waist and thrust himself against her in long, rapid strokes. Jessie's body shuddered. Her head snapped rapidly from side to side, lashing fiery hair across the bed. Morgan plunged inside her again and again. She could feel her orgasm mounting, surging through her veins. It was there, ready to take her over the edge. "Now...now... *NOW!*"

Jessie screamed, letting the searing fires consume her. Suddenly, Morgan went rigid and filled her like a flood. Jessie thrashed uncontrollably under his grip. Liquid fire licked her loins, coursed through her belly, and sent her reeling. Morgan gave a strangled cry and thrust deep inside her in a final burst of desire—

Jessie felt the slender columns of her legs turn to water. She sighed and fell on her belly and gasped for air. Morgan fell beside her, gently turned her on her back, and took her in his arms. Their bodies were slick with moisture. The heady scent of their love filled Jessie's senses with pleasure. A slight breeze from the open window tickled her flesh. She started to speak, to whisper in his ear. Instead, the words came out as a sigh and the lids fell heavily over her eyes...

When the sound reached her senses, she came fully awake at once. Something was there. In the room, close by. For a long

74

moment she forced herself to relax, let the rapid beating in her throat grow still.

The sound came again, a faint shuffling noise, scarcely audible at all.

Don't yell, damn it, stay calm ... reach over real easy and wake Jeff ... just touch him gently and roll toward him like you're asleep, then whisper in his ear ...

Jessie edged her hand slowly across the sheet. An inch, and then another. *Where the hell is he? Why's he so far away?*

Turning her head slightly, she risked a look. He was gone! The bed beside her was empty! Panic gripped her and knotted her belly. She was alone—alone in the dark room with the intruder. Instinctively she reached for the holster on her thigh, then remembered it was somewhere on the floor where their lovemaking had begun.

Taking another calming breath, she forced herself to turn her head slightly and search the room with her eyes. The faint light from the street cast a narrow yellow path across the floor. In another instant she saw him, moving quietly across the carpet, past the bulk of the sofa. He paused in the middle of the room, then moved silently to the window.

Jessie stared, and nearly cried out in relief. It wasn't an intruder at all, it was Jeff! The light from the window showed her his naked figure, the lines of his face and the—

Jessie froze. Something cold touched the back of her neck. Jeff Morgan was standing at the window, straining to read against the feeble glow. At once she recognized the slim leather folder in his hand, the Circle Star brand clearly visible in the light from outside.

Damn you! Damn you, you son of a bitch!

Anger, then the hot flush of humiliation filled her veins. He was calmly and deliberately going through all her papers, scanning each page at his leisure.

It took all the control she could muster to keep from sitting up and shouting, letting him know what she thought of his betrayal. Reason, and then the sudden touch of fear, held her back. *He's one of them, he has to be. And if they don't want me dead, they've got a reason. Raising hell right now could change their minds ...*

After a moment, Morgan returned the papers to Jessie's valise and came quietly back to bed. Jessie didn't move. After a while his breath fell into the slow, easy rhythm of deep sleep.

75

Jessie decided it was well after three. For another long hour she stared at the ceiling, trying to forget that she'd given herself to him, offered him everything she had and taken him eagerly into her body.

Before the sun rose, she slipped out of bed and dressed quickly in old denims and a worn cotton shirt. Feeling about on the floor, she found the pearl-handled derringer and slipped it behind the buckle of her belt. She hesitated a moment, then took another weapon from her valise. It was a double-action .38 Colt on a .44 frame, the gun her father had given her, and taught her how to shoot. It was a finely crafted weapon with peachwood grips and a slate-gray finish. If she ran into trouble, the .38 would prove a lot more useful than the tiny garter pistol. Jaybird Baxter didn't seem like much of a threat—the old man was trying to help her, not hurt her. Still, there was no use taking chances. Ki had proven that the cartel had its people in Jefferson.

You ought to know, Jessie Starbuck—you pleasured half the night with one of the bastards!

Picking up her boots and Stetson, she walked quietly to the door, glancing back once at the sleeping figure. *By God, that's a night you'll pay for*, she promised him silently. *You'll wish you'd never touched me, Jeff Morgan!*

Chapter 11

Jaybird Baxter was as good as his word. Jessie found him squatting beside the road, a little less than a mile north of town. He rose as she approached, coming to his feet with a painful grimace, one hand bracing the small of his back.

"Sorry to make you walk a piece," he said shortly. "Wouldn't have been wise, meetin' in town. 'Specially after the way things has been going." He raised a shaggy eyebrow to show her he had his finger firmly on Jefferson's pulse.

"I appreciate your caution," said Jessie. "And I don't mind the walk at all." Baxter gave her a patient look and didn't move. Jessie suddenly remembered. Reaching into her denims, she drew out three double eagles and dropped them in his open palm. "There's your fifty for expenses, Mr. Baxter. And ten more in the bargain. I appreciate what you're doing."

Baxter nodded and pocketed the money without a word. "Come on off the road, but watch your step. I got a couple of horses out in the trees."

Jessie followed the old man into the woods, through a patch of heavy brush. Baxter was wearing the same rumpled suit of the day before, and she guessed it was the only one he had. From somewhere he'd salvaged an old Danbury beaver hat. Half of the high crown had been gnawed by bugs or mice. It was at least a size too small, and perched atop his hair like a stovepipe on a sod house's roof.

A dappled gray and a chestnut mare were eating grass beneath a tall white pine. Their saddles were worn, and the mounts themselves had seen better days.

"Take the gray," Baxter offered, stooping to hand her the reins. "They're both sorry animals, but the gray's some better."

"She'll do fine," said Jessie.

When they were mounted, Baxter led them east across the

77

road, then turned abruptly south. "We'll hit the bayou in 'bout a quarter-mile, then follow it on east. The Injun woman's got a shack on a little creek."

Jessie brought the gray up close. "It seems kind of peculiar to me, you know? Her husband was murdered right in Jefferson. The people who killed him likely know he had a woman—"

Baxter held up a hand. "I know what you're saying," he told her bluntly. "What the hell's she doing out here?" The rheumy blue eyes blinked once. "Answer is, she don't have nowhere else to go. *He* had the runnin' money, remember, not her."

Jessie was silent for a long moment. A patch of red flickered through the branches. An instant later she heard a woodpecker drumming against a tree. To the left, a lone blue heron took to the air.

"You know about the money—the gold he had on him," Jessie said evenly. "I suppose you know a great deal more. I don't know what kind of business you and Mr. Pike were up to, and I'm not going to ask. It seems real clear to me that Pike told you a lot more than he had a right to. *My* business wasn't his to tell. You have any idea why he might have done that, Mr. Baxter?"

Baxter shrugged. "Sure I do. Two good reasons, Miss Starbuck. One, Tobias was scared. And two, he was a drinker. A gentleman drunk, if you want to put it plain. Scared men and drunks got to have someone to tell their troubles to. Tobias had me."

"I see," said Jessie. After a moment, she asked. "How do you know Black Jack Morgan?"

"Who said I knew him at all?"

"No one," Jessie said calmly, "but I think maybe you do. I think you saw him across the street, the time you and I first me."

"Got a real good eye, for a woman," Baxter muttered.

"Then you *do* know him?"

"I know who he is, and I know he's pure poison."

"What exactly does that mean, Mr. Baxter?"

"Means just what it means," Baxter said shortly. He kicked his mount's flanks then, and showed Jessie his back.

At noon, Baxter brought them to a halt on the edge of the bayou. Starting up a low fire, he cooked wild onions and

78

potatoes in a soup, dropping in a pinch of salt and a few peppercorns. There were two skinned squirrels in a sack across his saddle, wrapped in wet green leaves. Jessie guessed he'd shot them just at dawn—probably with the old Henry repeater he carried in a buckskin scabbard by his leg.

Baxter cooked the squirrels on a forked stick, under a thick slice of fatback stuck just above. As the squirrels cooked, the fat melted and sizzled over the meat. When the game was nearly done, the old man pinched pieces of dough off a ball, stretched it in his fingers, and wrapped it around a stick. A few minutes over the fire, and he had a tin plate full of hard little rolls. Jessie liked the bread and the soup, and didn't complain about the squirrel. The fat that Baxter had used for his drippings had gone rancid, and soured the taste of the meat.

The morning had started hot and sultry. By noon, the humid air was a nearly visible pall above the dark bayou waters. Jessie's hair was limp and wet, and her cotton shirt clung tightly to her. The forest was thick with tupelo and water oak, and the ever-present cypress. Spider lilies, wild azalea, and swamp buttercup added color to the hundred shades of green.

"Not too far," Baxter told her. "Couple of miles, maybe."

"There's something I'd like to know," said Jessie, "if you can give me an answer. If this Caddo woman's hiding out from her husband's killers, how do *you* know where to find her?"

"Circles I travel in, I hear things other folks don't."

"And Pike knew about this? Because he didn't tell me."

Baxter shrugged. "Couldn't very well have done that."

"And why not?"

"'Cause *I* didn't tell *him*," he said bluntly.

Jessie reined in her mount, forcing him to stop. "Why, Mr. Baxter? You thought it was important enough to tell me."

"I was going to," he snapped. "Just didn't get around to it, is all. Come on, we're wastin' time and it ain't goin' to get any cooler!"

Baxter jerked his horse angrily aside, kicking the mount through a thick stand of fern. Jessie stared at his back. *My God*, she said to herself, *he was selling what he knew to Pike, one little piece at a time. Pike's dead, and I'm the new customer* . . .

The land rose slightly ahead. Enormous cypress boles flared into the dark bayou water. Spanish moss bearded the low

79

branches, dripping nearly to the surface. Jessie saw a cotton-mouth twisting its way across the water.

"Pines get thick a ways to the left," said Baxter. "Ol' Davy Crockett hisself used to hunt bear 'round here, they say. Got a dozen in one trip."

Once, Jessie started and jerked the mare off the path as something with a dark and scaly hide rolled heavily in the water. "God, what was that?" she gasped.

"Alligator gar," Baxter told her. "Big bastard, too. Eight foot, maybe four hundred pounds. Ugliest fish you ever saw. Got gills and lungs both. Can't figure what they want to be." Reining in the chestnut mare, he pointed south. "Our Injun lady's just ahead, but I don't want to scare her, comin' in the front door."

Jessie nodded and gripped the horse with her legs. The gray plowed up a slight rise, clearly glad to find higher ground. In a moment Baxter eased up beside her.

"Just ride easy after me," he said quietly. "I'll leave you in the grove up there and go on in." He stopped and gave her a studied look. "Only reason this woman's going to talk is for runnin' money. I figure twenty, twenty-five dollars ought to do it."

"Offer her fifty," said Jessie. "You get another fifty for yourself when this is over, Mr. Baxter. She gets her money when I hear what she's got."

Baxter frowned but kept his peace. He led the chestnut mare a few steps farther, then eased himself out of the saddle with a sigh. Looping the reins over a branch, he turned and squinted at Jessie. "Don't do nothing till I get back. Stay where you are."

"I will."

"Won't hurt to get off and stretch, I don't guess. But don't wander off. Can't never tell with Injuns. Sometimes they'll jus—*Great Jesus Christ!*"

Jessie started as the man walked soundlessly out of the trees, not three yards from Baxter. Baxter cursed, turned, and grabbed for the Henry at his saddle. The man calmly raised a pistol and shot him in the back. Baxter clawed at his horse and fell to the ground. Jessie jerked her mount around and grabbed for the butt of her Colt. In an instant the man was on her, strong hands dragging her to the ground. Jessie cried out as he slapped a hand roughly over her mouth. She caught a quick glimpse

80

of a lean, wiry body, a face with sharp features and dark eyes. His hand left her mouth and she gasped for fresh air. A heavy rag came out of nowhere and covered her face. Jessie inhaled a sweet, powerful odor, screamed against the cloth, and pounded the man with her fists. Her thoughts grew hazy and her limbs began to go numb, then the smothering darkness closed in swiftly around her. . . .

Chapter 12

Ki woke to the pungent smell of burning wood. He turned over in his bedroll and saw Silas poking with a stick at a small fire halfway down the knoll. Surrounding the bedroll was a tent of mosquito netting suspended from an upright stick planted in the ground. Ki lifted the netting and stood and stretched. The world came to an end less than fifteen yards away, shrouded in heavy fog. The knoll was a high spot on the edge of the marshy terrain—"high," as he'd learned the day before, meaning anything over a foot above the dark, sluggish water. The small patch of reasonably dry ground was a tangle of swamp grass and second-growth willow. A narrow creek choked with vines and rotting logs led off to the left. Ahead, lost in the fog, the marsh stretched off to the south. "Four inches deep and a million miles wide," Silas had said.

"Smells good," said Ki. "What is it? Catfish?"

Silas nodded. "Caught me a couple just after sunup, 'bout half an hour ago. Creek gets deeper a ways back."

Ki squatted by the fire and ate his meal in silence. The fish was covered in cornmeal and coarse black pepper. Gnats stuck to the meat before he could get it to his mouth; the tiny bugs matched the flecks of pepper and Ki ignored them. The coffee was hot, and there were biscuits left from the night before.

"How soon do you think the fog will burn off?" he asked Silas.

"'Bout midmorning. No use gettin' moving till then."

"And how much farther is it to the settlement?"

Silas grinned at Ki's expression. "Hell, man, we just gettin' to the *good* parts. You ain't seen the Big Thicket yet."

"That's good to know," Ki said soberly. "Nice to have something to look forward to."

"Ain't that the truth?" Silas dumped the lard from his skillet. "Answer to your question is 'bout dark tonight, if I know what I'm doing. If I don't, we see 'bout tomorrow."

Ki nodded, then helped his companion clean and pack the cooking gear. A day in the Thicket had taught him the wisdom of Silas's answer. No man living could say he knew even one small part of the tangled wilderness. Silas knew where he wanted to go, and roughly how to get there. If he was wrong, they'd back off and try again.

"Came here once," Silas had explained. "Got myself plumb lost in the swamp for two days. Come to find I'd circled the same damn place 'bout two dozen times. Wasn't never more than a hundred yards away."

The pair took their time getting the site in order and packing their belongings. When they were finished, they sat down to wait. Ki stared at the fog, and Silas spread his worn pack of Steamboat playing cards between his legs. He had a running game going with himself, two-handed high-stakes poker. Ki had asked him once who was winning, and Silas muttered, "That other son of a bitch . . ."

By about ten, the sun began to burn the fog away. Wisps of cloud retreated rapidly over the water, baring the ghost forest of dead and bearded pines. It looked to Ki like the graveyard of a thousand abandoned ships, stark white masts and tattered sails against a shrouded sky. When the last of the fog was gone, the sun broke through and beat on them like hammer. Ki mounted his mule and silently followed Silas out.

They'd left Annie's riverboat early one morning, south of Caddo Lake, then walked halfway to Marshall, skirting the town until they found a place to get a horse. Since he was supposed to be dead and buried, he didn't figure the cartel would follow Annie and Silas. Still, after all that trouble, there was no sense in taking chances. They kept to the backroads south, making decent time. After stopping for sleep twice, they finally traded the exhausted mounts for a big bay stallion and a clayback gelding and rode hard for the last half-day. Ki guessed they'd covered a good hundred and sixty miles, all told. If anyone had noticed them at all, they'd done a damn good job of keeping their cover.

When the land began to change, tall pine and hickory giving

way to sycamore and willow, Silas found a small town and traded their horses for mules.

"These animals used to pickin' their way through the Thicket," he explained. "Been doin' it all their lives. Ain't going to break a leg in no hole, or shy ever' time they see a snake."

Ki cursed the big creatures the first day out—and blessed them the second.

The way ahead was flat water the color of slate. The muddy bottom seemed to be an inch or so deep as far as the eye could see. So why was Silas wasting time, cutting a curlicue pattern across the marsh instead of slogging straight ahead? He stood the plodding pace as long as he could, then veered the long-eared animal off its course and took after Silas at an angle. Nothing happened for the first few steps. Then the mule abruptly came to a halt. Ki kicked the beast soundly in the ribs, but it balked and refused to budge.

"What the hell's wrong with you?" he said sharply. "Let's go, damn it!"

"Nothin's wrong with *him*," drawled Silas. Ki turned to see that his friend had ridden up behind him. "Ol' mule just don't like quicksand, is all." Without another word, he turned and left Ki to his problem. Ki frowned at the gray water, then dismounted, and let the mule back off. When it was where it wanted to be, he mounted once again.

"All right," he said evenly, "you're smarter than I am, mule. I won't say another word."

Toward noon the marsh, with its forest of skeletal trees, came to an end. Yellow iris dotted the shore ahead. Silas led them out of the water onto slightly drier ground. At once they were lost in a tangle of willow and sharp-leaved holly. Farther on, the willow gave way to a steep hammock of pine and welcome shade. Silas eased himself to the ground, stretched, and peered through the trees. Ki heard a sound behind him, turned, and saw a hundred white herons rise out of the marsh.

"We passed the Big Sandy late yesterday afternoon," Silas said to him. "Bound to have crossed the Cypress and Bad Luck Creek. Reckon we be all right."

Ki nodded. Silas mounted again and turned to face him. "Gets real bad from 'bout here. Don't advise no exploring. Keep back of me, and don't argue with that mule."

"I won't," Ki said soberly, "don't worry."

On the other side of the hammock, the land turned abruptly into a hot and lifeless swamp. Past tupelo and green palmetto fans, the dense growth closed in around them in a tangle of big-boled cypress and choking vines. The sluggish water on either side was mirror-black, cut off from the light above. When sunlight managed to pierce the thick canopy overhead, it struck the water in muted shafts of ochre green, as if the sun had passed through panes of colored glass.

The heat was unbearable, the air almost too thick to breathe. Dark clouds of mosquitoes found the pair at once. Ki and Silas smeared their hands and faces with rancid fish oil. The smell was strong enough to choke a bear, but the mosquitoes stayed away.

The path through the swamp grew more treacherous with every step. Even the mules were unsure of themselves now. One moment the tussock was solid, the next the animals sank clear up to their knees. Gallberry bushes grew thick, and over ten feet high. Black gum, bay, and water oak choked the way. Color seemed out of place in the gloomy bog, yet bright flowers abounded in a dozen different shades. Hundreds of snow-colored and snakemouth orchids clung to the vines and trees.

The air was strong with the smell of mold, and it seemed to Ki that everything around him was falling apart with rot. Touch a wet leaf, or snap a piece of bark, and something white and wriggly crawled out. It took Silas a good three hours to guide their mules two miles to drier ground.

"Call those places baygalls," Silas told him. "'Cause of all the bay trees and gallberries. Awful goddamn place to get stuck. Kinda pretty, though. There's flowers in there ain't but a few men ever seen."

"Are we going to hit any more fine spots like that?"

"Not if I can help it," said Silas. He slapped a bug on his neck. "This is *spring,* man. Ought to see this place 'bout August . . ."

Late in the afternoon, Silas signaled them to a stop and sat quietly in the saddle. Ki listened, but heard nothing other than the constant shriek of birds, the far off grunt of a bull 'gator. Silas motioned him forward and told him to wait. Ki nodded, and watched his friend guide his mule between two heavy oaks. In less than a breath, Silas vanished as if he'd never been born.

85

Now that he knew the place better, Ki had mixed emotions about the Thicket. You could hide all the gold in the world in there, stack it right in the open, and it was likely that no one would ever find it. But the Thicket worked two ways—for you and against you. It would hide you and swallow you up all at once. He recalled the brief journey just behind them—two men on mules, traveling light. Christ, if the cartel was running gold through the Thicket, they had to have a full battalion of outlaws to support their operation. Most likely, there was a good-sized community back in the swamp—shelter, supplies, mounts, probably women and liquor to keep the men happy.

The magnitude of his task suddenly struck him. He'd have to find the cartel's base without the cartel spotting him first, then get out, find a telegraph west of the Thicket, and try to get Jessie and an army of marshals or Texas Rangers back into the tangled wilds. Maybe they'd bring in help up the Trinity to Liberty, or take one of the better roads. Ki remembered that Bremond's rails ran up from Houston—

He swept his thoughts aside as Silas suddenly reappeared. "Did better'n I thought," the man said with a broad grin. "The settlement's through the trees 'bout half a mile. Walked right right up on it." Silas's face went solemn. "Ki, these are good people here, and you'll be treated just fine. But don't expect anyone to run out and greet you."

"All right. I understand."

"There's not many black folks in the Thicket—never was no plantations or nothing else in here callin' for slave work or cheap labor. White people that live here is just as poor as us, and that ain't always too good. Most white folks don't take kindly to being as poor as blacks. Lot of times, they take out their mad on us. People in this place don't cheer or nothin' when they see a white man coming."

Ki waited. "There's something else, Silas. What is it?"

Silas shrugged. "Good news or bad, depends on the way you want to take it. Jacob Mose has been around. Folks has seen him here less than three days back. Got a burr up his ass 'bout something. Whatever it is, he ain't going to be too happy 'bout *you*."

"You're saying there's some kind of trouble. Something to do with Jacob Mose."

"There's always trouble where Mose is. Man *lives* on trouble. And he don't much care for whites."

86

Ki forced a grin. "Tell him I'm half white and half Japanese."

"Uh-huh, I'll do that," Silas said soberly. "Thing is, half's likely white enough for Mose."

Chapter 13

Men and women looked up as Ki and Silas rode into the village. Ki nodded, and some nodded back. The men were dressed in faded cotton trousers, patched many times. Their shirts had been bright calico patterns when they were new. Now the colors were faded by too many washings. Each man wore a tattered straw hat pulled low over his brow. The women wore dresses that matched the men's shirts. Straw hats or bonnets hid their features. Men and women alike were gaunt and lean-featured. If there were any portly citizens around, Ki didn't see them.

The settlement was a hodgepodge of ramshackle dwellings built from driftwood and whatever else was available. As they rode through, dozens of children gaped and pointed. Most of them, Ki noted, were big-bellied and spindly-legged, small ribs clearly visible under arms as fragile as sticks.

Silas stopped before a house nearly covered with pepper vines and Virginia creeper. Ki eased off his mule and joined his friend.

"Noticed you watchin' the young'uns," said Silas. "Told you folks was poor in the big Thicket. Eat mostly fried meat and lots of lard—whatever the hell they can get. Can't see it in these chillun here, but the white babies all got skin as yellow as tallow. Folks from outside calls 'em 'clay eaters.'" Silas shook his head. "Lots of little ones die of chills and fever— black and white the same."

"The Thicket doesn't make you real welcome."

"No. For a fact it don't."

Silas disappeared inside, and returned with a short black man with frizzy gray hair and rheumy eyes. "Ki, this is Mr. Loomis King," he said solemnly, "he's kindly lettin' us use his place. Movin' in a night with his daughter."

Ki shook the man's hand. "We're grateful, Mr. Loomis."

88

King looked solemnly at Ki. "You beat the shit outta that feller on the boat, like this boy says? That really true?"

Ki glanced quickly at Silas. "Uh, yes sir. It's true."

King grinned, showing the few teeth he had left. "You make yourself at home. Yes sir, you're welcome as long as you like."

Silas smiled when the old man was gone. "He'll be tellin' that story to everyone in the place. Be a dozen men and a bear you took on, by the time he's finished."

"All right, it was a good idea," Ki admitted. "Maybe it'll impress Jacob Mose."

"Maybe," said Silas. "Wouldn't count on it much, though."

Before the evening settled in, Ki asked Silas for directions and walked north past the village to a point where the sluggish creek deepened to relatively clear water. Following a hard-packed dirt path, he passed a marshy inlet where weathered planks and old bricks had been laid to cover the mud. Dugout canoes and larger, flat-bottomed pirogues were pulled ashore. Two black men patching their boat looked up and nodded.

Farther upstream he found the shore lined with sycamore and cherrybark oak. A frayed rope dangling from the water told him he'd found the swimming hole. Making certain he was alone, Ki stripped and washed the grime and sweat of travel from his body, scrubbed his clothes, and laid them out to dry in the lowering sun. Dressing, he sensed someone behind him, turned swiftly, and caught a small boy peering at him from the brush.

"Hello," Ki said quietly. "What's your name?"

"Franklin Lincoln Smith," the boy announced. "Mistah, you sure got funny-lookin' eyes."

"I know," said Ki. "Can't help it, though." The boy nodded gravely, ducked through the foliage, and disappeared.

Taking a shortcut back, he passed wooden pens made of rough-cut timber. He could smell the big razorback hogs long before he saw them. They snorted as he passed, rolling in the mud to send clouds of swollen blue flies into the air. The animals were enormous. One, an old meat hog, looked three hundred pounds or more. Tusks curved up from its bottom jaw, met strong upper teeth, and clicked menacingly at Ki.

As he approached the settlement again, a pack of short-haired curs barked at his heels. Ki smelled woodsmoke and food, and his belly reminded him he was hungry. Silas was

89

gone, but a tallow candle burned on the wooden table, lighting two corners of the room. There were straw-mattressed beds and two keg chairs. The mattresses were covered with tattered quilts, bright with indigo and red-oak dyes. The floor was hard-packed dirt. A stone fireplace with a mudcat chimney was centered on one wall.

On the table, Ki found an empty plate scraped clean. Beside it was another, covered with a cloth. Ki lifted the cover and found bread, a piece of smoked pork, and some sweet potatoes. Clearly, Silas had eaten and he wasn't supposed to wait. Drawing up one of the chairs, he wolfed down the meal. The pork was wood hog, butchered and smoked the fall before, and heavy with salt. Ki ate every bite, and wiped his plate clean with the last piece of bread. He thought about looking for Silas, and decided that wasn't a good idea. The people here knew who he was, but there was no use pushing his luck. No one cared for strangers poking about in the dark. Leaning back and stretching his arms, he wondered how Jessie was faring. Wherever she'd decided to gather her forces, she was likely already there. There were plenty of trains to Fort Worth and Dallas, or down to Galveston and Houston. By now, she'd—

Ki sat up straight and forced himself not to turn around. "Evening," he said. "Come on in."

The voice behind him chuckled. A shadow darkened the table, moved past Ki's shoulder, and turned to face him. "Got a pretty good ear on you. Most folks don't hear me coming."

Ki looked up. The man's voice was a rich rumble that came from deep within his chest. The voice matched the thickset frame, bull-like neck, and almost perfectly square head.

"You'd be Jacob Mose," said Ki.

"Yeah, that's who I'd be. And they call you Ki." He stood before the table, big fingers hooked in a leather belt, openly studying Ki from head to toe. His shirt and trousers were old but sturdy, and a faded denim jacket was stretched tight over heavily muscled arms and a powerful chest and shoulders. His broad, flat features seemed chiseled out of stone. Ki thought his flesh was as dark as any he'd ever seen, with a sheen like highly polished wood. His eyes were deepset, and clearly missed nothing he wanted to see.

"Wasn't a good idea," Mose said abruptly. "You comin' here."

"No? And why is that?"

90

"'Cause you're not welcome is why," Mose said harshly. "'Cause I don't want you here, and neither does anyone else."

"Maybe. But you're the only one who's said it."

Mose's face went hard. "Anyone bother to tell you who I am? Shit, you don't *look* all that dumb." He spread his denim jacket to bare his belly. Ki had already noted the long-barreled pistol jammed in his belt. It was a Peacemaker .45 with a cutaway trigger guard.

"Yeah, I know who you are."

"You don't talk like you do."

"I talk the way I do because I'm a man, just like you. I don't work for you and take your pay. That means we start off even, unless you want it some other way. You come on mean and hardnosed, I'll get the picture."

"You figure you can handle that, do you?" Mose said shortly.

Ki shrugged.

Mose made a face. "Folks is sayin' you fought for a black man on the river. Beat up a couple of whites."

"I helped Silas out of a scrape."

"Well, don't count on it buyin' nothing from me."

"You're the one pinning on medals. All I'm doing is listening."

Mose eyed Ki with open disgust. "If I was you, I'd feel some pushed. Looks to me like you'll bend pretty far."

"I will. You're getting there, though."

"Well, now—" Mose looked encouraged. "That's something, I reckon. You ain't *all* white, are you?"

"No. I'm not."

"Which is it? Part Chinaman, or what?"

Ki didn't blink. "I'm half Japanese. My mother. What about you? Are you a full-blooded darky?"

Mose stared in disbelief. His broad features twisted in rage, and his chest swelled up like a bear's. Then, without warning, he threw back his head and gave a great, booming laugh that shook the room.

"By God, I know how far you'll go now, don't I?" The smile vanished as quickly as it had come. "Ain't sayin' I won't kill you for that, mister. But you ain't short on guts."

Ki let out a breath. "I gave you back the same as you handed me. A word about as useless as those you were throwing around. If you want to try to take me, that's up to you. I didn't come here for that. I came to the Thicket looking for something. If

91

you want to listen or tell me to go to hell, just let me know which. If you don't want to fight or talk either, I'm going to bed."

Mose licked his lips and scowled. "Long as I'm already here, go ahead. Not promisin' a damn thing."

"I wouldn't ask you to," said Ki. Leaning forward across the table, he told Jacob Mose who he was and what he was doing in the Thicket. Mose didn't bat an eyelash at the news of the missing gold, or the murder of the Caddo or Tobias Pike. An ugly frown creased his brow when Ki told him what had happened to James Cooper and Charlie Clay.

"Didn't know this Clay," he said evenly, "but James Cooper, he's some kinda family. Don't rightly know just what. Lord, that is a bad thing to do to a man."

"I've come up against these people before. More than likely, they took pleasure in killing Cooper that way."

Mose stood, found an old briar pipe in his jacket, and filled it with shag from a pouch. "James Cooper said I'd lend a hand in this, did he? I sure ain't bound by what another man says."

"No." Ki shook his head. "Cooper didn't say that at all. He told Pike you were the man to see about anything in the Thicket."

"He was right about that," Mose said flatly. "Dead *wrong* 'bout me helping you."

Ki waited, then stood and held out his hand. "Your privilege, Mr. Mose. I thank you for your time."

Mose scowled at Ki's hand, then turned to strike a light to his pipe. "You tell me, mister half-Japanese. Why would Jacob Mose want to help some rich white lady get back her gold? What the shit difference does it make to me whether her or someone else got a million or two more? *Damn*, man!" His big fists tightened and his eyes flared with anger. "You got any idea what *three* dollars means to these folks who's feedin' you tonight?"

"I've been poor," Ki told him. "I know."

"Maybe you do and maybe you don't," Mose growled. "Can't answer my question, though, can you?"

"Why you should give me any help?" Ki shrugged. "I doubt if it'll do much good, but I've got an answer. I know the people who are stealing that gold. Sooner or later they're going to run into folks living out here. A man fishing, a woman or a child hunting berries. If it hasn't happened already, it will. When it does, someone minding his own business will just up and dis-

92

appear. These people don't *care* whether a six-year-old saw something he shouldn't. They'll just kill him on the spot without blinking. Black, white, or whatever. It's like a weasel living close to your chickens, Mr. Mose. If you know he's there and you don't do something about him, don't be surprised when you find the bloody feathers."

Mose frowned at the ground, then turned and stared into the night. "Folks you're looking for are maybe ten, twelve miles southwest of here. Don't know exactly where or how many, but they're there. Hard spot to find, too."

"Could you show me the place?"

Mose's laugh exploded in his chest. "Likely. But I won't." He faced Ki again. "There's a man got himself a little settlement down the creek. Him and his brood. Five mile or so in the direction you're going. Name's Josh Biggers. You want to go in, Biggers could take you where you want to go—*if* it was what he was of a mind to do."

"And you know this Biggers?"

"Oh yeah." One corner of Mose's mouth curled in a grin. "I sure do know Josh Biggers. He's the meanest white man I ever saw. Hates everything living. 'Specially black folks, and me in particular. We been trying to kill each other 'bout ten years now. 'Fore I die, I'm goin' to catch him, cut off his head, and stuff it up his white ass." Mose looked straight at Ki. "You got any sense, you'll forget what I'm saying, and leave Josh Biggers alone."

"Thanks," said Ki, "I appreciate what you've told me."

Mose lumbered to the door and spoke over his shoulder. "When you leave this town, pay for what you ate and where you slept."

"I don't guess I need you to tell me my manners."

Mose nodded, and disappeared into the dark.

★

Chapter 14

Ki was on his way as soon as the first pale patch of gray light touched the sky. For a good half hour, the trip was almost pleasant. The slim canoe slid effortlessly downstream under a tangled canopy of green. An unexpected breeze dimpled the water and kept the mosquitoes at bay. A gray squirrel scampered up a loblolly pine, sending a lark sparrow into flight. A snake slid through the water and disappeared.

The change came almost at once. The sun rose over the swamp and turned the Thicket into a furnace. The cool breeze sizzled into steam, and the bugs came out with a vengeance. In an instant Ki was soaking wet, choking on gnats and mosquitoes. Letting the dugout drift, he smeared himself with fish-oil repellant. This morning the awful stuff seemed to have no power except to stink. Ki stuffed wads of cloth in his ears and up his nose, and kept his mouth and eyes shut.

South, and maybe five miles, was all Mose had said about the home of the mysterious Josh Biggers. Ki, though, needed no more help than that. There wasn't a man, woman, or child in the backwater settlement who didn't know exactly where Biggers's place was, and how to avoid getting near it.

"Keep straight to the creek, and don't wander off in no branches," advised Loomis King. "It's awful easy to do, and you ain't real used to the place." Wandering outside, King came back with a clump of dry straw and told Ki to stuff it in his pocket. "There's a trick to most everything," he said with a grin, and told Ki how to use the straw to find his way.

Now, less than a mile from the settlement, Ki knew exactly what King had meant about keeping straight to the creek. Dark, clear water suddenly turned to silt. The stream ahead forked in a dozen directions, each looking exactly like another. The

94

channels moved sluggishly through a maze of dead logs and saplings as thick as cane.

Ki pulled himself along, carefully testing each channel. Sometimes the straws came to a stop the minute they hit the water. More often they drifted at the very same speed on every branch. The trick might work for Mr. King, who'd spent his whole life in the Thicket. For Ki, it was just another way to get lost.

Near noon, he glanced up and saw a red-tailed hawk circling the matted growth. Ki wondered what it looked like from there. Every way he turned seemed the same—stagnant black water clotted with weeds, twisted trees heavy with hanging moss. The heat sucked every breath of air out of the swamp. Ki's body cried for water, and he forced himself to ration small swallows from his canteen.

More than once, the way ahead simply ended, the channel too thick with mud and vegetation to let him through. He could turn back, or get out and walk—slog his way through the mire and hack out a path to better water, then come back and drag the dugout through. He was glad he'd worn a pair of the good snakeboots he and Silas had purchased with their mules.

Ki was no longer sure he was headed due south. Until the bright haze drifted off, he'd have to trust his sense of direction.

"What you're going to do," Silas had warned him, "is get yourself *lost* out there, damn it. You don't know the Thicket. It'll swallow you up fifty yards from where you started."

"I can't take you in, and you know it," Ki told him. "Hell, Silas, this Biggers or one of his brood's likely to shoot me on sight just for practice. What do you think they'll do if they see a black man coming?"

Silas wasn't happy, but he had no answer for that. "I see a big 'gator with slanty eyes 'bout Christmas," he said soberly, "I'll figure you maybe ain't comin' back."

The haze drifted off close to two in the afternoon. Ki was surprised and pleased to see that he was still headed south. The way ahead cleared, opening to dark water under the shade of thick-boled cypress. The dugout seemed suspended in a cavern underground. Ki could see dry land on two sides, boggy hammocks lined with swamp grass and willow and stunted oaks.

How far have I gone? he wondered. Mose had said maybe five miles. Ki felt he'd taken enough turns to more than double

95

that. Letting his gaze sweep the murky water, he searched for some sign that the creek flowed out of the lake. Soggy knolls blocked the way south and west, which meant the creek was east, if it left the lake at all. Ki plunged his paddle in the water, and set the dugout gliding off to the left. A jay chattered overhead. A swarm of gnats clouded the water. He was nearing the far side of the lake when he heard a girl laugh.

Ki sat up straight, letting the dugout drift. Sound was deceptive in the swamp, but wherever the girl was, she was close. He gave the paddle a stroke, and let the canoe nose ashore among the willows. Keeping low to the ground, he climbed the shallow knoll and peered cautiously through the brush.

The pool was long and narrow, sheltered by willows and the mossy branch of an oak. The girl was laughing and swimming in circles, tossing sparkling water into the air. Ki sucked in a breath and held it. She was young, no more than seventeen, a rangy, big-boned girl nearly six feet tall. Ladies that size could look peculiar, but Ki found no fault with this one. Every naked curve and hollow on that big, magnificent frame was sized just right. Pale yellow hair the color of corn spread out on the surface of the water. Her eyes were summer-blue, set wide over a broad, generous mouth and a saucy little nose. Gold coins of light dappled the water and danced off the full swell of her breasts. As Ki watched, the girl arched her back and let herself float across the pool. His grip tightened on the branch beneath his hands. The girl closed her eyes and swept her arms over her head. Droplets of water clung to her belly and glistened in the silky yellow patch between her legs. At the end of the pool she stood, grasped her long hair in both hands, and walked up the bank. The action gave Ki a breathtaking view of the curve of her back, a tight little bottom, and impossibly long legs. With her back still to Ki, she squeezed a handful of hair, letting water drip down her back.

"Ain't nice at all, mister, peekin' at girls in swimmin'. Didn't your ma never tell you?"

Ki's face colored. The girl turned and looked right at him. Her eyes seemed almost colorless in the harsh light of the sun. Ki let out a breath and walked into plain sight. She watched him come, her legs spread slightly apart, her hands loose at her sides. She made no effort to turn away or cover herself.

"Sorry," Ki said quietly. "I heard you laughing and walked up there to see who it was. I didn't know you were—how you are—"

96

"Uh-huh. Kept on a-lookin', though, didn't you?"

Ki forced a smile. "Yes, I guess I'm guilty of that."

"No harm done," she said flatly. "I been seen before. Go on and get a good look.

"Uh, listen—" Ki cleared his throat. "I meant what I said. I just happened on you, and I—"

"What?" The girl's eyes narrowed and the sleepy drawl went flat. "What the hell are you doin' here, mister? Where you think you're goin'?"

"South," Ki said blandly. "South and a little west."

"Nothin' there to see, 'cept a lot more of this."

"Just what I'm looking for," Ki smiled. "More of this. I've never seen this country before."

The girl didn't believe that at all. She wet her lips and crooked her left hand up to her waist. The motion raised her right hip at a jaunty angle, putting all her weight on one leg and thrusting her flat belly forward. The big, tawny body looked at ease, sleepy and relaxed. Ki knew better. There was an animal sense about her, a feral, untamed glint in her eyes. If he made a wrong move, she'd bolt and disappear like a doe. Now he understood how she'd known that he was here, though he hadn't made a sound leaving the boat or climbing the knoll. She was as much a part of the Thicket as any other wild creature. She'd sensed him, smelled him, known what he was. Ki's samurai training had taught him such talents over the years. The girl had been born knowing everything he knew, and likely a great deal more.

"You shittin' me, mister," she said abruptly. "Ain't nobody fool enough to come in here without no reason."

Ki decided that lying to this girl would get him nowhere at all.

He'd planned to try to get a close look at Biggers's place before showing his hand, but now that was out of the question.

"You're right," he told her. "Got to be careful who you tell your business to. I'm looking for a man named Josh Biggers."

"Uh-huh. What for?"

"I need to talk to him."

"'Bout what?"

"Well now, that's between him and me, isn't it?"

"Not if you don't *find* him, it ain't," she said bluntly. "Tell me what you want, I might take you to him."

"You know where he is?"

For the first time, the girl almost grinned. "Hell, mister,

97

anybody you meet down here on two legs is goin' to be a Biggers. We don't 'low no one else."

"Thought that's who you might be."

"Reckon you're thinkin' right if you did." She licked her lips again and let her eyes flick boldly over his body. "Listen, fella—you any good at stickin' a woman?"

"*What?*" Ki's mouth fell open. "Did you—say what I thought you said?"

"Goddamn, you got mud in your ears? I *asked* if you was—"

"That's what I thought," Ki finished. "Look, I, uh—don't think I got your name. Mine's Ki."

"Mine's Amanda Biggers. What's *that* got to do with anything? Are you any good or not? Lord God, mister, you're kinda slow in the head, you don't mind me sayin' so. Whyn't you quit talkin' and just swim or fly or whatever it is you do, and get yourself over here fast."

Ki could think of a dozen reasons why accepting the girl's invitation was a terrible idea. Number one on the list was that she was Josh Biggers's kin—daughter, niece, or cousin, it didn't matter which. Men like Biggers didn't take kindly to outsiders wandering in to sample their women. On the other hand, she was a fine-looking young lady, as slim and sleek as an otter, all that honeyed flesh glistening wet and naked—

"You know what I was thinking?" Ki said quickly. "Might be a good idea if you took me to see Biggers first. We could get our talking done and you and I could have more time to spend together."

Amanda's blue eyes flashed. "Friend, you don't get your ass over here and pleasure me fast, you ain't even gettin' *close* to Josh Biggers."

"Well now, if you put it that way—"

"That's the way I'm puttin' it." She grinned. "You do somethin' nice for me, maybe I'll do somethin' for you."

"Seems, ah—fair enough," Ki said soberly. He didn't care for the tangled roots and high grass that bordered the pool. The water looked good, and he jumped in and waded across. It was only waist-deep, but he stopped in the middle to let his body sink to the bottom. The layer there was cool, untouched by the blazing sun. The girl braced her legs and offered a strong hand.

"Damn it," she said irritably, "didn't figure you was goin' to take a bath."

98

"I've been traveling all day. Gets hot out there."

"'Course it gets hot. What'd you think it'd do?" She came to him then, locked her arms around his neck, and pressed her body wantonly against him. "My, my, you ain't a bad-lookin' man. Hard as a rock, too. All *over,* seems to me." She giggled and ground her belly playfully against him. Her hard little nipples burned like brands against his shirt. Her flesh smelled wet and musky, like a small wild animal in heat. The scent excited him further, and swelled his erection against her.

"Oh Lordy, let's do it," she gasped. "Let's do it right now!"

Ki was more than willing. Any caution he'd felt before vanished abruptly when her supple young body touched his. Her breath came in rapid little bursts against his throat. Her thighs pounded frantically against his legs while her fingers busied themselves with his trousers. Ki cupped her cheeks between his hands and raised her lips to his. Amanda sighed and closed her eyes.

"I'm goin' to like you a lot," she cried. "I'm goin' to like you somethin' fierce!"

"I'm going to like you, too," Ki laughed. "I like you already, Amanda."

"Haven't—haven't had me a real good man since John Henry got kilt by a bear last fall."

"Who's John Henry?"

"He was—he was my second-oldest brother. Sure good with a woman."

"Uh, your *brother?*"

Ki heard the unmistakable click of two hammers and felt cold steel between his shoulders.

"Climb off him quick, you little slut," a voice behind him said harshly, "'less you want to meet the buckshot comin' through!"

99

Chapter 15

When she awoke, everything hurt...

A dull, steady pain throbbed at the back of her head. Her body was numb, arms and legs as heavy as lead. She felt as if she'd slept in some terribly cramped position for a week. Her belly was hollow and empty, but the thought of food made her gag. The sickly sweet taste in her mouth took care of that.

Chloroform. She knew that was what they'd used. The taste and the smell brought the moment racing back to fill her thoughts. The man's sharp features, the narrow bridge of his nose, the slash of his mouth, as cruel as an open wound. And the eyes— Jessie shuddered and tried to forget the way they'd bored right through her in that instant before the rag covered her face.

It happened so fast. My God, no one can move like that! Baxter was dead and the man was on her before she could blink, before her hand could close fully about the grips of her Colt. He'd simply *been* there, swallowing the distance between them and wrenching her off her horse to the ground.

He's fast. Fast and incredibly good... you don't pick up talent like that off the street...

Ki's words struck her like a rush of cold air. Of course, it *had* to be the same man, it couldn't be anyone else! The cartel had her—they'd watched and waited, bided their time and then taken her when they chose, netted her like a fish. They knew everything about her: Jaybird Baxter, the Caddo Indian woman—

A sudden rush of shame and anger coursed through her veins. They didn't *have* to know where she was going or who she planned to meet. They just kept her busy and waited. Black Jack Morgan took care of that.

Damn you, Jeff! How could you make love like that, and then do this to me, you cold-blooded bastard! The question

100

gave way to another, one she didn't care to answer. *How could you be dumb enough, Jessie, to let a man like that take you in?*

She forced herself to relax, let the deep, calming breaths bring her back to reason, as Ki had taught her. Her hands and feet were bound. It was dark. Nighttime dark. A thin band of light from a kerosene lamp streaked the bottom of the door across the room. The motion and the rhythmic droning of the engines told her she was on a river steamer. Going where, and what for?

Forget it, she told herself grimly. *You don't much want to know the answer to that . . .*

She slept, woke, and slept again. When the key clicked in the lock, her body jerked in sudden alarm. The man squatted down and brought the lantern close to her face. Jessie turned from the harsh circle of light. She smelled clean linen and lavender water as he turned her on her belly and cut her free.

"Get up, Miss Starbuck. On your feet, please." The voice was firm but calm.

"Can't," Jessie said sharply. "You tied me so damn tight, I'm all numb."

"No," the voice corrected, "that's not so. Sit up and rub your ankles and wrists. You'll be just fine."

"I will, huh? That's a real comfort." She brought herself up and did as she was told. For the first time she noticed that her boots were gone, along with her belt. The man made no effort to rush her. When her hands and feet were working better, she pulled herself erect against the wall. Her head swam for a moment, but she gritted her teeth and held on.

"Are you all right now?"

"Don't bother to be helpful," she snapped. "I don't think I could stand it. Now what?"

"Out this door, please. Climb the stairwell straight ahead, a few feet down the deck."

The night was hot and humid. Darkness closed in around the boat on either side, and she could see nothing at all. The idea of making for the railing and jumping over struck her at once. Apparently her captors had thought of that, too; there was a man in shadow between Jessie and the water. She shrugged and climbed the steps and waited at the top.

"In there, Cabin Two." The man reached past her to open

101

the door. She caught a glimpse of a round, kindly face with ordinary features, hair thin and silvered at the temples. "You'll find a bath and a clean dress. I'll come to take you to breakfast in half an hour."

Jessie almost laughed. "Breakfast, is it? Just a bunch of old friends getting together on the river."

The man pretended not to hear. "Just knock when you're ready, Miss Starbuck."

Jessie bathed and dressed as quickly as she could, keeping one wary eye on the cabin door. It was foolish, she guessed; if the man wanted to watch and bring a dozen friends with him, there was nothing much she could do.

Still, she was relieved when she was ready. The garment they'd furnished was a simple calico dress, the cheapest you could buy ready-made. The sleeves came down to her wrists, and the collar covered her throat. There were no undergarments, and no shoes.

For a moment she studied herself in the mirror. The effect was almost startling, and she knew at once what they had in mind. The cheap cotton fabric was so thin that it clung to every curve and hollow of her body. Her nipples poked boldly against the cloth; she could follow the line of her ribs past the indentation of her navel to the thrust of her pelvic mound. Turning around, she could see where the cloth followed the cleft between her buttocks. She looked more naked and vulnerable than if she'd worn no clothes at all.

All right then, that's what you're after. You want Jessica Starbuck barefoot and humble....

Why, though? That was the part that sent a chill through her.

The sky was gray, the river still murky and indistinct, when they came to get her. Leading her forward, they crossed the upper deck from starboard to port, past the dark stack and the skeletal masts of the derrick. The man opened a door and ushered her in.

"Sit down, Miss Starbuck. Someone will be joining you shortly."

"Oh my—" Jessie's frown was a parody of disappointment. "You mean we're not dining together?"

"Perhaps another time," the man said solemnly. He motioned her in, and closed the door behind her.

Jessie inspected the room. The dining salon was much like those she'd seen before, on a dozen sternwheelers. Not quite as nice as the *Texas Star*, but clean and well kept. There were two places set, one at each end of the table. She walked to the far end and took a chair. Almost at once, the outer door opened again. A man in butternut trousers and a faded blue shirt stepped in. Jessie started and gripped the arms of her chair. Lord, it was him! The man who'd murdered Baxter and brought her here, the man who'd nearly killed Ki!

The man looked past her, his muscles standing out in startling relief against his clothing, his black eyes moving restlessly about the room. Another man entered behind him. He was tall, closing on sixty, elegantly dressed in charcoal gray and a fine silk shirt. Jessie didn't miss the stickpin in his tie—a stylized gold crown, the cartel's unmistakable symbol.

The man looked straight at Jessie and smiled. "Miss Starbuck, a pleasure. My name is Dietrich. I hope you rested well?"

"You know damn well I didn't," Jessie said sullenly.

Dietrich waited while his shadow eased back a chair, then took his seat. The portholes were covered against the dawn, but the kerosene lamp on the wall turned his deeply lined face the color of parchment. He had a thin, aristocratic nose, a full and sensuous mouth, and ice-blue eyes. His hair was faded blond, swept back harshly across his skull.

"We'll eat now," he said quietly over his shoulder. "Tell them, please, if you will." The man nodded and disappeared through a galley door. Jessie's host caught her following him with her eyes. "His name is Malik," he told her. "Malik al-Kamil. He comes from a village in Syria, near the Wadi el-Harir. His father was a French soldier and his mother was an Egyptian whore. He can speak, but he seldom does. His silence is his penance for the shame of his birth." Dietrich paused, then leaned forward and smiled. "His only talent is killing. Your, ah—late friend was quite good. Malik is obviously somewhat better."

"Damn you!" Jessie exploded. "What do you want with me!" She didn't have to reach too far to find the anger to convince him that she thought Ki was dead.

Dietrich sat back, clearly pleased with her reaction. "Everyone has to die, Miss Starbuck. You should be quite proud of your man. He bested a great many of our people."

"There aren't enough of what you call your people to begin to pay for him," Jessie said sharply. She looked up then, as a portly young man in denims brought food out of the galley: hot bread, muffins, cold melon, bacon, chops, sausage, scrambled eggs, and peach preserves. Finally the man set steaming coffee on the table, and a carafe of chilled water.

Jessie decided this was no time to be stubborn. Whatever she was in for, a good meal couldn't hurt. Dietrich watched her eat, taking only a piece of melon on his plate.

"Do you mind if I talk while you enjoy your breakfast?"

"This is your party," said Jessie. The man called Malik padded noiselessly back into the room and stood dutifully at Dietrich's back. Jessie wished he'd go away. The sight of his dark eyes and cruel mouth didn't help her appetite at all.

"I'll try to make this as clear as I can," said Dietrich. "You know who we are, there's no use wasting time on that. We are taking you on a trip downriver. At the end of that journey, you will do a great many things we ask you to do. I'll be quite honest, Miss Starbuck. Whether you'll survive after you've served our purpose is still in question. But even if you do not, you have a very clear choice while you're alive. Do as you're told at all times, young lady. Do *exactly* as you're told, or I can promise you'll suffer a great deal—pain and indignities I'm certain you can't imagine. You've met us many times before, so I hope there's no doubt that I mean exactly what I say. You do understand me, don't you?"

"Oh yes. You've made it real clear." Jessie looked right at him and fought to keep the tremor from her voice. It was a foolish gesture; Dietrich would know she was smart enough to be scared. Still, she was damned if she'd let him see it.

"I guess the next question is just what do you want me *for?* I mean, besides all the pain and indignities and such."

Dietrich raised a brow. "I think that should be obvious, Miss Starbuck. The gold robberies, the very rapidly diminishing credibility of the Starbuck interests." He made no effort to hide the pleasure behind his smile, the triumph in his eyes. "You've been a thorn in our side for too long. We're simply removing that thorn. Finally and completely."

Jessie forced a laugh. "And how do you intend to do that? Starbuck isn't just me, and you know it. If I sink in a hole in the river after breakfast, the business doesn't grind to a sudden halt. If it was *that* easy, Dietrich, all you'd have to do is murder

104

a couple of Astors and Vanderbilts and Goulds, and the country'd fall into your hands." Jessie's green eyes blazed defiance. "You killed my father, and Starbuck didn't fall apart. I didn't quit, either."

Dietrich calmly dabbed his mouth with a linen napkin. "No, not that time, Miss Starbuck. This time, though, I'm quite certain you will." He looked at her and his eyes turned suddenly cold. "Breakfast is over," he said flatly. "Malik, get her out of my sight."

The lock clicked behind her, and Jessie sank wearily to the mattress in the corner. A quick glance in the growing dawn had told her nothing at all. They were headed downriver, but where? Shreveport, Natchitoches, or Alexandria, on the Red? Or past that, to the Mississippi and New Orleans?

A sudden thought chilled her to the bone. God, was that what they had in mind? Sneak her aboard a ship down in the Gulf and haul her off to Europe, to the cartel's lair? Why, though? What would be the purpose in that? Whatever Dietrich and the others had in mind, it centered on seizing the Starbuck holdings—one more step toward running the country itself. They were crazy if they thought they could pull that off, but that wouldn't stop them from trying.

Also, of course, she knew there was no way she'd get out alive after the cartel had finished with her; long experience had taught her that wasn't the cartel's way. Her only chance was to bide her time, try to keep her mind clear, her senses alert. There might come a moment, a second or two, when her captors' vigilance would relax. When that moment came, she hoped she'd have the strength and courage to take it.

Closing her eyes, she tried to relax, to gather what strength she could. The noises of the boat became familiar. The heavy thump and wheeze of the engines, the churning of the paddlewheel . . .

Chapter 16

Amanda's eyes went wide. With a quick gasp of surprise, she loosed her hold on Ki and backed away.

"Go ahead," the voice behind him said tightly, "just try somethin', mister. I'll blow your ass from here to Houston."

"Lady, I wouldn't dream of moving an inch," Ki said quietly. "Just take it easy with that thing."

"Don't you tell me what to do, you son of a bitch!" The barrels jabbed into his back. "Just turn aroun' slow, so's I can get a look at you. Amanda—get yourself decent."

"Ma, I wasn't doin' no harm," Amanda whined. "Me an' this fella was jus—"

"I *know* what you was doin', girl. God ain't struck me blind yet."

Ki turned slowly. The woman backed off, holding the shotgun steadily on his navel.

"Ain't seen you before," she said warily. "Who the hell are you, and what d'you want? 'Sides this little whore, I mean."

Ki stared at the woman in open wonderment. She couldn't possibly be the girl's mother—she didn't look five years older than Amanda herself! Even the tall, lanky figure was a copy of her daughter's. Or, he guessed, the other way around. The faded sack dress that came to her ankles failed to hide long legs and luscious curves. Except for the coal-black hair and hazel eyes, they could pass for sisters. Which meant Amanda was what, for God's sake? An extra-ripe fifteen? He'd forgotten how fast things grew in the Thicket.

The woman caught his eyes roaming, and her face went hard. "Better stuff your dirty thoughts back in your pants," she said flatly. "You in about all the trouble you can handle. Amanda—he's got a boat over yonder, past the willows. Drag it over here an' tie it to mine."

106

Amanda muttered under her breath and pranced behind her mother around the pool. The calico dress flew up around her legs and Ki tried not to look. When she returned, paddling his boat around a bend, her mother motioned Ki past the pool. He walked through scrub a few yards and saw the dugout boat pulled up on the flats. It was bigger than his own, a pirogue that could carry several people and some goods.

"Git in the back an' row, an' don't try nothin'," the woman commanded. "Girl, get that goddamn thing tied on and shove us clear."

Moments later the pirogue was moving quietly under veils of Spanish moss. The woman sat with her legs crossed, facing Ki in the stern of the boat, the shotgun on her lap. Her daughter sat behind her, in the prow.

"That's a nigger boat you was usin'," she said suddenly. "I seen a couple cut just like it. What you doin' with it?"

"I stole it," said Ki.

"You 'spect me to believe that?"

"Believe whatever you want. It's the truth. I'm looking for Josh Biggers. I needed a boat, and that one was handy."

"That's the truth, Ma," Amanda piped up. "He tol' me he was lookin' for the Biggerses."

"Shut up," the woman said wearily. "I *saw* what he was a tellin' you, gal."

"Ma!"

"Hush, Amanda. Gawd A'mighty, your pa's right as rain. You got all your brains between your legs."

Amanda stuck out her tongue behind her mother's back. Arching her shoulder, she let her dress fall fetchingly over one bare arm and shot Ki a wanton smile. He pretended to count the branches overhead. Dark water wound through a maze of somber cypress, wet islands of grass and rotting wood. The endless lagoons were strangled with weeds and a solid wall of vines. The air was almost too thick to breathe. When the sun broke through the tangle above, the feeble shafts of light were as pale as butter. Rounding a bend, Ki saw a dozen big 'gators slide off the mud flats and vanish under the water. Two of the creatures were monsters, well over fifteen feet from snout to tail.

"Me an' my brothers sat out here in the pee-row last summer," said Amanda. "You play the mouth-harp to 'em, they'll come right up to you."

107

"Shut it up, girl."

"Ma, I can *talk,* can't I?"

"Pearly Rae seen you an' your brothers out in that boat. What you was doin' with your mouth wasn't callin' no 'gators."

"Wasn't doin' nothin' with those boys you ain't done first!" Amanda shouted.

"Girl, you courtin' hell and eternal damnation for lying!"

"Ain't any lie to it, and you know it!"

"Amanda Biggers, if you don't—" The black-haired woman suddenly stopped. Color rose to her face, and her hazel eyes snapped at Ki. "Shut your ears, mister. This ain't no concern of yours."

"Yes, ma'am," said Ki, and earnestly tended to his rowing.

He smelled it before the settlement came into view around the bend. Woodsmoke, burned meat, hog droppings, and the odor of refuse. The town looked much like the one he'd left that morning: wooden shacks with roofs of dried palmetto, split-rail fences sagging in every direction. Hard-packed yards were filled with litter, yelping hounds, and dirty-faced children.

Ki gave the scenery a passing glance as the pirogue slid to a halt. His eyes were locked on the men watching him silently from the shore. There were five of them, dressed nearly alike in washed-out shirts and trousers. Each sported long greasy hair and a tangled beard that hid his features. Ki didn't need to see their faces; pale eyes narrowed in stubborn hate told him all he needed to know. He was as welcome in Josh Biggers's town as a basket of canebrake rattlers.

Amanda jumped lightly out of the boat and stood aside, pretending she hadn't ever been aboard. Amanda's mother stepped barefoot into the water, brushed dark hair over her shoulders, and handed the shotgun to one of the men.

"Found him down to the Hole," she said flatly. "Come in a nigger boat."

The oldest boy in the group glanced sharply at Ki. His eyes were closer to yellow than brown, and his beard was encrusted with food. "He was at the Hole? With *her?*" He nodded over his shoulder at Amanda.

"Don't have nothing to do with her," Amanda's mother said calmly. "He was just there, is all." Ki breathed a silent sigh of relief. He had a good idea the woman had just saved his life.

108

"What'd you bring him *home* for, Ma?" one of the boys called out. "Whyn't you shoot him out there?"

"'Cause I felt like it!" she snapped. "Mind your mouth, William T., or I'll wash it out with lye. John Lewis, see if he's got anything on him worth keeping. Henry, go and fetch your pa."

One of the boys scurried away. The man with yellow eyes stepped up and grinned at Ki. "Skin out of them clothes, slant-eye. Let's see what kind of pretties you got in your pockets."

Ki returned the grin. "Never took my clothes off for a man. I don't plan to start now."

The man stared, then solemnly shook his head. "Shit, that don't trouble me. I can go through your clothes just as easy when you're dead." He pulled an old Walker Colt from his belt and aimed it at Ki's head. Ki's right hand came up in a blur and sent the weapon flying. His left grabbed a handful of shirt, jerked the man toward him, and flipped him deftly over the point of his hip. The man yelped and hit the ground hard. A big fist struck Ki's back like a hammer. He lost his balance and started to fall forward, but rolled on his shoulder and came to his feet. The second man bellowed and tried to kick him in the crotch. Ki moved aside and came in fast, dug his shoulder into the man's gut and lifted him high, then turned and tossed him into the muddy water.

"All right, goddamn it—*hold 'er right there!*"

Ki froze and turned around slowly. The man holding the shotgun had red-rimmed eyes, a broken nose, and matted hair down to his chest. He was three inches taller than Ki, and fifty pounds heavier. He stared at Ki in open wonder.

"Mister, you plumb crazy or jus' tired of living?"

Ki wiped dirt off his face. "I don't suppose you're Josh Biggers?"

"Yeah, that's who I am." The man gave him a nasty grin and raised the shotgun to his shoulder. "Those your last words, boy?"

"You mind if I reach in my pocket?"

"What the hell for?"

"Save you the trouble of going through 'em when I'm dead."

Biggers laughed aloud and the others joined in. "Hell, that makes you feel better, go ahead!"

Ki reached in his pocket, brought out two gold coins, and tossed them to the boy closest to him. The boy opened his

109

palm and his eyes grew big as saucers.

"Glory be," he gasped, "they're—ten-dollar eagles, Pa. There's two of 'em, so that, uh—that makes—"

"Twenty dollars, you stupid bastard," growled Biggers. "Give 'em here, Henry." Biggers studied the coins and looked narrowly at Ki. "That all? You got any more of these?"

"I have three hundred dollars," Ki announced calmly. "It's yours if you'll take me where I want to go."

Biggers stared, then burst out laughing. He winked at the others and grinned at Ki. "You goddamn fool, I don't got to do *nothin'* . 'Cept shoot you and pick up my wages."

"Fine," said Ki, "go ahead."

"What'd you say?"

"I said go ahead. You think I'm stupid enough to bring that kind of money in here? It's out there. In the swamp. Tied in a little leather sack. Your wife and daughter got to talking and I dropped it in some roots. I know right where it is, too. You want to talk, fine. You want to kill me, get to it. I figure my clothes are worth about a dime. Are you willing to settle for that?"

Biggers's chest swelled and his face filled with color. "You're lying, you bastard. There ain't no three hundred dollars out there." He shot a dark look at his wife. "He get a chance to do somethin' like that? Don't tell me no story, Lou."

Amanda's mother worked her lips and looked at her feet. "I was—talking to Mandy. Yeah, he coulda slipped something over."

"Shoot him, Pa," urged one of the boys. "We can *find* the goddamn money!"

"Sure you can," growled Biggers. "Ain't more'n fifty zillion trees out there." He looked at Ki, then eased down the hammer of his weapon and tossed it angrily to one of his sons. "Come on, mister—reckon you and me better talk."

He stomped off in a storm, and Ki followed. Biggers led him past the settlement to the shade of a big oak. Notched in a limb was an ivory-colored crock. Biggers pulled out the wooden plug, took a deep swallow, and handed the jug to Ki. Ki started to shake his head, then realized that was a bad idea. Biggers was watching him closely, and he knew he couldn't fake it. The homemade hooch seared his throat and burned his belly. He could feel its tendrils surging clear to his toes, down the length of his arms, and out the top of his skull. It took

110

every ounce of control to keep from howling and breathing fire.

"Thanks," he said calmly, handing back the jug. "Real nice and smooth."

Biggers raised a brow with some respect. He set the jug aside and squatted on the ground. Ki joined him.

"All right. What kinda shit you feedin' me, mister?"

"I'm looking for some men," Ki told him. "They're in the swamp, past your place. Probably a camp of some size, twenty or thirty men, maybe more. They'd have pirogues coming in and out. Before that, mules and wagons—maybe traveling down through Polk and Tyler counties, past the Big Sandy. They're bringing something out farther south. Probably down near Liberty and the Trinity River."

Biggers looked right at him. "What kinda something?"

"What?"

"You said they was maybe bringing something out. You didn't say what."

"No? You're right, I guess I didn't."

Biggers scowled. He snapped off a blade of grass and slid it between his lips. "Who sent you in here to see me?"

"An old friend of yours. Jacob Mose."

Biggers spat out the grass and laughed. "That goddamn nigger. Meanest son of a bitch I ever saw. I'm goin' to kill that bastard one day. You wait and see if I don't." His eyes flicked to Ki's "What'd he say about me?"

"He says you're the meanest white man alive. That he's looking forward to cutting off your head and stuffing it up your ass."

"He is, is he?" Biggers grinned from ear to ear. "God*damn* his ugly black hide."

"He also said you could take me in deep if you had a mind to do it."

"Uh-huh. Reckon I could." Biggers paused and chewed his beard. "If there *was* anyone in there, like you say. And I ain't sayin' there is."

"Come on, Biggers." Ki made a noise in his throat. "If there was an extra bull 'gator out there, you'd know it. Don't take me for a fool."

Biggers scowled and looked at the ground. "All right, goddammit. They're in there, all right."

"That's better."

111

"I can show you where they are. But you're giving me that three hundred first, or there's no damn deal."

It was Ki's turn to laugh.

"I mean it, you bastard!"

"Good. So do I. You get the money when we get back out."

"Hell with that." Biggers shook his head. "Ain't no *we* to it. If I was to take you in, I'd point the way to go and that's all. Gettin' out again's your problem. Which is why I aim to get that money up front. Might be those fellers'll want you to stay, and then I'm shit out of luck."

Ki looked at him. "If I don't come back, it means you made twenty dollars for pointing me in the right direction and not risking your hide at all."

"Huh-uh. No deal."

"Whatever you say."

Biggers stood. "Which means you're 'gator meat, friend. I got no reason to keep you around."

"Suit yourself."

"Shit! You think I'm playin' with you?"

Ki stood and looked the big man squarely in the eye. "Quit talking about it and do it."

"You're a plain fool. You know that?"

"More than likely. Dead or alive, though, I've got three hundred and you haven't."

"Fuck the three hunnerd!" Biggers raged. "You got any druthers? I can do it with this old Colt or go and get the shotgun."

"How about another swallow of that whiskey? If that doesn't kill me, nothing will."

Biggers cursed under his breath. "You slant-eyed little shit. Anything I hate more'n a nigger, it's a slant-eyed little shit. Lou'll find you a place to bed down. We'll leave first thing in the morning. And leave my goddamn daughter alone, you hear?" He muttered into his beard and stomped off. Ki waited till he was gone, then walked back to the settlement.

Chapter 17

"Pa ain't ever goin' to let you walk out of here," said Amanda. "I guess you know that, don't you? Ain't no one gets the best of Josh Biggers. Anyone ever did, them boys'd be all over him."

"I'll bet they would, at that," said Ki.

Amanda walked beside him by the river, watching her bare feet make tracks on the path. "He'll worry it over like a dog with an old bone, is what he'll do. Chew on that thing till somethin' starts to workin' in his head. He's goin' to get that three hundred dollars, and you in the bargain."

"I know he's going to try. And I'm grateful to you for talking to me like this."

"Shoot"—Amanda made a face—"I wouldn't do nothin' to favor him." She shot him a shy smile from under a tumble of yellow hair. "Wouldn't want no one to ruin a fine-lookin' man like you. Ain't even had a chance at you yet."

"Yes, well—" Ki cleared his throat and, glanced anxiously over his shoulder. "It's not going to be that easy. We ought to think before we get ourselves in a whole lot of trouble."

Amanda threw back her head and laughed. "Lord, if you ain't a-squirmin' like a rabbit in a trap. 'Spect you'll chew off your leg in a minute."

"Amanda—"

"Still want to stick me, don't you?" Her blue eyes flashed with sudden mischief. "I can tell you do. Bet you're all hard, just *thinkin'* 'bout me spreadin' out wide."

"Yes," Ki said soberly, "I am. Now stop that. Teasing's a lot of fun if it doesn't get you shot. Just *talking* to you is trouble, Amanda. Everywhere I look, one of your hairy-faced brothers is looking back. And if it's not one of them, it's your mother."

113

"They ain't goin' to hurt you," she said solemnly. "Not 'less Pa tells 'em to."

"That's a comfort."

"You're not mad at me, are you?"

"No, I'm not mad, Amanda."

"Good," she said brightly, " 'cause I'm sure not mad at *you*." She turned to him then, and repeated her cute trick of letting her dress slide down to bare her shoulder. Ki raised his eyes to the sky and the girl laughed and twirled in a circle, long legs flashing under her skirt.

The Biggers settlement was larger than Ki had imagined. A dozen or so houses were clustered in the shade of ancient oaks. Many were hard to spot until you were nearly to the door; a thick carpet of Virginia creeper flowed out of the woods, and ran up the sides of the houses, over the roofs and into the windows.

"They're cousins and uncles and aunts and I don't know what-all," Amanda explained. "They're all Biggers, though. Ever' one."

You didn't have to tell me, Ki thought with a shudder. The men, women, and tallow-faced children looked disturbingly alike.

Amanda spoke to a woman boiling clothes in a big iron kettle. Nearby, a vacant-eyed youngster beat shirts and trousers with a paddle on a worn cypress block. Amanda seemed to guess Ki's thoughts. After they'd passed the spot, she spoke without meeting his eyes.

"You don't much like it here, do you?" she said.

"Why do you say that?"

"I know what's in your head. I seen you lookin' back there. Some of the Biggerses ain't smart. *I* know that. Don't guess I'm real bright myself."

"There's nothing wrong with you, Amanda."

"Uh-huh." Amanda gave him a stony look. "Every girl's *smart* 'tween her legs, right?" She kicked up dust and stopped to lean over a fence and peer inside. "That tusker's been right there since he was a couple of weeks old, and he's still wilder'n hell. See that big ol' scar on his back? That's where a bear got him. They can't outrun a woods hog, but they dearly love to catch 'em. What they'll do is sniff around and find hogs in a bed holler. They'll bite the backs of their necks and start eatin',

114

and hold on till they chew right through. Pa killed the critter that got this hog. Wasn't no good, 'cause it was right in the middle of August. Summer bear ain't fit to eat at all."

Amanda swept back her hair and jumped to the ground. Down the path, she picked a wild honeysuckle blossom and sucked out the sweetness.

"Preacher come by once and told us it weren't good for one family to be stuck out here alone. Said weddin' your own kin ain't right. Pa told him this place had belonged to Biggerses since the War, and wasn't no one else welcome." She looked up curiously at Ki. "He was right, wasn't he, the preacher feller?"

"Yes, I guess he was, Amanda. It's better for people to mix."

Amanda shrugged. "Guess what'll be is goin' to be. Always has and always will."

"Doesn't anyone ever leave?"

"Well, sure they do," she said crossly. "I been to Saratogie and Votaw and Kountze, and down to Sour Lake. Went clear to Cleveland once, and saw the railroad and ever'thing. That's near forty mile, I guess."

"No, I mean do any of the Biggerses ever leave here and *live* somewhere else?"

"You mean to *stay?*"

"Yes, to stay."

Amanda looked puzzled. "Why'd anyone want to do that? This here's where the Biggerses *belong*."

At supper, Ki ate at a big plank table between two burly members of the Biggers clan. The women and children kept quiet, and the men all talked at once, each shouting to make himself heard. More than once Ki felt watchful eyes upon him. Each time he glanced up, Amanda's mother was scowling his way. She was a damned attractive woman, but Ki couldn't settle on her looks. The smoldering hazel eyes sent a message he didn't like: *I can still tell them what you were doing with Amanda. I can, and maybe I will . . .*

Ki ate fat smoked ham, pumpkin yams, boiled hominy grits, cucumbers, and turnip greens. There was bread to use for a fork, and lard to spread for butter. After the platters were cleared away, the men broke out their pipes and chewing tobacco and talked about the best hounds for chasing wood hogs.

115

Josh Biggers told a story about catching wild ponies at Batson Prairie—a little blue dapple and a buckskin with a black mane and tail. There'd been some drinking and fighting and at least one killing. It was clearly one of Josh's favorite yarns, and the others listened with solemn respect.

A Biggers cousin was just back from a trip into Liberty, and said there was talk that Jesse James was still on the loose. The other news was that they'd given Ben Thompson a marshal's star over in Austin.

"That true?" Josh turned to Ki, the first time anyone had appeared to notice his presence.

"I've heard it is," said Ki.

"Well, shit," growled Josh. "If they'll make Ben Thompson a marshal, might as well run Bill Longley fer pressy-dint."

"Bill Longley got hanged, Pa," one of the boys volunteered.

"Now who the fuck asked you!" Biggers turned on the boy in a rage. "Talkin's finished," he announced, and pushed himself away from the table.

Ki was given quarters in a cramped, windowless structure, a log shed chinked with mud and straw. The walls and ceilings were lined with hooks, telling him the shack had been used to smoke meat. The night was still and humid, and the inside of the shed was a furnace. Still, it wasn't much better outside, and if anyone poked around, he'd know they were coming.

Ki wished he had his *tanto* blade, but it was lost in an alley near the waterfront in Jefferson. He had a wooden-handled knife Silas had bought up in Marshall, and there were still four *shuriken* throwing stars wedged in the lining of his waistband. The knife was dull, and the *shuriken* were next to useless for close fighting. If anyone bothered him, he'd meet them with his hands and his feet. They'd served him more than once, and they were weapons that never got lost.

He was thankful he'd brought the roll of mosquito netting, wrapped tightly in a hand-sized bundle. He kicked his feet through the dirt to scatter scorpions or spiders, then spread the blanket and draped the netting off the wall, holding the loose ends down with rocks. The instant he doused his candle, the mosquitoes arrived in droves. They sounded as big as birds, but the net kept them away.

Ki closed his eyes and listened to the night. A big 'gator grunted in the swamp, and locusts sawed in the trees. Some

116

of the Biggerses were up, and he could hear the discordant twang of a cigar-box fiddle. A man with more whiskey in him than song was doing "Molly Darlin'" and "Bring My Blue-Eyed Boy Back to Me."

The 'gator went silent. A sound like the eerie wail of a panther came from far across the swamp. Ki listened, but didn't hear it again. The man with the fiddle went to bed. A child wailed at the far end of the village, a sound very much like the big cat's cry. Ki relaxed, let out a breath—and jerked up at once, every sense alert.

"It's all right, it's me," the voice whispered softly. "I ain't a 'gator or nothin'."

"Amanda?" Ki's mouth went dry. "Are you out of your mind? If anyone catches you in here—"

"Shhhh. No one's goin' to catch me, all right?" Her shadow bobbed once against the night, then she slid under the net and nestled snugly in his arms. "Oh Lordy," she whispered, "now I'm goin' to get me what I missed back there at the pond."

"Amanda—" Ki slid his hands along sleek and naked flesh. "Where the hell did you leave your clothes?"

"Hush—don't need any clothes for this, and neither do you." Her fingers worked hastily in the dark, undoing his fly buttons and peeling his trousers over his ankles. "Oh my, yes, that's a good'n all right. It sure as hell is!"

Before Ki could move, her hand circled his erection. He felt himself swelling further under her touch. She rubbed her fingers gently along his smooth flesh in an easy rhythm. Then, without warning, her tongue flicked out to tease him, stroke him with rapid little thrusts. The moist flesh of her mouth was as hot as a furnace.

Ki drew in a breath and caught his hands in a tangle of hair. The girl groaned and opened her mouth to take him in, letting him draw her to him until her brow pressed hard against his groin. Her fingers raked his thighs and she pounded her face frantically into his belly. Long hair lashed his flesh like a whip. The strokes grew harder and faster until Ki felt a storm churning violently within him. It swept through his loins, shuddered into his member, and exploded in the warmth of her mouth.

The girl groaned and dug her fingers into his hips, eagerly drinking him in. Her slender body trembled with excitement. Ki filled her with coursing fire again and again, until she moaned and fell away, moist lips gasping for air.

Ki reached down and brought her into his arms. Her body was sleek and wet, musky with the sharp animal scent of their pleasure. She writhed against him like a snake, caressing his flesh wantonly with her own. Ki tried to hold her, but she slipped out of his grasp. Her breath came in rapid little bursts, her body trembling with a need she couldn't contain.

An instant before, she'd brought him to pleasure, drained him, and left him empty. Now he felt himself swelling again, his hunger unabated. She was a wildcat in his arms, an untamed creature with a wicked fire smoldering in her belly.

Ki grasped her shoulders hard, lifted her off him, and slammed her back against the ground. The breath burst out of her lungs. She tried to cry out, but Ki stilled her lips with his own. Her hands slid quickly between their bodies, grasped his shaft, and thrust it joyously inside her. Ki felt the surging heat of her loins, the warm flesh closing about him. He thrust himself against her; her hands found his neck, tore at the hard muscle of his shoulders. Ki felt the thunder building again. They were both poised and ready, balancing on the thin edge of their pleasure. Suddenly he came to his knees and lifted her off the ground. She bit the flesh of his shoulder and scissored her legs around him. Ki grinned and let her guide their pleasure. Her silken thighs slapped against him again and again. Her hands slid down his neck until she was hanging loosely beneath him, hair trailing the ground. She thrust her warmth around him, the hunger in her belly driving her to a frenzy. Once more, fire surged through Ki's loins; the girl felt it too, and thrust the wedge of her silken mound against him even harder. Without warning, he loosed himself inside her. She buried her cries in his throat and let her own sweet release take her under. A joyous burst of pleasure spasmed her slender frame. A sigh escaped her lips and she fell limply to the ground.

Ki bent to kiss her, tasting the sweet spices of her mouth, the hard points of her nipples. She drew in a breath and pushed him away.

"Can't," she whispered. "Got to . . . go now or I never will . . . just stay here and let you do that to me again and again."

"You're probably right," Ki said softly. "It's a good idea and a bad one too. Amanda—"

"No—" She placed a finger on his lips and slid out of his grasp. "By God, mister, I never had any better—" Ki reached out to touch her but she was gone.

118

Falling back on his blanket, he took a deep breath and let it out slowly. Lord, the girl had left him as empty as a husk. There wasn't enough left in him to even matter...

"Ki— you still awake?"

"Huh?" Ki opened his eyes quickly and strained into the dark. He could just make out the tousled head of hair. "Amanda! You're going to get us both killed!"

"Oh, Ki," she whispered, "I just *had* to. I can't help it." She slid under the netting, into his arms.

Ki chuckled. "What do you think I am, girl? You took everything out of me—I haven't got a thing left to give."

"What?" Amanda pulled away and stared in the dark. "Mister, don't you go sayin' such crazy things. I been all hot and wet since I laid eyes on you, and I'm damned if you're going to make me do without!"

"Do without?" Ki echoed, puzzled. "We just—"

"We just *what?*" the girl said, then stiffened and exclaimed, "Oh my Gawd!" She gripped Ki's hair and pulled him erect. "It's Ma," she said harshly, "just as sure as I'm alive. Goddammit, I can smell her. That *bitch!* That goddamn bitch has done it to me again!"

"Wh-what? Amanda, that's not possible."

"It ain't, huh?" Strong hands came up and pressed him roughly to the ground. "I'll take seconds, friend, but I'm damned if I'll do without. You better *find* somethin' big and hard right quick, 'less you want to hear how loud this little girl can holler!"

"Amanda," Ki said calmly, "it wasn't my fault. I didn't know. Maybe tomorrow you and I could, uh—"

"Hell with tomorrow," she said flatly, sliding the cotton dress off her shoulders. "You and me both know Pa's goin' to take you out first thing and try to figger how to git that money and cut your throat. Now just where the hell does that leave me?"

119

Chapter 18

"You sleep good last night?" asked Biggers. "Don't look real bushy-tailed this morning, you don't mind me sayin'."

"Mosquitoes," Ki said with a shrug.

"Uh-huh. Skeeters can keep a man tossin'." If Biggers's words held any further meaning, his eyes didn't show it. Ki was more than pleased to let the subject die.

Biggers had stomped into his shed before dawn, less than twenty minutes after Amanda slipped away. They'd shared a breakfast alone at Biggers's table. Neither Amanda nor her mother was in sight.

The day was less than an hour old, but the settlement was already far behind. Ki sat in the pirogue's stern and dug his paddle through murky water. His own smaller dugout trailed behind them on a rope. Josh sat facing Ki, the shotgun cradled in his arms. Moments before, they'd passed a baygall swamp, a spot even darker and more tangled than the one he and Silas had encountered. The place was alive with wild orchids and clouds of bugs, and Ki was thankful they'd skirted all but the edge.

Biggers scratched his head and squinted at the sun. "Here's what we got now, boy. Like you figgered, there's a bunch of folks up to somethin' where we're going. They come in and out with pee-rows and mules. Sometimes carryin' stuff, sometimes just travelin'."

"And you can get me in close? Won't they have guards out watching?"

"Shit." Biggers shot him a dismissing look and spat over the side. "Place they're at does all the guardin' a feller needs. What's goin' to sneak up an get 'em? 'Sides 'gators an' me?"

The pirogue was starting to drift, and Ki edged it back in the shade. "Where will you be when I come out?"

120

"Right where I leave you," Biggers assured him. "God-damn, boy, don't expect you to trust me. No reason why you should. But I'm damned if I can figure how to get that three hundred without you. So I'm goin' to take care of you the best I can. Without getting my own hide burnt, you understand."

"Right. That's fair enough."

"Good. Now let's stop jawin' and get moving. We got a fair piece yet to go."

The way was easy enough, the water dark and as smooth as glass under a canopy of thick leaves and dripping moss. Some-how, Ki had imagined the cartel's retreat would be surrounded by a nearly impenetrable swamp, strangling vegetation and muddy bogs that would hide the gold raiders from the world. But now he saw that the spot they'd chosen made far better sense. You could get in and out with relatively little trouble—if you knew where you were going. If you didn't, you could float about and look at black water and fat 'gators.

Color flashed through the trees, and Ki saw an ivory-billed woodpecker settle on a branch overhead. This part of the swamp seemed alive with the bright birds. The creatures were as big as hawks, with jet and white feathers and a startling red crest. Below, the water boiled with fish, and now and then the sleek shape of an otter.

Passing a hammock of land, Ki saw the high dark crowns of magnolias. The green waxen leaves seemed to thrust above the trees near at hand. Biggers caught his eye and grinned.

"They're a sight, ain't they? I could show you a magnolia'd put these here to shame. Two hundred feet if it's an inch. Coushatta Injuns say it's a thousand years old, and I believe 'em."

"Are there very many Indians around?" Ki asked, recalling the Caddo who'd worked for the cartel.

"Some. See one now and then," Biggers said glumly. "Worthless bastards, most of 'em. Just another kind of nigger. Can't trust a one of them."

Ki didn't pursue the subject. Josh Biggers's tolerance didn't stretch beyond the last house in his settlement—and his trust didn't go beyond his nose. Ki figured that the only reason Biggers was tolerating him was that the man's prejudice took a back seat to his greed.

●　●　●

121

Toward late afternoon, Josh sat up straight and took notice of the scenery. "We're gettin' in close," he told Ki softly. "Just paddle where I tell you, and don't make any noise."

The endless stretch of dark water and bearded trees looked no different to Ki than any others he'd seen. Biggers, though, stopped to sniff at every clump of swamp grass and rotten log.

To Ki's right, a big cypress had fallen years before. The enormous trunk lay half submerged, the cluster of broken roots choked with weeds and dead vines. Nestled in the midst of this tangle was a sight that sent a chill up the back of his neck. Twenty or thirty water moccasins lazed in a dappled patch of sun. They were twisted together like something disemboweled, the heat warming their slick grayish brown hides and white bellies.

Ki looked away and slid the pirogue silently over the water. Biggers motioned him left and right, through one dark channel and then another. Finally he turned to Ki and spread his hands flat. Ki brought his paddle out of the water and let the dugout drift.

"Bring your own boat in, and don't let it bump," warned Biggers. "Sound carries good out here."

Ki nodded and pulled the smaller boat alongside.

"Where you're goin' is about fifty yards through there," Biggers said, pointing to a small waterway branching off the one they were on. "There's a little finger of land with good cover. You hide the dugout there, and the camp's just ahead. The shadows'll be long, and if you're good they won't spot you. If'n you're smart, you'll see what you want to see and git out fast."

"And you'll be here?"

Biggers showed his irritation. "Said I would, didn't I? I'll sit real quiet till dark, then hide this thing and take me a snooze up a tree. You won't see me, but I'll see you. Now give me your paddle and get movin'. I don't like jawin' in the open this close."

Ki handed Biggers his paddle and crawled carefully from the pirogue into the smaller boat. Both hands were steadying the sides, and one knee was in the boat, when Biggers swung the paddle and hit him solidly in the back.

Ki cried out and went flying. Muddy water closed over his head. He came up spluttering, and saw Biggers gazing down the shotgun's length at him.

122

"Jus' stay where you are, boy. Don't come no closer than that."

Ki shook his head and stood. The water wasn't more than three feet deep. "I don't know what the hell you're doing," he said tightly. "This isn't going to earn you much pay."

"Well now, we'll see if it don't," Biggers drawled. "Jus' hold her real steady there, friend."

Ki started to speak. Motion caught his eye and he turned and saw two pirogues gliding toward them from behind a stand of cypress.

Josh gave him a wink. "Over here, boys," he called out cheerfully. "I got your froggie all gigged."

The first boat held two men Ki had never seen. They were solid, hard-eyed fellows in faded denims and worn Stetsons. One paddled, while the other carried a Winchester .44-40. The second dugout was smaller. Kneeling at its center was one of Josh Biggers's bearded sons. Ki felt anger rising in him, and cursed himself for a fool. He'd figured Biggers would wait until he got his hands on the money. Instead, Josh had left their meeting the day before and sent his son on ahead. The son of a bitch had never intended to keep the deal!

The man in the pirogue's bow gave Ki an appraising look. "All right, Mr. Biggers. Your boy didn't tell us all that much. What you figure we're gettin' for three hundred? Who's he supposed to be?" The man's face was pale, his eyes empty of emotion. He spoke in a flat West Texas drawl.

"What you're gettin'," Biggers said smugly, "is a feller willin' to spend good money to learn where you boys are, and what you're takin' in or out of the Thicket. *Real* interested in your business, he is. Likely a lawman, you ask me."

The man looked narrowly at Ki. "That right, mister? You lookin' for us?"

Ki shifted his feet to keep from sinking further in the mud and stagnant water. At the moment he couldn't think of an answer...

Jessie woke and pulled herself erect.

Her head felt empty and hollow, her body sluggish and heavy. Reaching out blindly, she found the jug and brought it to her lips. The water tasted awful. She made a face and set the jug on the floor. Her bare feet touched the deck. She braced her hands on the bed and tried to rise. The dizziness swallowed

123

her up and she sagged back onto the bed.

My God, what's wrong with me? I can't even stand!

She rested a moment, then took a deep breath. The air in the small cabin was thick and hot. The thin dress clung to her flesh like a second skin. She listened a long moment, ran a hand through her tangled hair, and tried to gather her senses. She gripped the edge of the bed to keep from shaking. Christ, what was wrong with her, what was *wrong?*

"Miss Jessie, you all right?"

"What?" Jessie started. "Wh-who's that, who's there!" Her eyes darted warily about the shadowed room. The little girl stepped up and laid a cool hand on her arm.

"It's all right, it's just me. I think you been dreamin' again, Miss Jessie."

Jessie stared. The girl was pale and awkward, growing too fast for her age. Thirteen or fourteen, she guessed. The simple dress that hung from her shoulders betrayed the beginnings of womanly hips and budding breasts. Her hair was straight and brown, eyes dark and enormous in a china-doll face.

"Wait, now. Wait—" Jessie reached out and held the girl's face between her hands. "You're—you're *Louisa*, right?"

The girl showed her a patient smile. "I'm *so* glad you remembered. You forget things a lot, you know."

"Oh yes, I know," Jessie sighed, and let her hands fall to her sides. It was coming back now—some of it, at least, in little bits and pieces. Fragments of days and nights. The man. The cabin. The girl.

God, what did they give me? Laudanum? Something else? I can't even think straight anymore!

There was breakfast with the man named Dietrich, and that was the end of the cartel's efforts at being social. No more meals outside the cramped cabin, nothing to eat at all, except watery soup and bread.

And somewhere in there, Louisa. Louisa helped her, stayed with her, talked to her and kept her from getting lonely.

"Louisa—" Jessie grasped the girl's small hands. "Louisa, do you—do you know how long we've been here? Do you, darling?"

Louisa let out a sigh. "You *always* ask me that. Every time."

"Do I? I'm sorry, really. I'm—not thinking real well."

"I know," Louisa said solemnly. "They give you some kinda medicine."

124

"Yes, yes, that's it," Jessie said intently. "You understand that? Good, Louisa. That's why I can't remember what I ask you."

Louisa smoothed Jessie's hair. "It's been three days, is all. Not more'n three."

Three days? God, it seems like years!

"Next, you always ask me who I am and where I came from," said Louisa. "I got stole, is what happened. 'Bout a month ago. My pa's got a place on the Guadalupe."

"Oh Lord. Near where, dear?"

"'Bout five miles from Gonzales."

"Yes, I've been there," Jessie said gently, bringing the girl into her arms. "I know right where it is." She bit her lip to keep from crying. The bastards! If they'd had this child a month, what did they want with her, what was she doing here? Jessie didn't like to think about that. Not now. And if she asked Louisa, it might frighten her even more.

"We've stopped awhile," Louisa announced. "I think we're taking on wood."

"Yes, that's probably what they're doing," said Jessie. "It looks dark out. Is it night?"

"About seven, I reckon. They'll be bringing us something to eat real soon."

"Are you hungry, Louisa?" Jessie studied the girl's pale features in the dark.

"Some, I guess."

"I am too. Real hungry." She thought for a moment, then brought the girl closer. "Only this time I'm going to try not to eat. Maybe we can get rid of my food somehow, all right? I don't want to take any more of that medicine. Not if I can help it."

Louisa gave a helpless little shrug. "You already tried that. Don't you remember?"

"Did I? No. No, I guess I don't."

"They always watch us eat," Louisa explained. "'Cause right after that's when they take you off to talk."

"What?" Jessie sat up straight. At once, memories came rushing back to fill her head. The stifling cabin next door, Dietrich asking her one damn question after another, patiently writing her answers in an open ledger. Long, tedious questions about Starbuck business. How much money was invested in shipping interests? What were the returns from Asian trade?

125

From Europe? From South America? What were Starbuck's plans for land development in the Territories?

"Lord, I remember," Jessie sighed. "I'm sorry, Louisa. That's why I've got to find some way to quit swallowing whatever they're poking down my throat."

"Oh, you don't have to worry about that," said Louisa. "'Least I don't *think* so."

"Oh? And why's that, dear?"

Louisa screwed up her face. "Remember? The tall man got real mad at the other one? Said it—said it didn't do any good to talk if you didn't make any sense?"

Jessie sighed. "Well, he's right. But—no, I don't remember that at all."

That would help, she decided. If they didn't keep her drugged, she could give them answers close enough to the truth to throw them off. And if her head was clear, she could think of some way to get off this damned boat and get help. Ki was down there in the Thicket right now. Maybe he'd already found the spot where the cartel was hiding the gold. Somehow she *had* to break free and help him before the—

Louisa's small hands dug into her arm as the cabin door burst open. The wiry figure of Malik stepped in, then Dietrich, holding a lantern.

"Supper will be late this evening, ladies," he said bluntly. "We've wasted a lot of time, and we have a lot to talk about."

"I could say I'm not real interested," Jessie said, "but that wouldn't matter much, would it?"

"I'm afraid not," Dietrich said coolly. He put his hands behind him and studied Jessie. "And wrong answers won't help either, if that's what's on your mind. *Please* don't waste my time with that, Miss Starbuck."

"Wouldn't think of it," Jessie said shortly. "Lord, I couldn't lie to an important man like you."

For an instant the gaunt cheeks flushed with anger. "Miss Starbuck, you must not even consider playing some foolish game with me. Don't let such a thought enter your mind. *Malik!*"

Dietrich's head snapped up, and Malik moved. Louisa screamed as the man wrested her from Jessie's arms. With one motion he tore the girl's dress away and tossed it aside. Louisa stood frozen, too frightened to cover herself. Jessie went to her at once and swept the cringing girl behind her.

"Don't you *touch* her!" she snapped, green eyes blazing with anger. "Don't you let that bastard *near* her, you understand?"

"I'm sure that won't be necessary at all, Miss Starbuck."

Jessie went cold at the man's easy smile. She knew, now, exactly *why* Louisa was here.

Chapter 19

The man in the checked shirt took a healthy slug of rye, wiped his lips, and set the bottle on the table. Glaring at Ki, he left the circle of light and spoke to one of the players. Both men laughed. The rye drinker walked purposefully up to Ki and hit him solidly on the jaw. The blow snapped his head sideways and turned the chair half around. The man grinned, hooked his boot under the chair, and sent it crashing to the ground. Ki cried out as his shoulder struck the floor. The pain licked down his arms and across his back.

"You keep that up, Sam, you goin' to kill him sure."

"Well now, who the hell cares if I do? Set the bastard up, Jimmy. I'm going out to take a piss."

Jimmy laid down his cards and brought the chair upright again. "Son of a bitch is sure mean when he's drinking."

"He's mean when he's *not* drinking, too," Ki said. He tried to relax, force back the pain, and fill his lungs with air. Every breath was an effort. His hands were bound tightly behind the chair, stretching his arms until his shoulder blades nearly touched. He could still feel his fingers, but his feet were completely numb. He didn't like that; he could take the beating, but if they left him bound too long, he'd lose his feet. The man called Sam had run out of rope and used wire and a pair of pliers on his ankles. He knew it was too tight, and what would happen if the bonds weren't removed.

Sam worried him a lot. From the start, it was clear he wasn't looking hard for answers. He'd listen, but he didn't much care what Ki was after, or who he was. The hurt was what counted. Besides drinking rye, it was the thing he did best. The heavy leather glove that covered his fist was slick and clean, unmarred by calfing ropes or barbed wire.

Ki ignored the stinging sweat and forced his eyes open.

128

Besides Sam, there were three other men in the room, two playing cards and one watching. That made four, and he'd seen at least five others when they brought him in. Nine or ten, then. Perhaps a dozen, if some of the hands were out of camp. A few shacks set back in the trees, a couple of storage sheds and some dugout canoes. A hammock of dry land out in the swamp, and a handful of men who were clearly hired guns— drifters and small-timers you could hire by the gross in any bar west of St. Louis.

And that doesn't make sense, not with the kind of money that's moving through here. There's someone else around, someone who's not showing his face—

Ki glanced quickly at the door as Sam walked in, took a last draw on his smoke, and flipped it into the dark. Turning to Ki, he grinned and slapped a leather-covered fist in the palm of his hand.

"You get rested up, boy? Feel like doin' some more talkin'?"

"Mister," Ki said evenly, "I've *been* talking, you just haven't been listening."

Sam leaned down and brought his face close to Ki's. He had a three-day beard, and eyes as bright as marbles. "I don't want to hear the same damn thing all over," he said gently. "I want to hear the truth. I'm *tired* of listening to your lies."

"I'm not lying. You—"

Sam slapped him hard on both cheeks. Ki's eyes watered and he bit back the pain.

"You give me that same old shit once more, I'm goin' to kill you!" Sam roared.

"I'm—looking for work," Ki said doggedly. "I heard over in Liberty that there was a—a camp in here that'd hire a good gun."

"Fuckin' *liar!*" Sam hit him hard in the belly. Ki moaned and retched on his shirt. Sam stomped off, came back with a bucket of water, and tossed it in Ki's face. "You're a liar and you smell bad, too. You stink, mister, you *stink!*"

"I—heard there was work here and—"

Sam bellowed in anger and buried his fist in Ki's gut. Ki gagged, but nothing came up.

"Might be he's telling the truth, you know," said the man who was watching the game. "You got no way to say he's not."

"And you do, right?" Sam said shortly.

129

"What I'd do if I was you is keep him *alive* till the boss man gets here," the man said evenly. "You kill a feller shows up here, he don't get to talk to him first—"

Sam laughed. "Marty, this goddamn Chink don't know nothin' but his name."

"He knew we was in here." Jimmy said plainly.

Sam threw the man a look, and turned back to Marty. "I know what's botherin' you. You gave that fool Josh Biggers three hundred dollars. If this feller don't know something, you figure the boss'll have your hide. Three hundred goddamn dollars." Sam gave him a pained look and glanced slyly around the room. "Who you think this bastard is—Jesse Chink James?"

The two men playing cards laughed. Marty got up slowly and the laughter stopped. Ki looked up and saw him clearly for the first time. He had plain sandy hair, ordinary features, and no life in his eyes at all.

"I give the man money 'cause that's the way the boss wants it," he said quietly. "He thinks I gave too much, I'll tell him the truth—that you was too drunk to ask. Sam, you run the show here any way you want. But don't go fuckin' with me. I ain't exactly tied to no chair."

Sam's fists closed at his sides, and his features went rigid. The man named Marty didn't move. Sam faced him a moment longer, then shook his head in disgust. "Shit, I'm getting some sleep," he growled under his breath. "You all want to nursemaid the Chink, you can do it without me." He paused to grab the bottle from the table, then stomped out of the room and slammed the door.

Ki waited, listening to the night until he was certain they were gone. The empty shed was ten, maybe twelve feet square, with a high peaked roof and sturdy crossbeam rafters. There was no light at all, but he'd looked the place over while Jimmy held a lantern and a pistol and the other man tied him for the night.

"Jesus, you going to make him stand up?" Jimmy had complained.

"Yeah, I'm goin' to make him stand up," the man grumbled. "That goddamn Marty could stare down a grizzly, but I ain't ready to take on Sam. This feller ain't here in the morning, I don't want to be the one that made him comfy."

"Don't know where the hell he'd go if he got loose."

130

"Uh-huh." The man shot Jimmy a cold stare. "Don't know where the hell I'd go, either . . ."

The man had done a good job.

Ki's hands were bound securely, the rope tied to a crossbeam overhead. The beam was rough-hewn timber, four inches on a side. Standing flatfooted, arms stretched over his head, his hands touched the beam with less than an inch of slack between his knuckles and the wood. Even if he'd had the strength to try, there was no room to pull against the rope and try to break it.

The scene in the shack hadn't reassured Ki at all. Sam had backed off, and likely would again. Someday he'd get liquored up and shoot Marty in the head while he slept. Right now he'd be thinking about Ki, and about finishing the job he'd started. He'd seen the man's eyes and knew it was so. Sam would finish the bottle and take a snooze and come and find him. If Ki was still here, he'd beat him to death.

Ki closed his eyes and let his whole body relax. His heartbeat slowed; his breath settled down to an easy, shallow rhythm. Every disturbing thought began to melt from his mind like tallow. Bringing his samurai training to bear, he pushed the pain aside, let it stay with another Ki, a part of himself he left behind. There was no more time for pain now. Time was running out, and he needed every second he could buy . . .

Suddenly springing from the balls of his feet, Ki brought his legs up and wrapped them around the beam. His thighs gripping the beam, he was now hanging upside down, his wrists bent painfully under his body, his shoulders and head hunched forward to take off some of the pressure. Slowly he began to work his wrists against the loop that held his hands, shifting the portion of the rope that circled the beam. Sweat covered his body, but he was grateful for it, since it lubricated his arms and wrists and allowed them to slide more easily against the chafing rope. Eventually the rope began to move against the beam. Ki was glad the wood was rough-hewn, and therefore of unequal thickness. He began to move the rope gradually toward a place where the beam was almost imperceptibly thinner; even a little more slack might make all the difference.

He was keenly aware of precious minutes slipping away. The rope moved a bare quarter-inch, then another. Every movement eased the tension in his wrists and gave him more strength and leverage. His body felt as heavy as lead; his head was near bursting from the pressure of the blood that flowed into it in this upside-down position. He wished there were more light, but he knew that really it wouldn't help. There wasn't anything to see.

Finally the rope began to move freely against the beam. He rocked his body from side to side, building up enough momentum that he was eventually able to swing himself up so that he now lay atop the beam, on his belly. A groan of exhaustion escaped his lips and he sagged against the rafter. *All that effort,* he thought, *just to straddle a piece of wood!*

Ki dreaded the next few moments. From the start, he'd never been certain this would work. The angle was all wrong, the tension too great. Just getting started could take all night.

Placing the backs of his hands perfectly flat against the beam, he arched his back and tried to fold his body into a ball. The tips of his fingers grasped the waistband of his trousers. If he could slip his fingers into the concealed pocket behind the waistband, he was free. Four of his razor-edged *shuriken* throwing stars were hidden there. If he could get his hands on one, he'd cut through the rope in seconds.

Ki struggled to bring his wrists into position. To do the job right, he needed a keen touch and a steady hand. Instead, his wrists were scraped raw, the tips of his fingers ragged flesh. He had all the dexterity of a fiddler wearing mittens.

It has to be now. If I can't do it now, it won't happen—

Ki stopped and raised his head, suddenly aware of dim shapes around him in the dark. It was dawn. He'd worked the whole night and it was getting light outside!

The discovery stopped him cold, and he took a deep breath to calm his fears. If Sam didn't show up soon, someone else would. And he'd be sitting there, perched like a monkey in a tree!

The tips of his fingers parted cloth, and he found the *shuriken*'s keen edge. Stretching his arms as far as they'd go, he worried the object slowly out of his waistband. It was there, almost in his grip. A quarter-inch would do it, one more push and—

Ki's face twisted in horror as the throwing star slipped from his trembling fingers. He felt it slide off the beam, heard the metallic ring as it hit the hard-packed floor. For an instant he stared helplessly from his perch. It was so light now that he could see the *shuriken* below. Gritting his teeth, he jammed his fingers savagely into his waistband, trying desperately to tear the fabric away. A fresh surge of pain told him he'd found the second star. Ki closed his eyes and probed with bloodied fingers. Suddenly the sharp-edged weapon was in his grasp. There was no time now to try the cord around his wrists. Bracing the star against his palm, he began frantically sawing the rope that circled the beam. It was coming—he could see the tough fibers parting one by one. . . .

Dull gray light slanted through cracks in the roof. A hound barked, and Ki heard a man curse it. He slid the edged disk back and forth across the rope, his own sweat and blood now wetting the frazzled strands.

Ki froze and someone kicked a wooden door. A man laughed and said something he couldn't make out. Footsteps sounded on the narrow path behind the shed where they'd led him the night before.

Too late! Ki let the *shuriken* fall. Muscles corded in his neck as he jerked his hands desperately against the rope, trying to part the last strands with his strength. The rope held, refusing to let him go.

"Hey, Chink, you ready for breakfast, fella?" Sam's voice grated from the path outside. Ki reached within himself and drew forth the last bit of strength he could muster, closed his eyes, and jerked again. Suddenly the shed below blazed with morning light.

"Hope you slept good, you little bastard, 'cause I— Huh?" Sam froze, blinked, and then looked straight up. A curse died on his lips and he backed off fast, clawing for the pistol in his belt. Ki gave a ragged, high-pitched yell and thrust his closed fists at the sky. The rope snapped and sent him flying. Fire blossomed and seared his flesh. His body hit Sam across the chest and slammed him hard against the ground. The big man bellowed, chopping out wildly with the barrel of his gun. Ki leaped free of the tangle and lashed out with his foot. The blow caught Sam in the belly. He grunted and fired wildly. The roar of the shot was deafening in the small shed. Ki kicked out again and missed. Sam scrambled off and backed hastily for the door. Ki rolled, came up in a crouch, and rammed his shoulder in Sam's back. The gun exploded again, plowing a hole in the earth. Ki hit him again and the pistol fell free. Sam's dark face clouded and his big left fist swept out in a killing punch. Ki moved back, bent his knees, and brought his bound

133

hands up in a blur. The blow caught Sam on the point of his chin and sent him reeling. Ki sprang back, cocked his leg at the knee, and kicked out at Sam's chest. Sam screamed and went pale. Ki heard ribs snap as the force of the blow ruptured the man's heart. Sam's eyes went blank and he slid to the floor.

Ki ran to the door and peered out. Someone shouted, and a rifle exploded twice. Lead chipped splinters over his head. Ki leaped through the door and ran, putting the shed between himself and the man with the gun. The .44-40 cracked behind him once more. Ki sprinted down the path under the trees, weaving his way through curtains of Spanish moss. A man shouted, then another. Ki saw them coming straight at him, cutting off his retreat. Both gunmen stopped and emptied their pistols in his direction. Ki glanced desperately from left to right, took three quick steps, and dove off the path into the swamp water.

Chapter 20

Lead peppered the water all around him. The bullets made shrill, high-pitched gurglings as they punctured the surface. Ki didn't dare come up for air; the water was barely three feet deep, and they knew exactly where he was. Worse still, he was practically crawling along the bottom, and swimming with both hands tied together didn't help his speed at all.

His lungs were near to bursting when his hands hit something hard. A cypress—one of the thin-bladed roots that flared several feet from the base of the tree. Ki pulled himself quickly to the far side of the trunk, surfaced, and sucked air. A shout went up from the shore. An instant later a volley of lead thunked into wood.

For the moment he was safe. They could plunk away all day and never hit him. He knew, though, that they weren't about to do that. An instant later he heard them thrashing through weeds, and then a dugout hit the water.

Ki took a deep breath. What the hell was he supposed to do now? He wasn't a lot better off than he'd been in the shed. Gripping the smooth bark, he risked a quick look around the tree. The gunmen yelled and loosed another volley. Ki had seen all he cared to see. There were three large pirogues racing toward him. Three men paddled, while five armed gunmen lay prone in the bows. They were twenty yards off and gaining fast. Ki guessed it would take about three minutes for the men to kill him. Four, if they were all half blind.

Filling his lungs, he felt his way to the bottom along the roots, then pushed himself off. There was a thick stand of cypress some thirty yards away, low branches heavy with Spanish moss. If he could make it that far, the moss would screen him. Maybe the water would get shallow and he could run. . . .

For a moment he was sure they hadn't seen him. Then bullets

135

began to weave frothy patterns all around him. He pushed off desperately to the right, knowing at once that that was a mistake—they'd turned him from his goal and made him use his air. Too late, he kicked his heels hard, clawing frantically at the mud with useless hands. He sensed the dark shape just behind him, heard the paddles slap water. His lungs screamed for air, his legs had nothing left to give. Stopping dead in the water, he turned around and faced them, dug his feet in the mud, and launched himself straight out of the water. A terrible cry escaped his throat as he broke the surface, swinging his bound hands like a club. The gunman in the bow looked startled, hesitated an instant too long. Ki's fists hit his rifle and sent it flying. The second gunman sat up straight and cursed, lowered his pistol point-blank at Ki's head. A sharp clap of thunder rolled over the water. The outlaw jerked upward and clutched his chest. The man in the stern began paddling as fast as he could.

Suddenly a volley of gunfire ripped through the swamp. Ki kept low and made for the nearest tree. The men in the last two dugouts had lost all interest in where he was. In an instant they'd turned from the hunters into the hunted. Ki could see where the intruders had holed up. They'd stepped out of a dugout onto the roots of a big cypress. Shooting from cover, they picked off their targets one by one. The gunmen answered their fire, but their efforts were next to useless. They were caught in the open, with nowhere to go.

In less than a minute it was over. The pirogues were empty. Ki heard the sharp lever action of a Winchester echo over the water. From behind the big cypress, a barrel poked squarely in his direction.

"If that's you, Ki, you better holler out fast," a voice said shortly. "If it ain't, you deader'n stone, mister!"

Ki laughed aloud. "It's me, Silas. I give up, all right?"

A dugout nosed from behind the tree. Silas sat in the bow. Jacob Mose was in the stern. Silas grinned and waved at Ki, but Mose stared somberly over the water, looking for any targets still moving.

Ki wolfed down his sandwich and walked out of the shack. Silas had found some good salve, ripped up one of the outlaw's clean shirts, and bound Ki's hands. They felt a little better, but they'd take a while to heal. Silas stepped up beside him as

136

Jacob Mose ambled out of the trees.

"If you counted good, there ain't any left," he said shortly. "If any swum off, they goin' to wish they's dead soon."

"I'm grateful," said Ki. "I guess you know that."

Mose made a rumbling sound in his chest. "This goddamn Silas Johnson'll talk you to death. Said you was likely in trouble out by yourself. Shit, I tol' him, *I* know that. Told the man myself what'd happen. Finally figured I'd have to shoot him to keep him quiet, or else come out and get you."

Silas grinned and shook his head.

"Didn't happen to see Josh Biggers, did you?" asked Ki.

Mose's face clouded. "Wouldn't be bothering with you if I had. Be back there skinnin' his hide."

"Ki, you really stash that three hundred somewheres like you said?" asked Silas. "That money layin' in the swamp?"

"No, I left all the money with you, except the twenty I gave Josh. Mr. Mose here warned me about dealing with Josh Biggers." Ki looked up at Mose. "There's a lot of good stuff here. Clothes, food, lots of canned goods. Kerosene and guns and probably cash money, if you can find it. I imagine the people back at your place can use whatever's here."

"Yeah, they can, all right. I'll get some boats down here 'fore Biggers sniffs out the place is empty. He was doin' business with them, wasn't he? I mean, 'sides handing you over."

"They knew him," said Ki. "They likely did some trading."

Mose laid his rifle across his arm and wandered off. Ki went back inside, tried to open a can of peaches, and failed. Silas took over and opened two cans. Ki ate all of his and drank the juice.

"Did you look this place over?" he asked Silas.

"Some. Ain't a whole lot to see."

Ki sat on the edge of a bed and faced him. "That's just the thing, Silas. There isn't much to it at all. It's a place you'd *expect* to see in the Thicket—a spot for outlaws to cool off from the law. But that's *all* it is." He stood then, and scowled at the wall. "There's something wrong here, my friend."

Silas looked puzzled. "You not sayin' we got the wrong spot? This ain't the bunch you was after?"

"Oh, it's the right place. And I don't doubt they work for the people I'm after. But they didn't *know* anything, Silas. They didn't ask me the right questions because they didn't know what to ask. I've faced the cartel before. I can't see them

137

trusting millions in gold to men like Sam and his crew."

"Yeah, I see what you're saying."

"Maybe this place is here so that if anyone comes looking, they can find it."

"What's the sense in that?

Ki shrugged. "I don't know. Maybe nothing at all. I've got a bad itch, Silas, and I don't know where to scratch. I've got to get word to Jessie fast. There's something wrong here and I—Silas, now what's that look supposed to mean?"

Silas cleared his throat. "Been puttin' it off some, Ki. Wanted to give you a little time."

"A little time for what? I don't think I'm going to like this."

"Friend, I don't think you are, either." Silas let out a breath and handed Ki a folded piece of paper from his pocket. Ki frowned, opened it, and saw it was the front page of the Shreveport paper, dated three days back. At first he didn't realize what he was seeing. Then, suddenly, the headline leaped up and struck him like a blow.

"Wh-where'd you get this!" he roared.

"Jus' read it," Silas said calmly. "Read it an' I'll give you the rest."

Ki shakily spread the paper before him on the bed.

STARBUCK HEIRESS TO SELL HOLDINGS

Miss Jessica Starbuck, heiress to one of the country's largest business empires, stopped briefly in Shreveport today aboard the river steamer *John T. Moore*, bound for the port of New Orleans. In a short interview, Miss Starbuck revealed that she would sell the Starbuck interests within the next few days to the Wheatland Corporation, a business consortium based in Kansas City, Missouri. The Starbuck holdings include cattle, land development, mining, shipping lines, and international trade.

Miss Starbuck denied reports that the company is in financial trouble due to a series of recent gold robberies. "We suffered some losses," Miss Starbuck stated, "but the company is quite solvent. The Wheatland Corporation is buying the Starbuck holdings because we are a sound, solid organization. The sale has nothing to do with the recent robberies."

Miss Starbuck stated the reasons for the sale as "personal considerations." During her interview aboard the

138

John T. Moore, Miss Starbuck appeared in a black mourning gown and veil. Her attire reflects the tragic loss several days ago of a close friend and associate in Jefferson, Texas. Ki, a gentleman of Oriental extraction, was mysteriously murdered in a late-night incident on the wharves of that city.

A spokesman representing Miss Starbuck stated that the sale to the Wheatland Corporation would be completed in New Orleans within the week. He added that while Miss Starbuck's future plans are incomplete, she will very likely retire to property in Mexico or South America. Miss Starbuck is the daughter of the late Alex Starbuck and Sarah Starbuck of the Circle Star ranch, near Sarah, Texas.

Ki crumpled the paper in his fist. "Whoever's on that boat," he said angrily, "it sure as hell isn't Jessie!" His dark eyes turned on Silas. "They've got her. My God, they've got her and they think they can pull this off."

"Annie said she figured it wasn't Miss Jessie, either," said Silas. "Said she knew she wouldn't do nothin' like that."

"What?" Ki looked up quickly. "What's Annie got to do with this?"

"It was her sent the paper," Silas explained. "Minute she seen the story, she hired a man and got him ridin' down hard for Livingston. Tol' the man to spend some money and see if you and me was with Jacob Mose." Silas grinned. "Mose wasn't real happy he was that easy to find. I wanted to come in after you anyway, Ki. Gettin' this thing made my mind up fast."

"And where's Annie now? Do you know?"

"Waitin' for us. Over to— Hell, I plumb forgot." He pulled a scrap of paper out of his pocket. "The note's for you. You read it."

Ki took the short scrawled message and scanned it quickly:

Ki,
The clipping speaks for itself. Jessie's in some kind of trouble. I paid for fast service to get this to you. You owe me money, friend. I'll take it out in "services rendered" if you like. I'm leaving the *Annie B.* here in Shreveport and taking the train to Baton Rouge. Be at the Jackson Hotel near the levee. Hurry.
                                        Annie Brown

139

●　●　●

Ki felt a sudden gnawing pain in his belly, as if someone had stuck him with a knife. The thing that frightened him more than anything else was that they'd tied the whole thing up in a neat package. Jessie was still alive, but they'd already printed the notice of her death. The closest she'd get to "Mexico or South America" was ten miles out in the Gulf.

Silas stood and hitched up his belt. "Reckon we better get started," he said. "We got to try, Ki."

"We've got to do a hell of a lot better than that," Ki said darkly.

Chapter 21

Ki and Silas waited until the train was nearly empty, then left their car and walked quickly past the station. The rain that had followed them east across Louisiana had settled in to stay. Baton Rouge at nine in the morning was as dark and somber as late afternoon. In less than a block, both men were soaked to the skin. Ki shouted at Silas, and they left the muddy street to huddle under a storefront awning.

"You want to keep going or what?" Ki said wearily. "I don't have the slightest idea how to find the hotel."

"I been here once or twice," said Silas. "If it's by the docks, it's that way to the left. Hell, no use stoppin'. We ain't goin' to get any wetter."

"I could argue with that, but I won't. All right, let's start swimming. You lead the— What, what is it?"

Silas grinned and nodded past his shoulder. Ki turned and saw the long-legged girl running toward them across the street, clutching a soggy newspaper to her head with both hands. Annie bounded to cover and Ki took her in his arms and kissed her soundly.

"My God," he laughed, "what are you doing running around out in the rain?"

"Waitin' at the damn station," she said bluntly. "Met every train that came in for two days. Christ, you two look *awful!*" She stepped back and gripped Ki's shoulders. "Are you all right? Your face is all—Oh Lord, your hands!"

"Never mind that now, I'll tell you the whole thing when we've time. Where's this hotel of yours?"

"About four blocks. This isn't going to stop, so we might as well make a run for it."

"Annie—do you know anything more about Jessie? Anything at all?"

141

"Nothing you want to hear soaking wet. Listen—when did you two last get some sleep?"

"I heard the word before somewheres," said Silas. "Can't rightly remember what it means..."

Silas left them in front of the Jackson Hotel, saying he'd find a place in the black section of town to clean up, then buy a change of clothes and meet Annie and Ki no later than one o'clock at the livery. Annie tried to protest, especially after Ki had stripped off his clothes and dropped back exhausted on the bed.

"My God," she cried, "you're black and blue all over. What did they *do* to you, Ki?"

"Everything they could," Ki told her. "I'll be all right. Nothing's broken."

"Nothin's in one piece, either," she said tightly. It was hard to hold back tears at the sight of his body. He was bruised and cut all over, and when she soaked the old bandages off his hands, they looked like slabs of raw meat. He told her all that had happened, leaving out the parts that involved Amanda Biggers and her mother.

Annie swept back her hair and looked puzzled. "It just doesn't make sense, Ki. Everything pointed right to the Big Thicket. The murdered Caddo Indian with Starbuck gold, the information Pike passed along to Jessie—"

"I know. Something's very wrong with the whole business. I just don't know what. Right now I don't have time to figure it out. I've *got* to get to New Orleans and Jessie." He sat up and moaned, forcing himself to keep his eyes open. He'd slept some on the train, but that hadn't helped. The beating he'd taken from Sam, and then his struggle to get free, had drained him of his strength. Even with Jacob Mose's help, it seemed forever before he and Silas were out of the Thicket and on a train. Before they'd finally reached the railroad, there was a long day of dugout canoes, rough walking, and more hours atop a mule than he cared to remember.

Annie went out to buy him clothes and something to eat. Ki kept only his worn leather vest with its arsenal of concealed weaponry. While the girl was gone, he tried to grip a *shuriken* with bandaged fingers. Finally he gave up in disgust. A six-year-old could handle them better than he.

The food was good, and he ate everything Annie put before

142

him. She'd found denims and a blue cotton shirt and a pair of low-cut boots.

"Know you don't like shoes," she said wryly, "but this *is* the state capital, you know. Can't have you walking around looking like a bum."

"Don't worry. I won't be here long enough to get arrested."

"We," Annie said soberly. *"We* won't be here, Ki. You don't really think I'm staying behind?"

"No. I'd rather you would, but I know better."

"Good. That saves us arguing, then." She stood and came to him and laced her arms around his neck. "If you want some loving, Ki, you know I'm right here. I know there's no time for that now, but when there is—"

"When there is, you won't have to ask," he assured her.

Annie gave him a mischievous grin. "You don't think you're too beat up for such strenuous work?"

"I'm beat up," he told her. "But I'm not dead."

When Ki left, the rain had eased off to a steady drizzle. He told Annie to meet him with Silas in an hour at the livery. It was only some seventy-odd miles to New Orleans; they'd make it before dark and start looking for Jessie. In the meantime, he had a couple of things to do before they left town. Annie raised an eyebrow at that, but didn't ask questions.

Ki walked along the street, keeping his head low against the light spray of mist in the air. On the train coming east, he'd been determined to stomp right into the Starbuck office in Baton Rouge, tell the general manager who he was and that Jessie's sale of her holdings was a fake—that she was in the hands of men who'd surely kill her the moment their business was done.

Great—except that the man named Ki was dead and buried in Jefferson, and there was clearly nothing wrong with Jessica Starbuck. She'd given an interview, hadn't she? Stood up in front of a whole bunch of people, plain as day.

Annie had showed him the second story when the woman posing as Jessie had passed through. There was nothing much new—except a sentence that made his blood run cold. Starbuck officials, key men in Jessie's organization, would be present when she signed away the company. That told Ki a lot. Jessie herself would be on hand, somewhere he could reach her. They wouldn't dare risk a phony for that.

They won't risk her giving the whole thing away, either, he reminded himself soberly, not right there in front of a bunch of friends.

Ki knew the answer to that. It filled him with a rage he could scarcely contain. They were certain she'd do as they asked; they had her so frightened she was no longer a risk at all.

But they hadn't won yet, he told himself darkly. He still had a hole card in the game: He was alive, and they didn't know it. He knew some of the top Starbuck men quite well. He'd find them in New Orleans. They'd listen, and they'd believe him. They'd work something out together and he'd go in and get Jessie out. Wherever they had her, he'd get her out.

Stopping in a waterfront store, he asked directions to the Starbuck Shipping Lines offices. He didn't dare show his face inside, but it wouldn't hurt to get close. Maybe he'd recognize someone he knew, someone he could trust. One thing he had to do soon was get money. There were Starbuck accounts he could draw on, all across the country. But not without proper identification, and certainly not if everyone thought he was dead.

A block farther on he saw the broad, flat expanse of the Mississippi. Clouds hung low over the river, turning it the color of rusty iron. The dockside was a tangle of smokestacks and derricks. Big sidewheelers chugged along in midriver, blurred by a veil of dirty rain.

Stopping in a doorway across the street, he watched the entrance to the Starbuck offices. The day was dark and somber, and lights showed through the windows of the two-story building. After a good ten minutes, two men came out. Ki studied them closely, but neither one looked familiar. He was ready to leave, admit the whole thing was a bad idea, when a man walked quickly around the corner and hurried into the building.

Ki stood up straight, suddenly alert. There was something about this man, something vaguely familiar. He waited, moving a few doors closer. Almost at once, the man was back on the street, moving at a brisk pace in the direction from which he'd come. Black suit and black Stetson, long determined stride—

"Morgan!" Anger heated Ki's face at the sudden recognition.

Morgan disappeared around the corner, with Ki right on his heels. The waterfront was a warren of brick warehouses, shipping offices, and bars. Wherever Morgan was going, he was

144

in a hurry to get there fast. Ki matched his pace, keeping a good fifty yards between them. He'd only met the gambler once, the morning he'd arrived in Jefferson. He'd been with Jessie then, but she'd made it clear she didn't trust him.

You know what happened to Jessie, he thought. *You know what happened and you're going to tell me all about it, you bastard . . .*

The gambler stopped, glanced casually over his shoulder, and lit a cheroot. Ki quickly studied goods in a window. Morgan had spotted him for sure. If he had any sense, he'd do something about it.

Morgan tossed a match aside and walked on. Half a block later, he turned and walked casually into an alley between two brick buildings.

Ki grinned, reversed his steps, and sprinted rapidly around the block. Just as he'd imagined, Morgan hadn't come out. He was in there waiting, ready to ambush Ki as he passed by.

Peering carefully into the alley, he saw that it curved in a slight L. Crates and boxes lined the narrow brick walls. Rain-swollen skies added to the gloom inside. Ki slipped off his new boots and went in low, staying as close to one wall as he could.

A rat squealed and scurried over the wet stone paving. Flies swarmed up off an odorous pile of garbage.

Ki cursed under his breath and pressed closer to the wall. Crouching low, he moved another few yards, stopped still, and listened. Nothing. A slight scratching sound, but that was another rat. He moved from behind a box and slipped forward, searching the shadows. He was in there somewhere, and not far away. Behind the next barrel, the next pile of boxes—

Suddenly, Morgan loomed up out of nowhere, directly in his path. Ki leaped straight in the air and kicked out with one leg. Fire exploded past his face. Morgan staggered back from Ki's blow, but held on tight to the Colt. Ki twisted and lashed out again, his heel catching the gambler in the chest. Morgan went sprawling, rolled to his feet, and took off running in the other direction. Ki went after him, anger blinding his reason. Morgan turned suddenly, crouched, and aimed the gun at Ki's head.

"Hold it, goddamn you, or I'll kill you right there!"

Ki froze. Morgan straightened and took a step back. "All right, mister," he snapped, "you got business with me, let's hear it!"

"You *know* what my business is with you," Ki blurted.

145

"Where is she and what have you—"

"Ki?" Morgan's mouth fell open. "Jesus Christ, you're—you're supposed to be dead!"

"Not yet I'm not, you bastard."

Morgan shook his head. "My God, I saw you all stretched out and— Lord, what are you following me for? What the hell's going on here?"

"You wouldn't know that, would you?" Ki rose up slightly on the balls of his feet, gauging the time he'd have before Morgan pulled the trigger.

"Don't." Morgan caught his eye and backed off. "You wouldn't make it, friend, and I got no reason to want to kill you. Damn it, I don't know what this is all about, but you just stand right still and listen. If you're trying to find Jessie, following me won't help. I don't know where she is. New Orleans, I guess, but I don't know where. I've been trying to track her since Jefferson. Since—" He stopped then, and gave Ki a narrow look. "Just answer one question, all right? The lady who came through here—that's not Jessie, is it?"

"You know damn well it's not."

Morgan shook off his words. "I didn't. I do now. Look, Ki, I was, uh—I was with Jessie the night before she left town. I knew she was in trouble, but she wouldn't tell me what. I even went through some of her papers to see if I could figure something out. That didn't help. When I woke up again, she was gone. I didn't see her again until noon, waiting in a carriage while a couple of banker types checked her out of the Excelsior. She was wearing black clothes and a veil and I couldn't get near her. That wasn't Jessie, damn it. Now what the hell's going on here, Ki? If she's not selling her business, if that's not her on the boat—"

"What were you doing back there?" Ki asked curtly. "In the offices of Starbuck Shipping?"

"Trying to see if anyone knew where I could reach Jessie in New Orleans. No one in there knows a damn thing."

Ki looked intently at Morgan. "You're not lying about this? You didn't have any part in taking her off?"

"No, I didn't." Morgan's face clouded. "Then it's true, isn't it? You think somebody's got her. Shit, I can't— Look, you trust me yet or not?"

"Some. But you're still the man holding the gun."

Morgan made a face, flipped the gun over, and offered it

146

to Ki. "If that'll help, take it. I don't think you and me killin' each other is going to get us closer to Jessie."

Ki gave him a sheepish grin. "Guess you better keep it. I'm doing well to hold a fork and eat supper."

Chapter 22

The room was stifling, dark except for narrow slits of light from the boarded window. Jessie could hear dim sounds from the street below—a vendor hawking his wares, the rattle of a carriage or a wagon. It was a city, and a fairly large one at that—bigger than most waterfront towns along the Red or the Mississippi. Most likely New Orleans, Jessie guessed. They'd brought her ashore late at night in a closed carriage, rushing her quickly down one brick street and then another. She could see nothing at all, but the sounds and smells told her it had to be the Delta city.

Sitting up on the narrow cot, she used her skirt to wipe dirt and sweat from her face. Her hair clung to her cheeks and she could smell the strong odor of her body. The last bath she'd had was the one aboard the riverboat. Since then, no one had even offered a basin of water.

Louisa slept soundly on the cot nearby. A beam of light no wider than a blade touched the bare white flesh of her shoulder. The sight of that fragile figure brought a lump to Jessie's throat. The moment Dietrich's man Malik had ripped her dress to shreds and left her naked, Jessie knew that she was beaten. She'd seen the sheer terror in Louisa's eyes and known she'd do whatever they asked. The men of the cartel knew her all too well....

Louisa cried out in her sleep, and Jessie went to her quickly. The girl opened her eyes and clung fearfully to Jessie's neck.

"It's all right," Jessie whispered. "It's all right now."

"I had a *real* bad dream, Miss Jessie."

"I know. It was only a dream. It's all over, Louisa."

"Could I have a drink of water?"

"Of course you can. You wait right here." Jessie rose and padded across the room, poured the girl a cup, and brought it

148

back. Louisa drank it greedily, then settled in Jessie's arms.

"What's goin' to happen to us?" she asked suddenly. "Those men are goin' to kill us, aren't they?"

"Good heavens, no, Louisa!" She held the girl up and smoothed her hair. "Where'd you get an idea like that?" She was glad it was dark in the room, that Louisa couldn't see her face.

"I'm real hungry. And I don't feel too good."

"You're hot is all. There's not much air in here. Say, I've got a good idea. You want to know a secret—something no one else knows we know?"

"What kind of a secret?"

"You just wait right here and I'll show you." Jessie got up and walked to the high boarded window. There was room on the sill to stand, and stretching on her toes she could peer through one of the cracks outside. After the darkness, the harsh light seared her eyes. The view was instantly familiar. She was looking over an iron lace balcony, two stories above Chartres Street. The three spires of St. Louis cathedral were to her right, and closer still, the columned arches of the Presbytere. She was in the heart of the French Quarter, the Vieux Carré. St. Peter, Toulouse, and, farther down, Canal Street.

"Come here, Louisa," she said. "This is the secret. I'll show you where we are." She helped the girl up to the crack. "See the big church? We're in New Orleans, Louisa." Jessie eased her down and sat with her on the cot. "When we—when all this is over, I'll take you to that church and show you how it looks inside. Then we'll get some real good things to eat. Let's see—we'll have some shrimp and baked potatoes and a bunch of stuff I bet you never heard of before. You know what jambalaya is? Louisa? Oh Lord, child, don't!"

Louisa trembled in her arms, her tears scalding Jessie's cheeks. "Louisa, it's going to be all right. It's going to be all *right*." She said it over and over, but Louisa knew it wasn't true.

"This is how it will be," Dietrich told her. "The signing takes place tomorrow afternoon, in a suite at the St. Charles Hotel. Your people from across the country will be on hand. Your telegraph messages have been answered, and all will attend who can get here in time." Dietrich paused and toyed with the ledger on his desk. "They may wish to speak to you in private,

Miss Starbuck. Quite naturally, a number of them are disturbed by your sudden decision to sell. Talk to them. Tell them your decision is final. Assure them they will be well compensated for their years of loyal service. They will. And if you say anything more than that, the girl will suffer. We'll be listening and watching, of course. If you try to pass a message of any kind, or—"

"I know," snapped Jessie. "Damn it, I'm not a fool!"

"Good, good." Dietrich smiled and leaned back in his chair. The window behind him was open on a shaded New Orleans street. Jessie saw a stuccoed building, painted blue. White lattice doors lined the second-story porch.

"There will be people from the newspapers. Distinguished guests. Businessmen and bankers. It's a very special occasion. Would you care to see?" He reached behind him and tossed several papers on the desk. Reading the cartel's lies made her skin crawl, but she forced herself to finish every word. Maybe something she saw would show her a way to stop this madness and save herself and Louisa. God, if Ki knew what was happening, he'd see through it in a second; he'd know for certain the cartel had her. If he wasn't stomping around in the swamp three hundred miles away...

Suddenly, Dietrich laughed. It was an action so foreign to his manner that Jessie was startled for a moment.

"Don't look so intense, Miss Starbuck. You worry me when you think. There's nothing to think about anymore. It is over. Play your part, that's all you have to do."

Jessie's green eyes narrowed. "I don't suppose you'd give me a straight answer to a question."

"What is it, Miss Starbuck?"

"I know what's going to happen to me. Is there anything I can say that'll persuade you to leave Louisa alone when—when this is all finished?"

Dietrich's face betrayed nothing at all. "I think we've talked enough, don't you? Barbara—" He turned and glanced at the closed door to his right. "Barbara, would you come in now, please?"

The girl who entered the room had light hazel eyes and reasonably pretty features. She had Jessie's height and approximate build, though she was slightly thicker around the waist and hips. She nodded curiously at Jessie, put her hands behind her back, and looked respectfully at Dietrich.

150

"Is that enough?" Dietrich asked her. "Is there anything else you need?"

"No sir," the girl said evenly. "I think that'll do just fine. Wanted to make sure, is all."

"Fine. Then you'd better be getting back."

The girl nodded again, then turned and left the room. Jessie stared, unable to believe what she'd heard. The girl's voice was a dead ringer for her own—the pitch, the accent, the way she strung her words together. She didn't just *sound* like Jessie Starbuck—she *was* Jessie Starbuck!

"Good, isn't she?" Dietrich allowed a slight smile to touch his lips. "Behind a black veil, no one knows the difference. No one even thinks to question who she is. Her job's nearly done, but there's a very important banker here from St. Louis. A man who says he's met you before. We didn't think it wise to turn him away, and Barbara likes to do things right."

Jessie clenched her fists at her sides. "Someone is going to see through all this," she said angrily. "You'll make a mistake before it's over!"

Dietrich blinked once. "Why, then you'd better pray that we don't, Miss Starbuck."

Late in the afternoon, a guard came to take Jessie and Louisa out of their room, down a narrow iron stairwell to a walled courtyard below. It was the first time Jessie had been outdoors since they'd taken her in Jefferson, and she was grateful for the light and the fresh air. A gnarled oak shaded the patio, and flowered vines grew thick on the red brick walls. The guard stood under an arched doorway and built himself a smoke.

"It's pretty, isn't it?" said Jessie. "Look at all the flowers."

"Yeah, I guess," Louisa said quietly. She sank down on a bench and looked at the ground. Jessie sighed and paced the brick courtyard, trying to bring strength back to her limbs. Her heart went out to the girl. Louisa had simply given up trying. She'd lost all hope, and nothing Jessie could do would perk her up. Not that she much blamed her, but damn it, they couldn't just quit, not while they still had a chance! Ki had to know what had happened to her by now. Once he got help, they'd—

Jessie stopped and turned as angry voices came from the door behind her. The guard stepped aside and another burst through the portal under the arch, dragging an old man by the

151

collar. The man flailed his arms and cursed his captor loudly. The guard laughed and gave him a swift kick that sent him sprawling on the hard brick floor.

"Get yourself some air," he called out. "You're stinkin' up the place, you old bastard!" Grinning at Jessie's guard, he rubbed his hands on his trousers and disappeared.

The old man pulled himself painfully erect, turned and faced Jessie and gave her a broad grin. "Well now, if you ain't a sight for sore eyes. See they ain't did you in yet."

"*Baxter?*" Jessie's eyes widened in disbelief. "My God, you're alive! I thought—"

"Yeah, reckon *I* did too." Jaybird Baxter brushed himself off and sank wearily on a bench next to Louisa. Louisa gave him a wary eye, stood quickly and sat down a few yards away.

"Who's the little tyke?"

"I'll explain her later," said Jessie. "Mr. Baxter, I'm glad to see you're all right, but I *saw* that man shoot you in the back. I didn't imagine that!"

"No, don't s'pose you did." Baxter gave her a painful grin. "Keep a extry blade down my back, hangin' on a thong. Little trick I learned on the river. That feller's bullet hit my knife an' damn near busted my spine. Son of a bitch trussed me up, hauled me to a boat on the river. Some city dude startin' asking me a bunch of fool questions."

"What—what kind of questions?"

Baxter glanced over his shoulder and gave her a sly wink. "Questions 'bout *you*, Miss Starbuck. How long I'd knowed you, where we was goin' that day and why. I thought it out real quick. After that feller seen I was still alive, he decided he'd let his boss figure what to do with me next. Didn't take me long to learn the only thing keeping me alive was maybe I knowed a lot of stuff about you. 'Course I ain't told 'em any different, but I'm running out of stories."

"What exactly *did* you tell them?"

"Not a damn thing," he snorted. "Said I'd worked for you a long time, that I was trying to sneak you out before the folks that was after you could do you harm. All kinds of nonsense."

Baxter frowned in thought, and wet his lips and stared at the wall just past her. "Listen real close, lady," he said softly, "I don't know what this mess you're in is all about, but I got me a guess it's a hell of a lot more than that gold we was talking about up north. I'll tell you one thing certain—the more I see

152

of these characters, the more I'm sure ain't none of us gettin' out of this with our hides. Am I right or wrong on that?"

"Yes, Mr. Baxter." Jessie closed her eyes. "I couldn't have put it better myself."

"What I figured." He faced Jessie then, watching the guard warily over her shoulder. "We haven't got but maybe a minute, so I better get to it. They got me sweepin' up in the kitchen. Don't think I'm real smart, so they don't watch me close. I can't get us out of here, miss. But I can get *word* out anytime I want."

Jessie sat up straight. "You can? Are you sure? How on earth would you—"

Baxter scowled. "Just listen, all right? There's hired girls and little colored kids comin' in and out all the time. Nobody pays 'em any mind. I stole 'bout half a dollar off one of the guards. I slip that to one of those boys and he's off like a cat. Now—" Baxter's eyes nearly closed. "Is there anyone here— anyone in town we could go to for help? Ain't any use sending a message 'less we got someone to send it to."

"My God, Mr. Baxter—" For the first time in days, Jessie's spirits soared. It was all she could do to keep from grabbing the old man and planting a kiss on his grizzled face. "If you can do that—"

"I can," Baxter snapped, "but we ain't got all day to discuss it."

"Wait. Wait, let me think." She brought her hand to her mouth and pressed her lips. "All right. Tell your messenger to find Deputy U.S. Marshal Owen McCartey. Or his boss, Jack Fisher. Anyone in town can tell him where to find their office if he doesn't know."

"McCartey and Fisher."

"Yes. Just say Jessie's in big trouble and to come in fast, without knocking. I don't want that little girl harmed, Mr. Baxter."

Baxter frowned. "Uh-huh. Figured it was something like that. I'll write it all down so the kid won't forget it. Is there anything else I should tell him? Anyone at all those marshal fellers could get ahold of? What I'm sayin' is, these folks act like they've got everything sewed up tight. If those two marshals kick the kid out on his ass—"

"They won't." Jessie thought a moment. "Mention Ki's name. He and Owen McCartey got along real well."

"Ki?" Baxter raised a brow. "You're talkin' about the Oriental feller that got kilt?"

"Yes, I am." Jessie paused a moment and studied her hands. "Only Ki's *not* dead, he's alive."

"Huh?" Baxter looked startled. "What the hell kind of foolishness is that?"

"I can't go into it now. Just believe me, he's alive. Tell McCartey he may possibly be in New Orleans right now. He—" Jessie waved her words aside. "Let's get some doors kicked in here first. If Ki's around, I'll find him, or he'll find me."

Baxter's face split a grin. "By God, that's somethin'. How in the world did you pull that off?"

"What? How'd I do what, Mr. Baxter?"

"Fool ever'one into thinking your friend was dead. Where'd he go? After Jefferson, I mean."

"That's not important right now," Jessie said irritably. "When we get out of this place I'll—"

"You'll tell me right *now*, damn you!" Baxter's hand came up in a blur and lashed her savagely across the face. Jessie gasped and staggered back, staring at Baxter in horror and disbelief.

"You!" Baxter turned and barked a command at the guard. "Get her upstairs. I want her there *now!*" He stood and stalked quickly through the arch and disappeared.

For a moment Jessie was too stunned to react. The guard grabbed her arm and pulled her roughly across the courtyard toward the stairs. Louisa cried out and clutched at her skirts. The guard cursed and shoved her aside. Two men rushed out of the house and pulled her away, kicking and screaming.

Jessie's guard shoved her down the long hall, past the room that was Dietrich's office and on to another. The door opened before he could knock, and Jessie faced the flat, expressionless features of Dietrich's henchman. Malik took her from the guard, pushed her into the room, and stood against the door, arms folded over his chest.

Jessie stared at the men before her. They sat behind a long wooden table, shuttered windows at their backs. Besides Dietrich, there was the round-faced man she'd seen aboard the boat. There was a younger man with pale eyes and a neatly trimmed beard, in European-cut clothing. Beside him was an

154

older man with a perfectly bald head and thick tinted glasses. And at the very end was Jaybird Baxter. He stood and faced Jessie, hands pressed flat against the table.

"Listen to me now," he said harshly, "I'm going to say this only once. You told me downstairs that the man Ki is still alive. Is this the truth?"

"My God," Jessie shouted, "who *are* you!" Baxter's voice, his whole manner had changed abruptly. Beneath the rough, grizzled features was a man she didn't know.

"Who I am doesn't matter," Baxter said patiently. "It should be quite clear I'm not who you think. Now. Just answer the question, Miss Starbuck. It's important that we get the right answers. We received a very disturbing telegraph message this morning. Our people are missing from a camp in the Big Thicket. A woodsman who worked for us told our man he took an Oriental to the camp. He says the man was Ki, and that our people took him prisoner. Now it seems he's broken free. It *was* Ki, wasn't it? He didn't die in Jefferson. Explain that, please." Baxter's eyes flicked from Jessie to Dietrich, and then to Malik. "Our man says he killed the Oriental. What happened, Miss Starbuck?"

"I guess your man was wrong," Jessie said shortly.

"Damn it, then it's *true!*" Baxter exploded. He turned savagely on Dietrich. "This changes everything. The Oriental's out there and he *knows*. He can ruin the whole plan!"

"He won't." Dietrich's face blazed redly. "He won't risk *her*. He will try to find her, but he won't expose us in the open. He's too smart for that."

Baxter turned back abruptly to Jessie. "Tell me the whole story. Everything. How he got away, who was involved, what you think he'll do. *Everything,* Miss Starbuck."

"There's not much to tell," Jessie said dryly. "Your man thought he killed Ki and he didn't. I got him away and—"

"*Malik!*" Baxter's eyes blazed. "Get the girl. Get her up here."

"No!" Jessie shook her head in alarm. "I'll—I'll tell you, you don't have to do that!"

Baxter shook his head in disgust. "Don't waste my time, Miss Starbuck. It's going to happen, and you're going to watch it. We cannot afford any more surprises from you!"

155

Chapter 23

Black Jack Morgan slammed the door behind him and dropped the papers in front of Ki. "Well, if you want to read about 'the dissolution of the Starbuck empire,' it's all right here. I got the *Picayune* and the *Times-Democrat* both."

Ki squinted at the papers, then ignored them. "Anything new we need to know?"

"No. Nothing's changed. The signing's tomorrow at the St. Charles Hotel. All the papers say is that Jessie will meet with her company officers at noon, just before the signing. Most of 'em are staying right there at the hotel."

"Damn it, we've got to get into that place!" Ki stood abruptly, stalked to the window, and glared out over the alley.

"We'll get in," Morgan said evenly. "I'm working on it, and so is Silas. It's just a question of spreading a little money around."

"I'd help with that," said Ki, "but it's too big a risk to show my face at the banks. And I can't approach the Starbuck people. They'd lock me up for a lunatic, and word would get back to the cartel in a minute."

Morgan shook his head. "You can't risk meeting someone you know in the street. Maybe it's not likely, but it could happen." He grinned and pulled a cheroot from his vest. "Don't worry about the money, I can handle that. Gamblers have got their own bankin' system, Ki. It's called 'keep it where you can get to it and run.' I've already made a couple of hefty withdrawals." He drew out a handful of bills and a stack of double eagles and dropped them on the table. "Some of that's for Silas to spread around. You take the rest and hang on to it." He lit his smoke and studied Ki over the flame. "I know what you're thinking. You want to get out there and *do* something. Break arms and open some doors."

156

"I'm not used to sitting on my hands," Ki said glumly. "Not with Jessie in trouble."

Morgan leaned back against the wall. "I went over there just now, to the St. Charles. It's just like it was last night. You can't see the bastards 'less you're looking, but they're there. Very hard and very efficient-lookin' dudes. In the bar, in the lobby, just standing around watching. I didn't even try to get near Jessie's suite." Morgan raised a questioning brow. "Most of the people I saw looked local. Didn't see any enterprising Prussian businessmen."

"You won't, either. Just the hired help." Ki turned to face Morgan. "Jessie's not in the hotel. Not yet. I'm convinced of that, and I think you are too. They won't bring her there until tomorrow." He looked at the gambler, and saw that Morgan knew where he was going.

"I've thought some on it," Morgan told him. "Getting to her right when they bring her in would be good—if we knew just how it was going to happen. We don't, and there's too many points to cover. If we guess wrong, we kill her."

Ki had to agree. Morgan straightened his jacket and moved to the door. "I've got some people to see. I think maybe you and me and Silas and Annie ought to get together right before supper. That all right?"

"That's fine," Ki told him. The gambler nodded and left. Ki walked back to the window. There was nothing to see but the building next door and a squalid alley below. Morgan knew the city, and had picked their shabby hotel with great care. It was just off Basin Street, their only neighbors bawdy houses and bars. Ki heartily approved of the location. It was a place where no one asked questions, or cared to provide any answers.

Where are you, Jessie? You're out there somewhere, maybe only a few blocks away...

Ki knew exactly how the cartel would do it. The woman in the veil would be seen around New Orleans once or twice. Maybe she'd show up in New York or San Francisco. Jessie, though, would be dead long before that. She wouldn't last an hour after the Starbuck holdings had been signed over. If he and Morgan and Silas didn't handle it just right, if they made a foolish mistake—

Morgan pressed the map out flat with his hands. Ki and Silas leaned closer to the table to see. Annie turned up the kerosene lamp overhead.

"Silas, are your people all clear? Everyone's got to be in position by eleven forty-five at the latest."

"They will be," Silas assured him. "No problem 'bout that."

"You don't think it'll work," said Ki, "trying to get people on this floor in a food cart, the laundry?"

"Huh-unh." Silas shook his head firmly. "Tested that out to see. Had a girl roll some fresh sheets up on Miss Jessie's floor close to her suite. One of those muscle boys dressed like a banker stepped up real nice and sort of casual-like poked through the goods."

"They can get away with stopping hotel employees," put in Annie. "The hotel and the local law think they're helping to protect Jessie. But they don't dare push around guests. Not at the St. Charles. And they don't have the whole floor to themselves."

"No, they don't," said Morgan. "They've got six rooms in a row, including Jessie's. But they don't have the whole floor, and that's where they're vulnerable. We can get our own guests and employees real close to Jessie's door, take out the guards, and hold that end of the floor while our people go inside." Morgan exchanged a grin with Ki. "They made a mistake there. They should've taken the floor and cut us off."

"They're not expecting trouble," Ki reminded him. "Just guarding against it. It's still not going to be easy. I *know* these bastards."

Silas looked up, his dark features creased in a somber scowl. "They goin' to get to know us, too, and maybe wish they didn't."

The meeting went on for another hour. Then Morgan retired to his own room, and Silas left to tie up loose ends. Ki lay in the dark next to Annie and listened to the sounds of Basin Street. It was a good plan, and he was satisfied they'd done all they could. Still, that didn't ease the awful sense that something was wrong, something he couldn't control. He felt that if he got up now and roamed the dark streets, he could find her, get her out of their hands before it was too late.

We've got to do it right. We've got to do it right or she's dead.

"Ki, you still awake?"

"Yes. I can't sleep now, Annie."

"It's goin' to be all right. It's goin' to work, Ki."

"I know it is. I won't let it be any other way."

158

"Good. Just keep thinkin' that, 'cause it's so." She slid from the hollow of his arm and let her hair brush his belly. Her lips found the hard band of muscle above his groin, then the dark curve that led between his thighs. At first her touch failed to stir him. Then the tip of her tongue flicked lightly over his member, the heat of her breath burning him like a brand. She teased him with her lips, then very gently drew him into her mouth. Ki cried out and pulled her into his arms. Grinding his mouth against her lips, he spread her legs and thrust himself roughly inside her. Annie groaned as he drove himself relentlessly into her body again and again.

He stood in the doorway on the corner, watching the entrance to the hotel across the street. Morgan had lent him a big pocket watch and he took it out and glanced at it once again. The minutes passed at an unbelievably slow pace. It was twenty-one minutes to noon—a minute later than when he'd looked at the watch before.

At a quarter after eleven he'd left the hotel with Silas. Annie and Morgan were already gone. Silas walked with him down Conti as far as Dauphine, then left him and headed for Canal Street to meet his crew. Ki made his way to St. Charles Avenue, taking up his position on the corner of Common. The hotel was to his right across the street. A moment before, he'd seen Annie disappear through the entrance. She wore a fashionable pale blue gown and twirled a dainty parasol above her head. A black girl walked behind her, a large shopping bag over her arm. The girl wore a white starched dress and a red bandanna wound tightly about her head. Under the packages in the bag were five short-barreled .45 Colts. Both Morgan and Ki felt certain the cartel's gunmen would think twice before they stopped a well-dressed lady and her maid.

The moment Annie and the girl entered the hotel, Ki knew three of Morgan's recruits would leave Gravier Street a block down, cross St. Charles, and walk into the hotel. Two others were already inside. One of the men was a gambler, two were accomplished burglars, and two had left the U.S. Cavalry in Kentucky without telling their sergeant goodbye. For the moment, all five looked like respectable businessmen or drummers.

A black man in work clothes crossed St. Charles, passed Ki without meeting his eyes, and gave him a nod. Ki stepped

159

off the corner and walked quickly toward the hotel. He wore a brown business suit. A light tan Stetson was pulled low over his eyes. The flesh of his hands was still raw and tender. Annie had bound them well that morning, and gently encased his hands in leather gloves a size too big. Annie was still concerned, but Ki wasn't. If he needed to use his hands, he'd do it without thinking. He could worry about pain when he had Jessie out of that room safe and sound.

Out of the corner of his eye, Ki spotted the men holding saddled horses to the left of the hotel, another two riding mounts down Gravier. He'd leave with Jessie on the horses in front of the St. Charles. Three of Morgan's men would ride behind to guard his back. Morgan, Silas, and Annie would disappear in a delivery wagon waiting a block away on Canal.

She's in there right now. It's time, and they've smuggled her upstairs to the room. Maybe they brought her early, last night or right at dawn.

Lowering his head, he entered the hotel and walked straight through the lobby, past overstuffed sofas and potted palms. The lobby was crowded with guests, and he was grateful for that.

A batwing door past the desk was marked HOTEL STAFF ONLY. Ki marched through as if he knew where he was going. Three black men in hotel livery stepped out of a passage to Ki's right. One scowled and drew a pistol from his jacket. Silas put out a hand and shook his head.

"Hurry," he told Ki. "We're going up now."

Ki nodded and followed the three up a narrow flight of stairs. According to Morgan's map, the utility stairs would bring them out three doors from Jessie's room. The cartel would almost certainly have a man by the door, and maybe one inside, watching the stairs themselves.

If he's there, thought Ki, *he's dead. Anyone who tries to stop us is dead.*

While they climbed the back stairs, Annie and her maid would reach Jessie's floor by the main stairway. By then, Morgan's five men would have passed her in the lobby and lifted pistols from the maid's bag. They could have brought in weapons under their jackets, but Silas had learned that off-duty policemen had been hired to watch for anyone who might try to harm Miss Starbuck.

Silas reached the final level before Jessie's, waved the others

160

back, and climbed up slowly to take a look. In a moment he signaled Ki and the others forward.

"We're lucky," he said softly. "There's no one this side of the door. He'll be there, though, right inside. You can damn sure count on that."

"What time is it?" asked Ki. He pulled out his watch and compared it with Silas's.

"Eight after twelve," said Silas. "We're right on it." He glanced at his two companions and nodded.

The timing had to be right. The instant they stepped into the hall, Silas would take out the nearest guard with his knife. His two companions would draw their guns and cover Ki. Morgan and his men would burst into the hall from the main stairway and kill the men guarding Jessie's suite. Morgan guessed there would be no less than six cartel gunmen to stop. Ki would go straight for Jessie's door and kick it in, Silas's crew behind him and Morgan's men on their heels. Ki would go for Jessie, stop anyone in his way, and take her to the floor. The men with Morgan and Silas had their instructions: Anyone in the room left standing was fair game.

"All right," said Ki, thrusting the watch in his pocket, "it's time, Silas. Let's go. Morgan's in position."

Silas nodded, drew a long blade from his belt, and gripped the knob of the door.

"Now," Ki whispered harshly. *"Go!"*

Silas pulled the door open and went in low, the knife curved upward from his waist. Ki came in behind him, the black men at his side. A woman in a bright red dress and feathered hat bumped squarely into Silas, saw the gleam of steel in his fist, and screamed. Silas blinked and backed off, searching the hall for someone to fight.

"Damn it," Ki snapped, urging the black men to him, "let's get to that room! "A waiter with a tray suddenly blocked Ki's path. Ki pushed him angrily aside and sprinted for Jessie's door.

"Ki, *no!*" Morgan appeared out of nowhere, gripped his arm, and turned him aside. "Something's gone wrong," he said tightly. "Silas, get the others. Get them out of here fast."

Ki shook free and stared in anger. "What the hell are you doing, Morgan? Get out of my way!"

Morgan stood his ground. "She's not here," he said bluntly. "She's gone. No one's here, damn it. Ki, they've beaten us.

161

They changed the whole thing at the last minute. *The signing's on a boat in the Mississippi, not here. It's happening right now!"*

Ki wasn't listening. He was bounding down the main stairway to the lobby, taking four steps at a time. Guests of the hotel saw the terrible rage that twisted his features and scattered quickly out of his way...

★

Chapter 24

They left her in the boarded-up room the rest of the day. She wasn't surprised when darkness came and no one brought her food and water. They were angry—angry because they knew Ki was alive, that someone out there was aware of what they were doing. She was certain Baxter could easily have killed Dietrich on the spot. It was his man, Malik, who had failed, and Baxter had let Dietrich know it. And because there was trouble between them, Jessie would go hungry that night. As further punishment, they'd keep Louisa from her, let her wonder if the girl was all right.

Jessie pounded her fists in frustration against the bed. "Damn them—*damn* the bastards!"

What they'd done to the girl was, in its way, as cruel and heartless as if they'd raped her one at a time. Malik simply stripped her and made her stand atop a chair before the others. Through it all, Louisa stood frozen in horror, too frightened even to scream. Malik scarcely touched her, but the awful sense of his presence was enough. He could have used that fragile body, taken her in every way imaginable and driven her to madness. The men at the table understood this very well. Jessie saw that knowledge in their eyes, and it shook her to the very core of her being. They didn't care about the girl, scarcely saw her naked flesh. It was enough that she was theirs, that they could stop the beating of her heart whenever they wished.

When they took Louisa away, Jessie sank weakly into a chair. The thing they'd done had left her drained, empty— and, for the first time since they'd taken her, truly frightened of the men who held her. Baxter began to ask her questions, and Jessie answered them, one by one.

● ● ●

163

They came for her at dawn, and led her to a small room off the kitchen, where they set a hot meal before her—hot bread, fried ham, scrambled eggs, and strong Louisiana coffee laced with chicory. Jessie was half starved, and not ashamed to wolf down every bite. When she was finished the guard led her back upstairs, to a room she'd never seen. A steaming tub was in the corner. On a table nearby were thick towels and a bottle of perfumed liquid soap. A black linen dress and a black hat lay on the bed. On a vanity were fresh underthings, stockings, a new pair of shoes, and a comb and brush.

The guard closed the door and locked her in. Almost at once, another door opened to Jessie's left. The woman who entered through it was somewhere in her forties—short and heavy, but clearly as hard as nails. Her hair was drawn severely back from flat, expressionless features.

"Get your dress off and get in the tub," she said sharply. "Wash your hair too. I'll dry it and comb it out."

Jessie's green eyes smoldered. "I've been taking baths all by myself for a long time. I don't imagine I need any help."

The woman folded her arms over huge breasts and gave Jessie a nasty smile. "Don't sass me, lady, or I'll peel you down naked myself. Wouldn't mind at all, dearie."

Jessie flushed and turned away, then slid out of the soiled dress and sank hastily into the tub. The woman leaned against the wall and watched. The bath felt good, but Jessie couldn't enjoy it. Stepping out on the bare floor, she padded naked across the room, wrapped a towel around her head, and began drying herself with another.

The woman let out a breath. "Lord A'mighty, aren't you something! Be glad to help you with that, honey."

Jessie grasped a bottle of toilet water by the neck. "Try it, and I'll pretty up that ugly face of yours, *honey.*"

The woman's eyes went flat. For a moment Jessie was certain she'd come off the wall right at her. Instead, she stopped where she was as the hall door opened and Jaybird Baxter walked in.

"Damn it," Jessie said harshly, grabbing a towel to cover herself, "what is this, a public park?"

Baxter's expression didn't change. He walked straight to her, snatched the towel from her grasp, and shoved her roughly into a chair.

"Sit down, shut up, and listen," he said flatly. Moving a

step away, he thrust his hands behind his back. "In spite of what you may think, Miss Starbuck, your body doesn't impress me at all. If I want a naked woman, I'll have a bunch sent in—in assorted shapes and colors."

"Fine," Jessie said shortly. "If you don't want to look, give me back my towel."

Baxter ignored her and turned to the woman. "The clothes all right? She have everything here she needs?"

"Yes sir," the woman said respectfully. "Everything is fine."

"Good. Get out of here. I'll call you when I want you." The woman turned and left quickly. Jessie stared at Baxter. She was certain she wouldn't have known him in the street. Instead of a drunken drifter in shabby clothes, he was a dignified, freshly shaved gentleman with carefully combed hair. His suit was an immaculate white English linen, a perfect match for his pale yellow shirt, patterned cravat, and vest of golden Chinese silk. She couldn't believe the change—any more than she could believe he'd taken her in right from the start, led her like a dog on a leash wherever he wanted her to go.

Baxter turned and held her gaze. "We've made a few changes," he said quietly. "Your friend's been a danger in the past, and we don't underestimate our enemies. If he shows up here he could be a problem. We don't have time for that." He paused and gazed past her at the wall. "The signing will *not* take place at the St. Charles Hotel. You'll be taken from here to a boat on the river. We'll be isolated there, and considerably less vulnerable."

"What about the people from my company? You'll keep me from seeing them now, I suppose."

"Oh no, not entirely." Baxter shook his head. "They'll be represented at the signing, but there won't be any, ah—private discussions, as we'd planned." He saw the question in her eyes and went on. "You see, Miss Starbuck, you asked two of your people to come to your suite at the St. Charles early this morning. This was just after we discovered that a madman had tried to break into your rooms disguised as a waiter. He saw your name in the papers, it seems, and came very close to taking your life. There really *is* such a lunatic, of course, a man with a record of threatening newsworthy people. After all this, you broke down in front of your two employees. The pressure you've been under, Ki's terrible death, and now this . . . It's all been too much for you, I'm afraid. Your physician stepped

165

in at this point and said he thought the signing should be canceled entirely. You protested and said you wanted to see it finished, but that you were too frightened to stay in the hotel. One of our people agreed, and suggested the boat. Your employees thought this was an excellent idea. In fact it was *their* idea that you cancel the private meeting with your managers. So—these two loyal friends will be taken aboard to witness the signing. All legal and proper, you see."

"And they believed that nonsense, right?"

"You've met our Barbara, I understand. With the veil, she's quite an excellent performer. This afternoon, of course, your lovely face will be bared for all to see."

"You *bastards!*" Jessie stood abruptly, grabbed a towel, and covered herself as best she could. This time Baxter made no effort to stop her. Jessie turned on him, green eyes blazing. "What have you done with Louisa? Where is she?"

"The girl is perfectly safe. She hasn't been harmed."

"I want to see her, Baxter."

"No. That's out of the question."

"She goes with me on the boat," Jessie said firmly. "I want to know where she is."

"My God, woman." Baxter laughed aloud. "We'll do what we want with the damn child. And if *you* don't do exactly as you're told, I'll cut her up myself!"

Jessie faced him squarely. "Do you think I'm a fool? The minute I leave this house, you don't need Louisa alive. And *I'm* dead as soon as I sign those papers. So what have I got to lose? What's to keep me from giving the whole thing away in front of my two managers?"

"You're distraught," Baxter said evenly, "possibly even having a mental breakdown. We've already suggested that possibility. They won't believe your ravings."

"Oh. Well then, you don't care *what* I do, right?"

"Now look, lady—"

"I've got a better idea. Whose signature would you like on those contracts? If I'm going to be 'Mad Jessie,' let's make the most of it. How about Queen Victoria? Or maybe Jenny Lind?"

Baxter's features twisted in rage. Before Jessie could move, he slapped her savagely across the face. Jessie gasped and went sprawling onto the bed. The towel fell away and bared her naked flesh. For the first time Baxter's pale eyes touched her body with interest.

166

"Damn you," he said tightly, "what do you hope to gain by all this? You know how it has to come out!"

"I want to keep that girl alive as long as I can," she said simply. "That's all. You can take it or leave it."

Baxter's lips curled in disgust. "Fine. You can have her, Miss Starbuck. If it makes you happy, we'll drop you into the Gulf in the same sack. Now get some clothes on, bitch!" He turned and jerked open the door and slammed it hard behind him.

Ki bolted through the hotel lobby and out the front door. Morgan shouted behind him, but Ki didn't stop. The horses they had waiting were still there, a chestnut gelding and a stallion as black as tar. Ki chose the dark horse and threw himself into the saddle, biting back pain as his gloved hands gripped the saddlehorn. Holding the reins as best he could, he danced the horse in a circle, searching the street on either side.

"Goddammit, will you hold up a minute!" The gambler shot him a look and quickly mounted the chestnut. "It's that way, to the left. Quit chasing your tail. I know how to get around down here and you don't."

"Then move!" Ki shouted. *Show* me!"

Morgan kicked his mount, then jerked back suddenly on the reins. A teamster cursed the pair from atop his wagon and wrenched his mules out of the way. Someone yelled, and the gambler looked over his shoulder. Two plainclothes policemen burst out of the St. Charles, shouting at them to stop.

"Shit," Morgan growled, "we got help we don't need. Come on, let's go!"

The policemen raced toward them, drawing their revolvers on the run. Two of Morgan's men materialized out of an alley, hit them soundly, and sent them sprawling. Morgan waved the pair to horses across the street, and kicked the chestnut southwest down St. Charles.

"You said they're on a boat," Ki demanded. *"What* boat, Morgan? You know where it is?"

"I know where the river is," he said bluntly. "That's a start."

Ki looked appalled. "Morgan, even *I* can find the Mississippi!"

"Left, right here," said Morgan. He glanced back to make sure his men were still with him. Three were right behind, but he couldn't find the fourth. Suddenly a wagon bolted out of the street just ahead, sending pedestrians scattering for cover.

167

Ki spotted Silas bent over the reins, Annie on the plank seat at his side. Three black men in hotel livery clung desperately to the back. Ki shouted to Morgan and pointed, and the gambler spurred his mount after the wagon. They raced down Jackson to the southeast. In a moment Ki could see the muddy expanse of the river. Silas's wagon clattered over the cobbled streets, straight for the waterfront. Finally he brought the wagon to a stop and jumped down. Annie and the three men followed.

Ki stood in the saddle and let his eyes sweep the river. The sight of the place shook him badly. Christ, he'd never find Jessie in all that! The broad levee stretched to his left and right as far as the eye could see. Barrels, kegs, bales, piles of lumber and machinery and goods of every kind imaginable were stacked in endless rows. The place was packed with people; merchants, planters, rivermen, and dockhands swarmed over the levee by the hundreds. Teamsters jammed every open space with their wagons, cursing each other to make way. Berthed along the levee were the great sidewheelers, smoke from their high black stacks blotting out the sun. Ki guessed there were fifty or more giant vessels lined up along the shore, and nearly as many straining up and down the river.

"My God," he cried aloud, "the place is a madhouse, Morgan!"

"She won't be on one of those," the gambler told him. "No way to keep people off. They'll have her out there, Ki—" He pointed over the river. "Anyone comin' at them they'll spot easy."

"That makes sense." Ki took a deep breath. "That still leaves a river full of boats. She's out there, Morgan—and when those devils get through with her, she's dead."

"Ki—" Annie laid a hand on his knee and said, "Ki, we're going to get her. We're going to get her back."

He looked at the girl, but scarcely saw her. One of Morgan's men left his horse and ran up to the gambler.

"Isn't too good just sittin' here," he said. "Me and Zack drew flies coming over. Lost 'em, I think, but that fella and his wagon—"

"He's right," Morgan told Ki. "We're goin' to have New Orleans law on our asses real soon. And they aren't goin' to care to hear any wild stories about Jessie."

"Fine," Ki said stubbornly. "Let 'em come. I'm not leaving the river without her."

168

"None of us are leaving without her," Morgan said flatly. "All right? Just hold on to your—"

"Ki!" Both men turned as Silas and one of his men ran up from the crowd on the levee. "I found her," he said tightly. "It's got to be her. Come on, it's 'bout a quarter of a mile down to the left—hurry!"

Ki didn't stop to ask questions. Annie gathered her skirts and swung herself up behind him. Silas mounted behind Morgan, and his men ran to bring up the wagon. Silas led them to the far bend of the river. After a moment he called a halt, dismounted, and studied the water, shading his eyes against the glare.

"There," he said firmly. "That's got to be it."

Ki eased out of the saddle and came up beside him. "God, Silas, it's out in the middle of the river. A seagull couldn't get up close to that boat."

"How do you know that's it?" said Morgan. "You certain, Silas?"

"'Course I'm certain," Silas told him. "White man don't pay no mind to what's happenin' on the levee—black man makes it his business to know. I talked to three fellas that seen a couple of longboats rowin' out to that thing. Close to half an hour ago. Bunch of men in fancy suits, and some hired guns." He looked straight at Ki. "There was a lady along. Had kinda red hair and wore a black dress. There's a little girl with her too."

Ki looked puzzled. "A little girl? You sure the woman's Jessie?"

"You sure it ain't?"

Ki shook his head and turned to Morgan. "Silas is right. It's got to be her. We've got to get out there fast."

"Fine," Morgan said grimly. "I'm with you. Who gets to dive in first?"

"You're both a couple of fools," Annie said harshly. "Ain't anyone doin' any swimming. You forget you've got a real live riverboat captain right here?"

Ki stared, his mouth creased in a weary grin. "Hell yes, of course we do. Pick one you like, Captain, and it's yours."

"Already did," said Annie. "That sternwheeler right ahead is gettin' up steam."

Morgan sighed and nodded to his men. "Come on. Those fellas aren't likely to be real understandin' about this . . ."

Chapter 25

Silas manned the engines while one of Morgan's men stoked the boiler. Annie shouted from the wheelhouse, and the stern-wheeler belched black smoke. The paddles began to churn muddy water and the vessel chugged slowly away from the levee. When the boat was some thirty yards off, Morgan lined up the scowling captain and his crew on the larboard deck.

"Anyone here can't swim, you better tell me 'bout it now."

"This is piracy, you bastard," snapped the captain. "Your ass is in big trouble!"

"Yeah, I know," said Morgan. He drew his revolver and thumbed back the hammer. "Anyone else got somethin' to say?"

No one did. The men turned and dived hastily into the river. Morgan watched them for a moment, then slipped the Colt back under his jacket and walked forward. "Stealin' riverboats sure is easy," he told Ki. "Wonder why folks don't do it more often?"

"Maybe because they're too big to hide."

"Yeah." Morgan gave him a thoughtful nod. "Likely somethin' to that."

Ki squinted ahead. The big sidewheeler was sitting still in midriver, a good two hundred yards off, backpaddling to keep from making way. Their own vessel was headed downstream, speeding up fast as the engines and the current took hold.

"I'm going up to ask Annie how to do it right. I figure we ought to hold off turning as long as we can. What have we got, nine of us? Counting you and me?"

"My three and Silas's crew is six—yeah, you're right. That's not too bad. And they all know how to shoot."

Ki nodded at the boat up ahead. "So does everyone up there."

● ● ●

170

Jessie's hand froze.

The pen refused to put her name to the paper that would give them what they wanted. In one quick stroke she'd lose it all, everything her father had worked a lifetime to accomplish. Alex Starbuck had died protecting what was his. Now his daughter was going to hand it to his murderers on a platter...

No, damn it, I can't! It's not right!

"Miss Starbuck, is something the matter?" Dietrich leaned across the table. His voice and the furrowed lines in his brow showed his concern. Jessie alone could see the ice-blue eyes dart meaningfully at the door to his right.

Jessie took a deep breath and wrote her name. Again, and then again. One of the cartel's silent attorneys sat beside her and helpfully turned the pages. Another was near Baxter and the bald-headed man with tinted glasses. Dietrich faced her across the table, the young man with the beard by his side. Two old friends, Marcus Ferguson and Noah Cooper, watched from the far end of the table. Jessie could scarcely bring herself to face them.

They think I've betrayed them, sold them out. I can tell by the way they looked at me just now. If I could only tell them, somehow let them know!

"That's it, Miss Starbuck. Everything's done."

"What? Oh yes, of course." Jessie looked blank as the attorney deftly slid the papers from her grasp. Dietrich covered them with his hand, a gleam of triumph in his eyes. Baxter stood, grasped Jessie's arm firmly, and guided her to her feet.

"Well now, I know you're glad to get all that behind you," he said gently. "Gentlemen—" He nodded toward the two Starbuck executives. "Thank you so much for being here. I know it meant a lot to Miss Jessie."

"Wait—" Jessie turned and glanced desperately toward her friends. "I'm sorry, I—" The words seemed to stick in her throat. "It had to be done, you see. It was—something I had to do—"

Noah Cooper looked at his gnarled hands. "We understand, Miss Starbuck. We surely do."

"Dear lady, it's been such a trying day." Baxter's fingers closed around her arm like a vise. "Everyone knows what you've been through. I'll see you back to your cabin so you can rest."

"No," Jessie protested. "I—don't want to go back there."

171

"You'll feel better a little later, I'm sure," said Baxter. He opened the door and drew her into the hall. Dietrich came through on their heels and shut the door behind him. Baxter's smile faded and he slammed Jessie roughly against the bulkhead wall. "Goddamn you," he said between his teeth, "you had to try, didn't you!" His eyes blazed at Dietrich. "Get those Starbuck people in the dory and get them ashore fast. Tell Hellmann I want this boat under way. That ship's waiting in the Gulf— I want to be on it and out to sea before nightfall."

Dietrich looked at Jessie. "What about her?"

"I'll put her back in the cabin for now. And she's not to see the girl."

"Yes, of course." Dietrich nodded and hurried off.

Damn you!" Jessie wrenched free and jerked back her arm to hit him. Baxter stopped her clenched fist with one hand and slapped her across the face. Jessie gasped and staggered back. Baxter hit her again. Jessie's head rang from the blows. Baxter gripped her chin and held her flat against the wall.

"It's over, Miss Starbuck," he said sharply. "Don't you know that yet? We don't have to keep you pretty any more. Malik! Where the hell are you!"

Almost at once the silent figure appeared. He looked straight at Jessie, black eyes reflecting no light at all.

"Where do you have the child?" Baxter asked him.

"Cabin Four. The man Kruge is with her." It was the first time Jessie had heard him speak. His voice was like a boot on broken glass.

"Take this lovely *lady* to the girl," Baxter said flatly. He looked right at Jessie. "I've changed my mind, Malik. We won't wait till we get to the Gulf. Kill them both. Now. Do the child first. Any way you like. I want Miss Starbuck to see it."

"No!" Jessie cried out in horror and tried to pull free. Baxter pushed her roughly away. Malik caught her deftly, turned her around, and twisted her arm into the small of her back. Jessie sucked in a breath and came up on her toes. Malik marched her down the hall, onto the open deck, and up the aft staircase. Jessie could hear Baxter on their heels. Black smoke blossomed out of the tall iron funnels; the engines wound up to a high pitch as the boat got under way.

Dietrich stopped them as they reached the upper deck. He touched Baxter's arm and pointed excitedly off to starboard.

172

"Captain Hellmann says that sternwheeler's trying to catch us. It's laying on too much steam to be going downstream."

Baxter frowned at the approaching vessel. She was even with their stern, but still a good thirty yards abeam. "Maybe they're just in a hurry and trying to pass us."

Dietrich shot him a look. "You wait and find out if you like. I'm getting some people up on deck."

"Can't hurt. I don't want any— By God, the damn fool's veering right toward us!" Baxter stared as the sternwheeler suddenly angled to port, shuddered, and plowed swiftly across the current. "Malik, I'll take the woman," he said sharply. "You get below and help the others!"

Malik nodded and let loose Jessie's arm. Jessie let her legs fold and went limp. Baxter leaned forward instinctively to catch her. Jessie brought her knee up fast and rammed it between his legs. Baxter howled and folded like a sack. Malik turned on his heel and came at her. Jessie shoved Baxter in his path and ran aft as fast as she could . . .

Ki crouched low and sprinted toward the bow. The timbered deck shuddered under his feet as Annie shouted for more steam from the wheelhouse overhead. Ki hoped to hell she knew what she was doing—the engines were shaking so hard he was certain they'd rip off their moorings.

A sharp flash of light winked from the sidewheeler to port. Lead splintered wood at Ki's feet and he rolled for cover. One of Morgan's men dropped his rifle, grabbed his arm, and ran.

"Stay down!" Morgan bellowed. "Damn it, keep your cover!"

The boat loomed closer every second. Ki's crewmen answered the enemy fire. One of Silas's men squeezed off a single shot from his Henry .44. A man went limp on the sidewheeler's upper deck and tumbled into the river.

"Ki, look there!" Silas came up behind him and gripped his shoulder hard. "She's turnin' off—we've got 'er going now!"

"They'll run aground," Ki muttered. "They're headed straight for— It's *Jessie!*" Ki leaped to his feet and stared. Silas pulled him to the deck as a volley of bullets whined overhead. Ki broke free and bellowed at Morgan. Morgan saw her at once, running fast along the upper deck. His right hand pumped the Winchester's lever action as he loosed one shot after another at Jessie's pursuer. The man danced aside and kept going. For

173

an instant he turned and glared in Ki's direction. Ki saw the familiar face and went rigid.

"Hold on!" Morgan shouted above the noise. "We're goin' to hit!"

Ki grabbed the nearest iron stanchion, wrapped his arms and legs about it, and ducked his head. At the last instant the captain of the larger vessel turned his wheel hard a'port. Annie hit the starboard hull aft at a sharp angle, just ahead of the great sidewheel. The smaller ship's bow tore through the hull, snapping timber, moving at such speed that the shallow hull came out of the water and ground to a wrenching halt on the sidewheeler's decks.

Ki covered his head as a hail of debris rained down on the deck. A man screamed and landed at Ki's feet. Silas kicked him in the chest and scooped up the man's Colt. Ki leaped over the wreckage and made his way forward. Broken steam lines shrieked to his left. An enormous black shadow blocked his way, and he realized that one of the sternwheeler's twin stacks had snapped in two and snagged itself in the twisted rigging of the derricks. Black smoke billowed from the broken shaft and he plunged blindly through it to the big sidewheeler's cargo decks.

One of Morgan's men darted past him, emptying his pistol at the level overhead. A stairwell to port was still intact and he climbed quickly to the upper deck. Fire exploded to his right, and buckshot tugged at the billowing fabric of his shirt. Ki dived for cover as the second barrel chewed up decking where he'd just been. Scrambling to his feet, he saw the man frantically kicking out shells and poking new loads in the old Parker. Ki went after him as the man pulled the hammers back fast. His foot lashed out and smashed the weapon against the gunman's face. Blood streamed from his nose and the man sat down hard. Ki kicked him solidly in the chin and wrenched the Parker out of his hands. He had no love for guns, but this was no time to be choosy. It was a weapon he could hold without tearing all the raw flesh off under his gloves.

Gunfire sounded to his right. Ki went low and kept moving. Suddenly a terrible, piercing scream rent the air. "Jessie!" Ki cried, freezing in his tracks. "Jessie, hang on!"

Lead whined over his shoulder, but Ki ignored it. He raced along the deck, past smoke and howling steam. A cabin door hung at an angle on its hinges. Ki kicked it aside and ran on.

174

The forward deck suddenly opened up before him. Bullets tore up wood at his feet and he shrank back into an alcove. A pistol cracked twice. Splinters stung his cheek from a ricochet and he scampered to better cover. One was waiting ahead, and he'd let another sneak up behind. Jessie needed him now, and they had him pinned down like a rabbit.

Keeping close to the bulkhead wall, he moved quickly back in the direction he'd come. The open cabin door was just ahead. Ki stopped, sensing that something was wrong. Glancing quickly over his shoulder, he scooped up a piece of fallen timber and slid it across the deck to the door. A pistol roared from the dark cabin. Ki poked the shotgun around the corner and fired blindly into the room. A man cried out and went silent.

Ki turned and moved off without looking back. Heavy fire sounded again from the forward deck. Someone gave a shrill whistle behind him. Ki whirled around, saw one of Morgan's men, and lowered the Parker's twin barrels.

"Careful," the man warned, "there's three of 'em hunkered behind that downed stack. Maybe a couple more."

"Have you seen Jessie?" Ki asked quickly. "She's here somewhere, I *heard* her!"

The man shook his head. "Haven't seen a damn thing except fellers tryin' to chew up my ass." He paused and looked curiously at Ki. "Now what the hell are you doing, mister?"

Ki had laid the shotgun aside and was working painfully with his gloved hands to slip off his coat and pry his feet out of his shoes. "Can't do a thing, trussed up like a banker. I've got to have some room to breathe."

"Yeah, well, whatever you say." The man inched past Ki and peered around the corner. Lead chewed wood by his head. *"Shit!"* He jerked back and stared at Ki with surprise. "Son of a bitch out there tried to *kill* me!"

A man shouted to Ki's left. He thought it was one of Silas's crew, but couldn't be certain. Suddenly the scream came again— this time, choked off almost before it began. The sound ripped at Ki's gut. With a ragged cry of pain he bolted from cover. The man behind him shouted a warning. Gunfire blossomed from behind the downed stack. Lead hit the tangled steel derrick and sent sparks flying. A man leaped atop the stack to get a clear shot at Ki. Ki cut him in half with the Parker and kept going. A Winchester roared to his left, the shots so close together it sounded like a Gatling. A man cried out behind the

175

stack, and then another. From the corner of his eye Ki saw Black Jack Morgan's tall form striding deliberately across the deck, the Winchester blazing in his hands. Morgan ignored the fire from ahead and kept coming. Ki spotted movement to Morgan's left. A gunman suddenly appeared, leveled his Colt in both hands, and bore down hard on the gambler.

"Morgan, look out!" Ki bellowed. His cry was lost as the Colt exploded. Morgan stumbled and went down. Ki planted his feet on the deck, gripped the shotgun by the barrels, and sent it flying. The gunman had an instant to see the dark blur spinning toward him. His eyes widened in surprise just before the weapon caught him across the forehead.

Ki ran for Morgan and bent over him quickly. Behind him, his friend broke from cover and sent a deadly volley of fire at the stack. One of Silas's men joined in, and together they quickly cleared the decks.

"You all right?" Ki asked anxiously.

Morgan's face was pale and dripping sweat. "Yeah, sure. Hell, I get shot all the time, don't you?" Ki ripped Morgan's shirt and saw that the bullet had gone in the shoulder, just below the collarbone. He wrapped it quickly to stop the blood, and Morgan winced.

"You'll make it," Ki assured him. "And thanks. If it hadn't been for my damn fool charge—"

"Forget it. Get out of here and find Jessie. I heard her, just before y— Jesus Christ, Ki, look out!"

Ki turned in a crouch as the high-pitched scream came again. A gray-haired man stepped from cover near the bow. The slender girl whined in his grasp, and he jammed his short-barreled Webley in her face. Ki stared, trying to make sense of what he saw. It wasn't Jessie screaming at all—it was the child! Silas's friends on the levee had seen a young girl going aboard. What the hell was she doing in all this?

"Stand back and give me room," the man blurted. "Out of my way or I'll kill her!"

Ki didn't move. His two men across the deck stood perfectly still. The man glanced wildly about. His white suit was smeared with grease and there was an ugly cut on his brow. The young girl trembled with fear. She tried to scream again; her mouth moved but nothing came out.

"I'm leaving," the man said tightly. "D-don't come close. I'll blow her head off. I'll kill her right where she stands!"

"No one's stopping you, mister," Ki said carefully. The

176

man turned and stared at Ki as if he'd only just noticed he was there.

"You!" The word exploded from his mouth and his features twisted with rage. "This is all your doing, goddamn you!" Suddenly he jerked the pistol away from the girl's head and leveled it at Ki. A dark shape appeared on the railing directly behind him. Silas's big right hand grabbed Baxter's gun in a viselike grip and tore it away. In the same instant his left hand snaked out in a blur, passing quickly across the man's throat. Baxter's eyes bulged, and a bright red line appeared and began to grow beneath his chin. Silas wrenched the girl free and pushed Baxter's limp figure over the railing. Louisa gave a ragged little wail and buried her face against Silas's chest.

Ki glanced quickly at Morgan. One of his men ran to tend him and the gambler waved Ki off. The forward decks were clear. The gunmen left alive had quickly vanished over the sides. Ki smelled smoke, glanced over his shoulder, and saw fire licking the stern of the vessel. Most likely, he decided, one or both of the boats' boilers had gone up.

"Ki!" Annie ran forward with one of Silas's men and pulled him quickly to the railing. "Ki, I *saw* her," she cried. "Jessie, a—a man's got her. I saw them in the water!"

Ki followed Annie's shaky hand and ran aft. The big side-wheeler was aground, settling in the mud only a dozen yards from shore. A crowd had already gathered on the levee and he could hear the metallic clang of distant fire wagons. "Damn it, I don't see a thing," he said shortly. "Nothing!"

Annie clutched his arm. "There, look!" Ki spotted them at once. The man was wading ashore, clamoring quickly up the levee with Jessie draped roughly over his shoulder. Bare legs flailed the air below her skirts; her fists pounded desperately against his back. Men closed in around the pair. A uniformed policeman ran forward, trying to stop Jessie's captor. The man hit him hard with his free hand and kept going.

Ki cursed under his breath and jumped off the railing into the river. At once he sank up to his shoulders in muddy water. The bottom sucked at his feet and threatened to pull him under. He slipped, and silty water closed over his head. Pulling himself erect, he slogged ashore and climbed the levee. A man reached down to help him up. "Mister, what's happening out there? What the hell's going on?"

Ki didn't answer. He spotted Jessie and her captor to the left and started running. A policeman called out to him to stop.

177

Two burly men got in his way, and Ki brushed them aside. He lost Jessie for an instant, then found her again. A man in a gray frock coat was writhing on the ground, blood smearing his face. The cartel's killer was trying to hold the man's horse, jerking savagely at the reins to keep it steady. He tossed Jessie roughly over the saddle, then leaped atop the frightened animal. Ki took two quick steps and threw himself at the mount. The man pulled the horse aside and lashed out with his boot. The blow caught Ki in the chest and slammed him to the ground. The horse pawed air, then broke into a run. Ki picked himself up, turned, and spotted a wide-eyed young man on a chestnut gelding. The boy saw Ki and tried to turn the horse away. Ki caught the reins and pulled the horse to him. The horse bolted, and seared Ki's gloved hands with fire. "Sorry, boy, you have to get off," he said bluntly. He grabbed the boy and eased him to the ground. The young man cursed him, and Ki leaped into the saddle. A man shouted behind him and fired two shots over his head. Jessie's captor was moving south down the crowded levee, scattering everyone on his path. Ki leaned forward in the saddle and dug his heels into the horse's flanks.

Suddenly Jessie's captor glanced over his shoulder, saw Ki behind him, and bolted his mount to the right. Ki quickened his speed, trying to cut the man off. The killer lashed his horse and leaped a stack of crates. Ki groaned, certain that the gelding would balk and send him flying. At the last instant the horse bunched his muscles and took the leap. Hooves splintered wood and the animal hit the ground running, jolting every bone in Ki's body.

The rider ahead bounded off the broad levee, moving away from the river. Warehouses gave way quickly to busy streets and crowded shops. Ki lost sight of his quarry, then saw him again as he turned abruptly northwest up Jackson. A frightened team whinnied and shook their heads, wrenching the carriage behind them aside. A wheel snapped off and rolled free down the street. The carriage slid to a stop and the driver shook his fists in Ki's direction.

The rider ahead left the street and sent his mount flying over an expanse of green lawn. At once Ki found himself surrounded by great columned houses, well-tended gardens, and thick-boled oaks and magnolias. Jessie's captor plunged through a manicured shrub and disappeared. Ki lowered his head between his shoulders and kicked the mount through. Sharp branches

178

tore at his face. The cartel's man paused, danced his mount in a circle, and headed west through a grove of trees. Ki followed quickly on his heels.

Suddenly an expanse of trimmed grass loomed up ahead. Ki caught a glimpse of a vine-covered gazebo, a lawn set up for croquet. A dozen young ladies dressed in whites and pale yellows screamed and scattered for cover. Ki's foe tried desperately to stop, but the horse plunged ahead. The mount's hooves tangled in metal wickets and Jessie and her captor went flying. Ki's horse bolted aside and drove through the side of the gazebo. Ki cried out as vines and splintered wood jerked him from the saddle. He picked himself up and threw the tangle aside. The killer came through the greenery like a bull and hit him hard, driving him to the ground before he could get his bearings. Strong hands circled his throat and tried to choke off his life. Ki pounded the man's head with useless fists and twisted his body to shake free. The killer refused to give an inch. Fingers as strong as steel tried to tear Ki's windpipe from his throat. His vision blurred and his lungs cried out for air.

Ki fought the pain in his hands, sent all the strength he could muster into his arms, and drove both fists against the sides of the man's head. Ki's assailant roared and loosened his grip. His face twisted in pain and he rolled away, fingers clawing at his ears. Ki came to his feet in an instant, kicked the man in the ribs, and drove his heel solidly at the heart in a killing blow. The man twisted aside and Ki's foot glanced off his shoulder. He sprang to his feet in one fluid motion and lashed out with his fist at Ki's face. Ki's head snapped back and the man hit him again, the blow nearly knocking Ki senseless. His hands came up to ward off the deadly fists. The man knocked his arms aside and hit him again. Ki staggered, fighting to clear the blood from his eyes. Another blow caught him in the face. The killer drove in relentlessly, pounding with his left and then his right, working close to Ki's body so he couldn't use his feet. The sudden blaze of triumph in his eyes told Ki the man knew he was finished, that his hands were nearly useless and numb with pain. The cruel slash of a mouth split in a grin. A punishing right caught the side of Ki's head. He took the blow, letting it drive him to the ground. The man laughed as Ki's back slammed against the earth, twisted on the soles of his feet, and cocked his leg to finish Ki off. Ki twisted aside and took the blow on his shoulder, brought his knees together under his chin, and snapped his body out straight. His heels drove into the man's belly and bent him double. He retched and tried to straighten and get his bearings. Ki sprang to his feet, twisted in a quick half-circle, and lashed out with his heel at the man's head. The blow glanced off and the killer staggered back. Ki turned and kicked out once and then again at the man's chest. Bone snapped and the man coughed blood. Ki lashed out again. The man backed away, stared at Ki with dark hatred, and came at him with a strength born of killing rage. A terrible, ragged cry burst from his chest as he drove himself at Ki, slashing the air with deadly fists. Ki dug one foot in the grass, let all the strength he had flow into his thighs, and kicked straight up at the man's chin. The blow lifted the killer off the ground, arms and legs spread wide, and then he slammed to the ground, flat on his back. Ki swayed and sucked air into his lungs. He didn't need to look at the still figure. The awkward angle of his neck told him all he needed to know.

Wiping blood from his face, he searched frantically about the green lawn. His assailant's horse lay ten yards away. It raised its head and turned a fearful white-rimmed eye in Ki's direction. Jessie lay a few steps past the mount. Ki ran to her, went to his knees, and raised her head in his arms.

"Jessie? Jessie, damn you, *talk* to me," he shouted hoarsely. *"Talk* to me!"

Jessie opened her eyes, stared at Ki, and blinked in surprise. "Ki? Lord, you sure show up in the strangest places."

Ki laughed aloud with relief. "Jessie, are you—are you all right?"

"Yeah, I guess. Got the wind knocked out of me some. Did you—" Suddenly her eyes went wide and she stared fearfully past him. "Malik! Is he—"

"Take it easy." Ki held her shoulders. It was the first time he'd heard the killer's name. "He's not going to hurt you anymore."

Jessie relaxed, then fear tightened her features once more. "Ki—there's a—a little girl. Back at the boat. Do you know if she's—Oh Lord, I don't even want to ask!"

"She's all right," Ki assured her. "We've got her."

Jessie shuddered and let out a breath. Tears of relief welled in her eyes and she wiped them quickly away. Ki held her and helped her to her feet. Jessie blinked, startled at her surround-

180

ings. A stately, white-columned house stood under enormous oaks across the broad lawn.

"Oh, Ki, it's so—quiet and peaceful," she sighed. "I'd like to hole up in a place like this forever!"

"You would, huh?"

Jessie raised her chin in defiance. "Of course I would. That's what I said, didn't I?"

"I'd give you about a week," Ki said soberly. "Ten days maybe."

Jessie frowned and gave him a quick kiss on the cheek. "You know what, friend? You know me too damn well. Come on, let's get out of here."

★

Chapter 26

It was well after dark before Jessie was able to break free and get to the hospital. Jeff Morgan was propped up in bed, smoking a thin cheroot. A kerosene lamp was turned low on the table beside him. There were three other patients in the ward, but a high screen shielded him from the rest of the room. When Jessie entered, he looked up and gave her a weak smile. Jessie bent to kiss him, then pulled a chair close to the bed.

"Well, Mr. Morgan," she said wryly, "you look like a man who forgot to duck."

"It isn't real bad," said Morgan, "just got a shoulder that's sore as hell. I'm not goin' to feel like shuffling or dealing for a while. Jessie, I'm damn glad to see you again. Don't guess I have to tell you that."

"No," she said gently, "you don't. But I don't mind hearing it at all." She leaned closer to him and stroked his arm. "I owe you a lot, Jeff—including a couple of dozen apologies. I had no business suspecting you had a part in this. Especially after what went on between us. Hell, I mistrusted a man who was trying to help me, and swallowed Jaybird Baxter's lies hook, line, and sinker. Looks like I'm a fine judge of character."

Morgan shook his head and looked puzzled. "Jessie, I hate to sound ignorant, but I never *heard* of any Jaybird Baxter."

"I keep forgetting," Jessie sighed. "Of course you haven't. That's what Ki said too." Jessie told him the whole story from start to finish. When she came to the part Ki had told her about Baxter and Louisa, understanding dawned in Morgan's eyes.

"*That* was Baxter? The man Silas killed? Well, I'll be damned. Jessie, you mean that crazy old man was running this show?"

"He wasn't crazy at all," Jessie said soberly. "If it hadn't

182

been for you and Ki . . ." Jessie let her words trail off. "And yes—Baxter *was* running the show. Dietrich and the others had a hand in it, but I'm convinced Jaybird Baxter was one of the top cartel leaders on this side of the Atlantic."

"Sounds like he knew what he was doing."

"If he'd been any better, I'd be dead," Jessie said flatly. "They used me right from the start, Jeff, led me all the way 'round the barn. Ki says he's told you about the cartel, and what they're trying to do to this country. Stealing the Starbuck holdings would have brought them a little closer to their goal, given them more power and money to take over someone else."

"That's what it was all about, then," Morgan nodded. "Robbing the gold shipments and getting hold of you."

"Robbing the gold to weaken Starbuck was important, but yes—getting me was what they wanted. It's going to take a while to sort it all out. Maybe we'll never know the truth about everything that's happened, but I think I can make some pretty good guesses. Baxter fed that information to Pike to draw me to Jefferson. But unless I'm wrong, he probably never even *knew* Tobias Pike. What happened is that Baxter found folks who *did* know Pike, and used them. Like James Cooper, for instance. He had Dietrich's killer, Malik, do away with some poor Caddo Indian—a man who likely never even got close to the Big Thicket. Malik planted a little Starbuck gold on the Indian, and Baxter made sure a lawman in Jefferson got the news to Pike. Maybe they bribed that deputy friend of Pike's, or scared him half to death. They're very good at that. I'm pretty convinced that Baxter threatened James Cooper—told him his family would be killed if he didn't feed Pike the right information. Jeff, the only good that came out of all that business was Jacob Mose. Cooper was likely scared to death, and tossed Mose's name to make his story sound better. Or maybe Baxter found out he was related to Mose, and *told* him to drop Mose's name on Pike. Like I say, there's a lot we can only guess at now."

Jessie sighed and looked straight into Morgan's eyes. "I'm sorry, Jeff—and so damn angry at what happened that I can't see straight. Baxter was *good* at what he did. He used everyone he could to build up his story. You just happened by and we got together—so he threw you in the pot to confuse me a little more. You were following me that day to keep an eye on me after Pike was murdered. That was after Pike first approached

183

me. He saw you, and picked up the idea on the spot. Run off and look scared and I'd think you were part of the game. And of course that'd make me trust *him* all the more, wouldn't it?" She looked sheepishly at her hands. "Worked, too. I—I was attracted to you, but I sure as hell didn't trust you. Especially after I caught you going through my stuff—and right after you'd made love to me, at that."

"I don't blame you for what you thought," said Morgan. "Let's forget all the apologies again, Jessie. There's too much of that between us. I say we toss 'em all away."

"Yes, let's do that, Jeff." Jessie smiled and took his hand again.

"Ki kinda figured that whole business with the Thicket was a false trail," said Morgan. "Was it or not, do you know?"

"It wasn't *all* false," Jessie explained. "From what we can piece together, they'd used the camp for cartel operations before. Whether any gold ever passed through there I don't know, and likely never will. There was a real camp there, so Baxter tossed it in for good measure. The idea was to get me to take the bait. If he hadn't been able to take me in Jefferson, he would have tried it on the way to the Thicket or somewhere else. The overall plan was to steal Starbuck gold and weaken the company—but more important than that, make it look like I had a good reason to sell out. Then they'd get me away from Ki and make me sign over the company. When Ki came to Jefferson, they were ready. Of course, they *had* to get him out of the way before they could play their game with me. They knew it wouldn't work with him alive. And Ki's death would work for Baxter in another way as well—it'd give me an extra reason to want to sell. The company losing its standing, my good friend getting murdered—" Jessie paused a long moment. "Baxter was one of the most dangerous men I've ever come up against, Jeff. He never missed a bet. He saw everything coming and got ready for it."

"Not everything," Morgan reminded her. "He didn't see me, or Ki or Annie. He sure as hell didn't figure on Silas Johnson."

"No," Jessie said distantly, "he didn't." She turned and looked past Morgan. A window was open behind his bed, and she could see the street lamps outside, and hear the sound of distant music. "Jeff, Baxter's dead and he was a pretty big fish, but he was the only one we got, damn it. I mean, besides

184

Malik and a bunch of hired guns. Dietrich and the other two cartel bosses just disappeared off that boat. And there's *no* one in that house in the French Quarter where I was held. Even if we find any of them, you can bet they won't have the slightest idea who they've been working for. And big surprise. The Wheatland Corporation of Kansas City, Missouri, doesn't seem to exist anymore, as of late this afternoon. Of course, the papers are playing the whole thing down," she added bitterly. "They say the gold raiders are responsible for everything that happened. That, or a ring of confidence men." Jessie ground her fists together. "The law doesn't know what to make of it all, and of course no one wants to hear Jessie Starbuck's wild tales about conspiracies and mysterious international cartels. I'm just a hysterical woman who's been through a bad time!"

Morgan looked at her. "You think someone got to the press and the police, is that what you're trying to tell me?"

"I'm telling you it's happened before," she said darkly. Jessie leaned back, shook strawberry hair out of her eyes, and forced a smile. "I'm sorry, I don't guess I'm doing a real good job of cheering up the wounded. A couple of *good* things have happened, believe it or not. Remember all that gold the cartel stole? It's all right there in the boat Annie sunk—buried under two or three feet of Mississippi mud. A salvage crew's going to start going after it tomorrow. Baxter, Dietrich, and his friends were going to transfer it to an oceangoing vessel out in the Gulf, and take it back to Europe."

"Good," said Jeff. "And the little girl, Jessie? She's all right?"

Jessie beamed at the mention of Louisa. "I've got her family on a train, coming here. Time's the only thing that'll chase the demons out of Louisa's head. I think the sight of her family and a couple of weeks in New Orleans might be a good start. After that, I'd like them to come and stay at the Circle Star in Sarah for a while. Of course, that's up to them." She gave Morgan an impish smile and looked absently at the ceiling. "I don't guess I have to tell you Ki and Annie are managing to while away the time. And Silas seems to have found himself a friend. That pretty little girl who was posing as Annie's maid when you tried to raid the hotel? Seems she isn't a maid at all, but a schoolteacher who works right here in New Orleans."

Morgan grinned appreciatively. "I saw her. I expect she can teach Silas about all he can stand to learn."

185

"Lord," Jessie scolded, "you men are so vulgah, Mister Maw'gun."

"Please, no more Miss Annabelle Lee." Morgan laughed, then flinched and grabbed his shoulder. "I'm an invalid, lady. I need kind and loving care."

"Uh-huh. I know." Jessie gave him a lazy smile, pushed back her chair, and stood by the side of his bed. "See, that's why I really came to visit," she said solemnly. "I figured a girl ought to do what little she can to help our wounded boys, bring a little happiness into their lives."

Morgan looked at her. "And, uh—just what kind of happiness did you have in mind, Miss Starbuck?"

"Oh, something you could sort of just lie back and enjoy—without straining yourself too much." Jessie's green eyes flashed with flecks of gold in the light of the lamp. Without looking away, she lowered her hands to her sides and began gathering the thin material of her dress between her fingers. Morgan held his breath as the gown slid over her knees, past the lean curve of her thighs. Jessie paused an instant and teased him with her eyes, then drew the dress up slowly until it was a good six inches above her waist. Morgan's gaze wandered boldly from the flat little tummy to the lovely swell of her hips, his eyes settling finally on the soft amber nest between her legs.

Jessie peered down and bit her lip in surprise. "Lord A'mighty, Jeff, I'm getting real careless. I plumb forgot my underthings!"

"Uh, yeah," Morgan said dryly, "looks that way, doesn't it?"

Jessie slid his sheet down to his knees and grinned at what she saw. "Hey, friend, does the nurse know about that swelling you've got down there?"

"I don't think so. I'll show it to her if you like. She's a cute little—"

"Damned if you will!" Jessie leaned toward him, cupped one hand about the chimney of the lamp, and blew it out. Gathering up her skirts, she climbed carefully onto the bed, straddled him, and lowered herself gently over his thighs. "Now you just lie right still," she whispered. "I promise this won't hurt a bit, Mr. Morgan."

"Go ahead, doc," Morgan groaned. "Do whatever you have to do . . ."

Watch for

LONE STAR AND THE HANGROPE HERITAGE

twenty-third novel in the exciting
LONE STAR
series from Jove

coming in July!